MARION KUMMEROW

THE
BERLIN
WIFE

Published by Bookouture in 2023

An imprint of Storyfire Ltd.
Carmelite House
50 Victoria Embankment
London EC4Y 0DZ

www.bookouture.com

ISBN: 978-1-83790-963-6
eBook ISBN: 978-1-83790-278-1

1

MUNICH, NOVEMBER 1923

Early in the morning, Edith Falkenstein woke up, realizing her husband Julius had once again not returned home to sleep in his bed, because she couldn't hear him snoring in the adjacent room.

Fixing her eyes on the clear blue sky streaming in through the curtains, she gave a sigh. Julius had a habit of throwing himself into work, and with rampant hyperinflation, he was needed at the bank he owned day and night.

Another sigh escaped her throat. Despite all their riches, even they felt the desolation taking hold of the German population. After they had lost the Great War, the country had rapidly spiraled downward until it seemed like everyone was out of a job. Beggars and war invalids lined the streets of the formerly rich and beautiful city of Munich.

She rang the bell on her nightstand, and mere moments later her maid Laura entered the room in her freshly starched black dress, a white apron and white bonnet completing the outfit. At least some things hadn't changed.

Laura curtsied. "How may I serve you, *gnädige Frau?*"

It had taken Edith a long time to get used to having servants around, speaking to her so formally. In contrast to her husband, a rich and powerful man fifteen years her senior, who came from a long line of merchants and bank owners, she'd grown up as the daughter of an elementary schoolteacher on the outskirts of Berlin.

Five years ago, after their wedding, she had followed Julius to Munich, way down in the South of Germany, far away from her family and friends.

"Please prepare coffee for me, and advise the driver to shine the car, as I'm going to pick up my brother from the train station later today."

"Yes, *gnädige Frau*." Laura was an industrious girl, quite versatile in all household chores and a devout Christian. Unlike Edith and Julius, who were Protestants in name only, and rarely, if ever, went to church.

"Have you had word from Herr Falkenstein?" She only ever referred to her husband by his last name in the presence of staff.

"He called around three a.m. to advise the driver that he had been held up at work and wished to be picked up for breakfast," Laura said. "If you wait for another hour, you may eat with him."

"Thank you, I will wait then. Bring me the coffee now, will you?" Even without comprehending much about business, Edith understood that Julius was fighting for the survival of his bank. Nonetheless, she wished he would spend more time with her.

After moving to Munich she had barely made any friends. In all honesty, Edith was horribly bored. Brought up as the daughter of a teacher, she'd never been idle in her life. That had changed after marrying Julius, when she suddenly found herself with a plethora of servants taking care of her every wish.

At least in Berlin she'd had her friends to spend time with. Here, the days were endlessly dull. She could go shopping only so much, especially now that there was barely anything on display in the glamorous Maximilianstrasse.

In these unusual times the pendulum was swinging from a frantic urge to spend before the paid salary lost its worth, to not buying anything at all because the money wasn't even worth the paper it was printed on.

An hour later, her husband arrived home. She heard the car engine long before she peeped out the window to see his Mercedes limousine coming up the driveway toward their beautiful mansion, right next to the English Garden near the center of Munich.

Edith glanced in the mirror to make sure she looked her best. A habit Julius appreciated not only for himself, but also because he often brought unannounced guests with him.

"Good morning, Julius," she greeted him, since he'd long ago told her never to call him darling or some other term of endearment in public—their servants counting as public for him.

"Good morning, Edith," he responded, giving her a tired glance from bloodshot eyes. "Is breakfast ready?"

"Yes, I have ordered the cook to prepare scrambled eggs for you, and, of course, coffee."

"Will you join me?" he asked with a pleasant smile.

"I took coffee already, but waited with breakfast for your return," she said.

"You look beautiful this morning," he complimented her. "Have you slept well?"

"I did," she lied, not wanting to let him know that she woke up several times, listening for whether he would arrive to sleep at home.

He put his hand on the small of her back and led her into the dining room, where the maid had already served steaming hot coffee and two plates of scrambled eggs, each with a richly buttered piece of bread.

"How was your work?" she asked, once they settled at the table.

"Tough. The government has our backs against the wall with this inflation. You won't believe the amount of people storming our offices each morning to retrieve any money that was deposited overnight, for fear it won't be worth a thing by evening. It's stretching our cash inventory to the limit and we can't source the bills with the printed-on denominations fast enough. I've had to hire more security guards to keep customers from turning violent against the cashiers."

"Can't you do anything?" she asked, taking a tiny forkful of egg, the way her mother-in-law had taught her during the nine months of their engagement, when she'd lived with her in-laws in Berlin—obviously with Julius not sleeping in the same house. Frau Falkenstein senior had been a harsh mistress, teaching Edith exactly how a woman of society was expected to behave. Edith had never complained. Since she and Julius had been very much in love, she'd eagerly picked up every piece of advice, to be a perfect wife—and to make him proud.

Julius gazed at her indulgently. "It's not as easy as it might seem. Our bank has a duty to serve all our customers. At least that is the mission issued by the government, but when that same government isn't able to provide us with enough banknotes to satisfy the public's need, it really gets us into a bind."

Edith knew all about his dislike for the previous Reichskanzler Wilhelm Cuno, whose call for a strike against the reparations due after the defeat in the Great War had ruined the country. Three months ago he'd been replaced by Gustav Stresemann. "Hasn't the new chancellor tackled this problem?" she asked.

"Hmm," Julius puffed. "He's good for nothing. Almost got himself sacked by a communist coup last month. Can you imagine? The communists, of all people?"

Edith nodded, inwardly bracing herself for a lecture on the evil communists, whom Julius, a wealthy and powerful bank owner, loathed by default.

"God, I have no idea why all our politicians are a bunch of corrupt weaklings without a brain among them!" he blurted out.

"Perhaps you should go into politics?" she suggested.

"I should." He seemed pleased at her suggestion. "But then, who would run the Falkenstein bank? Father is much too old, and I'm his only son."

Julius was very fond of his younger sisters, Adriana and Silvana. He especially adored and indulged Silvana, a feisty woman who wouldn't allow anyone to tell her what to do. Yet, it was unthinkable that one of them should step into the family business, even if they had the inclination to do so. "What about your brothers-in-law?"

He shook his head. "While they both are good men, Florian has his hands full with his rubber factory and Markus doesn't have what it takes to run such a business."

Edith smiled. Markus Lemberg preferred the fine arts over business. He was a celebrated author and professor of literature at the university in Berlin. "Perhaps one of my brothers then?"

"Don't take it personally, Edith, but your brothers come from a middle-class background with no prior education in business. It would be a very steep learning curve for them." He emptied his plate and rang for the maid to bring him another one. After Laura was gone, Julius added, "No, what our country needs is a strong and honest man with the best interest of all people at his heart. Someone who won't be pushed around by communists, separatists and whoever else is leading our nation into bankruptcy with their unworkable ideas. Someone, perhaps, like this Hitler fellow, though I can't see him succeeding as his views are too extreme."

Edith didn't want to hear more about this supposed savior, who'd recently been elected to the German Battle League, since she considered him a man who offered nothing but the spread of hate. Not wanting to get into a political discussion, she changed the topic. "You do remember that my brother Joseph will be staying with us for a few days, don't you?"

"Of course I do, darling. When is he due to arrive?"

"This afternoon." Edith suspected that Julius had indeed forgotten about the visit. He was always too preoccupied with problems at work to remember such mundane events.

"I need to attend to business this afternoon. I assume the driver will pick your brother up from the train station? Have you arranged for a welcome dinner tonight?"

"Of course." Edith was in charge of their busy social life. Since his mother had impressed on her how important it was in their circles to mingle, she used every occasion to invite important guests. She immensely enjoyed the planning, scheduling and organizing of events. Julius often complimented her on how good she was at it, and that much of his success was due to her efforts in maintaining relations with a multitude of important people.

"Your secretary has it in your schedule. The mayor will be attending, as well as a few of your business partners."

Julius beamed with pride. "Always up to the game. I couldn't have wished for a better wife."

She looked at him, seeing the fondness he held for her shine in his eyes. During their courtship, she'd been impressed by the much older man with the impeccable manners and the charming attitude. He had given her his complete attention, showered her with gifts, opened a completely new and exciting world to her. The time passed as if in a drunken stupor, despite the four long years of the Great War when he'd served as an officer. Heartwarming, soulful letters had flown back and forth and, on their wedding day, she had truly been the happiest woman on earth.

Gradually, though, that had changed. Their passionate love

was gone, and these days it seemed their marriage was mostly a business affair. Edith often wondered whether things might have been different if she'd been able to give him the heir they both so fervently wished for. But after five years of marriage, her womb was still barren, which she attributed to his increasingly infrequent visits to her bedroom after her two heart-shattering miscarriages.

She pushed the quelling bitterness away. Despite them drifting apart Julius was an upright man; others in his position would have divorced her by now, replaced her with a younger, more fertile woman.

What would she do then? She certainly had no desire to join the army of jobless, hapless, penniless beggars on the streets. Living in a marriage devoid of honeymoon-passion was a small price to pay for the security of always having enough food on the table and a roof over her head.

After breakfast, Julius retreated to his bedroom to take a nap, whereas Edith headed into the kitchen to give the staff their last instructions for the reception tonight. When it was time to get ready to leave, she changed into a woolen two-piece costume, complete with matching hat and gloves, plus a great-coat against the humid cold of November. Being so near to the Alps, the temperature in Munich could get rather chilly this time of year.

The driver was waiting for her in the huge reception hall of their mansion on the prestigious Königinstrasse. It was not far to Munich Central Station, nevertheless she preferred to leave early. Julius' mother had taught her that a lady never arrived late, except when she wanted to make a statement.

Since picking her brother up didn't warrant making a statement, she told the driver, "I'm ready to leave."

"Yes, *gnädige Frau.*" He held the door open for her.

Before stepping through, she turned and told the housekeeper to make sure the guest room was in impeccable order to receive her brother.

Joseph was four years her senior and she had been looking up to him ever since she could remember. He worked as a tram driver in Berlin, where her family lived. He might be rough around the edges, definitely not the kind of man whom the Falkensteins usually mingled with, but he possessed a good heart and always fought for what he believed was right.

That was the way their father, a schoolteacher, had brought up his four children: Joseph, Edith, Carsta and Knut, in order from oldest to youngest.

The driver rushed ahead of her to hold open the passenger door.

"To the train station, *gnädige Frau?*" he asked, no doubt having been alerted by the housekeeper about Edith's plans.

"Yes, please. My brother will arrive on the afternoon train from Berlin. It's his first visit here." She noticed a tad too much excitement in her voice.

"He will love it in Munich," the sturdy man, a born Bavarian, said with unconcealed pride at his city.

"I'm sure he will." While they drove down the Ludwigstrasse, passing the venerable University of Munich, the Bavarian State Library, and other iconic buildings, Edith observed the huge number of beggars lining the streets and murmured to herself, "People are suffering so much."

"Shall I stop and pull down the shades on your window?" the driver helpfully asked.

"No. No. It's just, the newspaper this morning said there are dozens of suicides every day by people who are at their wits' end."

The driver glanced at her, his face unreadable. "It's all the government's fault. They betrayed us by paying all these reparations after the war."

Julius had told her that, despite popular belief, this wasn't the real cause of the depressing economic situation. Edith, though, didn't feel inclined to start an argument with the driver, who obviously rehashed what he heard at the regulars' table in the beer hall.

During her first months in Munich, Julius had taken her to a beer hall on several occasions. She'd found that she disliked the bitter taste of beer as much as the raucous atmosphere, and had been relieved when he'd discouraged her to step into a beer hall, even in his company, after the state of the German nation lapsed into chaos.

When the automobile reached Munich Central Station, she told the driver to wait for her outside by the car, relishing a rare moment of privacy. It definitely had its perks to be surrounded by servants at all times, but it also came with the constant need to present a certain image of herself.

At the platform she ascertained the train was running late, yet she was reluctant to walk back. If the driver got concerned, he'd come inside and check up on her. Therefore she decided to settle in a café next to the platforms, admiring the majestic structure of the huge station hall. Here, she had a perfect view across the platforms while being sheltered from the wind.

A waitress came to her table in a rather tattered uniform. "I'm sorry, we don't have cake or sweet pies, just buns."

Edith wasn't here to eat anyway, since she would have dinner later at the welcome party. "Just a coffee, please."

She had taken a purse full of bills with her, and yet, it barely sufficed to pay for the cup of coffee. This interaction drove the point of the rampant inflation home, as she remembered the conversation with Julius this morning, complaining about the lack of actual bills. Just a week prior this amount of money would have been enough to buy a hat and gloves.

Sipping her coffee, she heard a long whistle announce the arrival of Joseph's train. She quickly emptied the cup and walked toward the platform, waiting for her brother at the head.

Masses of passengers disgorged from the wagons and passed her by, until she spotted him: a tall, blond man who towered over most of his compatriots by half a head.

He noticed her in the same moment, waved and sped up his steps. "Edith! Good to see you."

Mindful of her mother-in-law's disdain for showing emotions in public, Edith took a step backward to avoid Joseph's outstretched arms and shook his hand instead. "It's all my pleasure. How was the journey?"

"Awful. We sorely need a government that brings back law and order," Joseph answered.

Edith had no intention of engaging in a political discussion, since there would be enough of that later in the evening, so she asked, "Are you tired? Julius has insisted I organize a reception in your honor this evening."

Joseph rolled his eyes. "Never misses an opportunity to do business."

Giving her brother a scathing look, she said, "It is because of men like my husband that Germany hasn't completely shattered. He is working day and night to provide cash to the population."

"Well, he's a Jew after all, isn't he?"

"That's not true, he's a Protestant just like you and me," Edith protested. Julius had converted to Christianity on the day he turned twenty-one, much to the chagrin of his rather religious mother.

"It's the lineage that counts, and your husband comes from a long pedigree of Jews, so it's only natural that he would have the business running in his blood." Joseph glanced at his sister. "That is nothing bad in itself. Banks are desperately needed to keep the economy afloat, as you said yourself. And to answer your question: no, I'm not tired. You can take me out on the town."

Edith laughed. It was just like her brother to spend a sleepless night on a train and still want to venture out. Perhaps understandably, because it was his first visit to Munich and he'd only stay for a couple of days before he had to return home. "Julius has given me the use of the car and driver for the entire afternoon, so where do you want to go?"

"I'd like to get a taste of that famous Bavarian beer."

"Then we absolutely must visit the Hofbräuhaus." Julius and his acquaintances preferred to gather in the fancy hotels and bars, but she reckoned her brother would rather visit the down-to-earth place that proclaimed to brew the best beer in all of Bavaria, and offered the folk music to go with it. They walked to the automobile, where she advised the driver to take them to Platzl Square.

Minutes later, they stopped in front of a huge stone building in the very center of Munich's old town. In front stood a horse-drawn cart, loaded with ten wooden barrels.

Joseph jokingly said, "Hey, don't carry the beer away, I'm dying of thirst."

"There will be enough for you," Edith answered her brother and beckoned him to follow her inside. At this time of the day it was rather empty, so they had a choice of tables and opted for one in a corner of the impressive beer hall.

"This thing is huge!"

"It is indeed. The *Schwemme*, which is what they call the ground floor hall, where we are currently, can seat around thirteen-hundred guests."

"Impressive. You often come here?"

"Rarely. If we do then we use one of the rooms not open to the general public, like the ballroom or the coats of arms hall."

"Well, I much prefer to stay with the normal people," Joseph said. "Hitler does the same, he's a true leader, going where the people are, not hiding in some fancy hotel sipping champagne."

"Everyone seems to be talking about him." Edith was reminded of her conversation with Julius this morning.

"That's because he's up and coming; finally, a politician who actually cares about us normal folks. Did you know that he recently founded his own party, the National Socialist German Workers' Party? It already has fifty thousand members." Joseph puffed out his breast, leaving no doubt that he was one of the fifty thousand.

"Let's not talk about politics. Rather, tell me how is the family doing?" She yearned to hear about her parents and her other two siblings, Carsta and Knut.

Joseph complied. Like most non-Bavarians he wasn't used to drinking an entire liter—a mass—of beer. So, after the first one, the alcohol did its work and relaxed Joseph's tongue. "I like it here. I might be staying for a while in Munich."

"How so?"

"It's nothing official yet. Things are in the works," he answered evasively.

"A new job?" He had worked as a tram driver for the Berliner Strassenbahn until recently when, due to the bad economy and the prohibitive cost of electricity, the communal company had declared bankruptcy and let go all of its employees. While the successor, a privately owned company, had re-hired about half of them, with less pay for longer working hours, Joseph hadn't been among the lucky ones.

"Probably."

Since he didn't elaborate, she asked, "What about your family? Are they going to join you?"

"Not at the moment. Sandra has taken the children to live with her parents in the country until the situation in Berlin improves." Joseph pressed his jaw tight.

"I'm sorry. That must have been a difficult decision for the two of you, but I guess you need to do what is best for the children. I have heard so many awful stories about people starving in the big cities."

It was clearly not a topic Joseph wished to discuss, because he suddenly seemed to be very interested in the orchestra on stage. Edith bit on her lip, unsure whether she should push it or rather change the topic. Finally she settled on middle ground. "Perhaps Julius can help. You should have asked him right away."

Joseph's gaze returned to her. "I'd hate to depend on the charity of my brother-in-law. So I waited to visit until I have something to offer him as well." Edith was intrigued, hoping he'd elaborate. Unfortunately, her brother showed his unwillingness to offer more information by taking a big gulp from his second beer, and she knew better than to ask. Men didn't like to be quizzed about what they considered men's business.

Finally, he broke the silence, asking, "But tell me about you? Are you finally pregnant?"

Edith stiffened inside. That question was a sore spot for so many reasons. She hated everyone asking her what was taking so long and why she hadn't given Julius the heir he desired so much. Obviously everyone assumed it was her fault, that five years after their wedding she was still without child. What did they know about the horrible grief of losing two unborn children, coupled with Julius' increasingly distant behavior?

A decade ago, at the tender age of sixteen, she had met him, a man of the world, at a dance event, and had immediately been smitten. She had not believed how lucky she was that Julius Falkenstein had taken a liking to her.

Unfortunately, their courtship had been cut short by the outbreak of the war, when he'd joined the army as an officer to fight for his nation. Nevertheless their love had deepened throughout the years of separation and as soon as he returned in 1918, plans for a wedding were made. If only back then she'd known how lonely being Frau Julius Falkenstein would be.

"You'll be among the first ones to know."

"Ah, don't be sad, little sister. God gives children to all who deserve, and you are very deserving."

She hoped he was right. Having an infant to care for would finally give her life a reason.

2

After a refreshing nap Julius was ready to tackle work again. Since Edith had use of the driver, he opted to use the office in his home. It was less stressful than braving the angry crowds in front of the bank anyway. People were livid, and rightly so, just that they were directing their anger at the wrong institutions.

The government had ruined Germany with their asinine call for strikes in the Ruhr area after its occupation by France, following several late payments of the monthly reparations due.

Julius understood the reasoning behind the strike; the execution, though, was a master example of economic ignoramuses at work. What other explanation could there be for paying the striking workers out of government funds, hence bankrupting the entire country and leading them head first into the hyperinflation that had run rampant since June?

He sighed, picking up the telephone to call his father, whose advice he valued very much.

"Ferdinand Falkenstein," his father answered the phone.

"Good afternoon, Father."

"Julius, what a delight to hear from you."

Not bothering to exchange courtesies, Julius asked the question burning on his tongue. "Do you think the recently installed martial law in Bavaria will lead to a rupture with the rest of Germany?"

His father, a great connoisseur of politics and business, weighed his answer carefully. "I think it's mostly a power play. Your newly appointed state commissioner Gustav Ritter von Kahr may publicly show his disdain for the federal government, nevertheless he must know that Bavaria on its own will be much worse off than it is now."

"Worse off than now?" Julius scoffed. "I don't know what's happening in Berlin, here the bedlam is frightful."

"This is the problem of all democracies. The commoners are simply not educated enough to know what is good for the country, they tend to put their personal benefit over everything else. We need a strong ruler in Germany to reunite the states."

"So you think it'll all blow over?" Julius leaned back in his seat, taking a sip from the freshly brewed coffee.

"Yes, my son, I do. I have experienced more crises in my life than I care to remember. All have passed sooner or later. Those who are prepared will profit, the rest goes under. Never forget that we as business owners have a duty to serve not only the government, but also our citizens."

Julius listened only with half an ear to his father's sermon, which he'd heard many, many times before. A good business owner had to care for his family, his employees, his customers, and every one of his compatriots—in that order. Especially the employees, house servants as well as business staff were considered extended family and, like any good patriarch, the head of the Falkenstein bank had to look out for each one of them.

Sometimes what was best for the immediate family might clash with the interests of the employees, which then required great consideration to find a fair solution for everyone.

"Have you acted upon my advice?" his father asked.

"I did." This was such a situation, where possibly

conflicting interests had to be considered. Julius had concluded that while the Falkenstein bank might be suffering from the irresponsible actions of the government, his personal wealth should not. It wasn't done out of a sense of greed, but to stay in a position where he could provide emergency funds to people in need, if the bank went belly up and had to let go of all its employees.

"I bought several prime pieces of real estate, all credit financed as you suggested."

"Good boy. You just sit back and let the inflation do its work. I'm quite certain a currency reform is the only way out of this depression, then you have got it made. With a single stroke of the pen, all your debts will be gone. It'll empower you to do much good after a reorganization of the economy."

"A brilliant gambit. I'll own half of the Maximilianstrasse debt free if what you predict comes to pass. None of our current employees have to worry about starving, we have even extended our fund for war widows to include women whose husbands died in the past year," Julius said eminently satisfied.

"Don't keep much cash at hand," his father advised.

"I am buying up as many antiques and jewelry as I can." Julius chuckled. Edith would be over the moon about his generosity, since he intended to regale his wife with the most precious jewelry.

"How's Edith?" his father asked.

"She's fine. Her brother Joseph is arriving today, to stay with us for a few days."

"I've heard he has joined the NSDAP."

"Has he?" Julius hadn't known this piece of information and wondered whether Edith knew. Probably not, or she would have told him. For the time being the NSDAP was insignificant, but with Hitler as the leader, it had the potential to become more popular. Being related to a party member might turn out to be useful. He made a mental note to ask Joseph about his stance on the current situation in Germany.

His father ended the call after Julius promised to travel to Berlin for Christmas, which was only six weeks away. Working for the rest of the afternoon, he was about to go to his bedroom and get changed for the dinner party, when he heard the main door opening and shutting, followed by Edith's clicking heels on the parquet floor. He walked into the foyer to greet her and Joseph.

"Good afternoon, Julius," Edith said, immaculately dressed as always. Even after a decade had passed, he vividly recalled the day when he'd first met her. He'd attended the dance only thanks to the incessant pressure of his friends who thought he was working way too much.

As soon as he set eyes on Edith's lithe figure, her beautiful face framed by shoulder-length blonde waves, he'd decided that this beauty would become Mrs. Julius Falkenstein. Due to the war, their courtship had been interrupted, although his time away had—as strange as it sounded—intensified their relationship. Through letters they stayed in contact, bared their souls to each other, fell deeper in love with every passing day until five years later she'd finally become his wife.

It hadn't been all sunshine and roses, though. His mother had fervently opposed the marriage, because Edith came from a modest background. In his mother's opinion she wasn't appropriate to become a representative of the Falkenstein family.

Julius had never in his life acted against the explicit wishes of his mother and he doubted that he would have been able to go through with his proposition, if it hadn't been for Father taking his side. Ferdinand Falkenstein had instantly taken a shine to the stunningly beautiful, if frumpily dressed, Edith, and only thanks to his intervention had Julius been allowed to wed her.

Five years later even his mother acknowledged that she

couldn't have found a more suitable candidate to fill the role of Julius' wife: elegant, sweet, never outspoken. Edith always smiled, had a kind word for everyone, never publicly showed anger or sadness, and welcomed their frequent guests as if they were her dearest friends.

Edith truly was the perfect Frau Falkenstein. He loved her dearly, although the fire of passion had considerably dimmed after her miscarriages. He didn't know himself how and why it happened. The fact that she had yet to bear him the heir he desperately needed to carry on the family lineage, and one day take over the bank, obviously played a role, but there was a much deeper root. It sounded ridiculous even to his own ears, but he had somehow been afraid to get her pregnant again. She'd been so utterly destroyed by the miscarriages, he somehow resisted the notion of her possibly having to go through that one more time.

"Good afternoon, Edith and Joseph. How was your journey?"

"Awful. The railway is in a frightening condition." Joseph shook Julius' hand.

"I know, I know. There's not enough money to keep everything in good shape," Julius answered.

"If the two of you will excuse me, I have to supervise the preparations for tonight's dinner reception," Edith said.

Julius gave her a grateful nod, since she was perceptive enough to realize that he was eager to talk to Joseph in private before the guests arrived. Then he turned toward his brother-in-law. "Are you up to a cognac and cigar in my office?"

"How could I say no to that?"

They retreated to his office, next to the library room, with a splendid view across the rose garden. Since Julius didn't like to flaunt his riches, the office was decorated in a classically under-stated way with a few pieces of furniture of the best quality materials. Dark mahogany wood shelves hosted the many law and economics papers he kept at hand, providing a nice contrast to a white-stucco ceiling from the last century.

After buying the mansion just a few years ago, he'd employed the best handymen to renovate the old house up to modern standards without destroying its antique charm. He led Joseph to a coffee table in the corner, flanked by two cozy armchairs.

"What do you fancy?" He opened a cabinet and pointed at the several dozen bottles that wouldn't be out of place at a fancy bar in town.

"Cognac." The first time Julius had asked this question years ago, Joseph's answer had been, "Whatever schnapps you have."

"A good choice." Julius mustered the cabinet for several seconds until he selected a bottle of Courvoisier. The refined taste would be wasted on his tram-driving brother-in-law, but Julius still wanted to show his appreciation.

He poured two glasses and handed Joseph one of them. "Here you go. This was purportedly Napoleon's favorite cognac."

"I hope that's not the reason he's dead."

Julius forced himself to chuckle at the tasteless joke. On occasions like this one he was amazed how much Edith had achieved to become the impeccable woman she was today. Then he returned to the cabinet to select two fine Cuban cigars, and asked, "So, what is new in Berlin?"

"Not much. The country is going to hell in a handbasket. Thanks to the stab-in-the-back by the Bolshevists."

That purported fact was nothing more than a conspiracy theory made up by the German Army leaders to shirk their responsibility at losing the war. It wouldn't do any good to lecture Joseph, so Julius nodded sagely. "The Treaty of Versailles is breaking our neck."

Encouraged, Joseph launched into a monologue about the

vices of the victorious Allies and how they wanted to enslave the German population.

"We need a strong chancellor to end this once and for all." Julius offered Joseph a cigar, before he picked up the enamel Fabergé lighter to light it for him.

"Hitler is our man," Joseph said as he took the offered cigar.

Julius shook his head. "I don't see how. He's too hotheaded, has no political experience, no allies, and, most importantly, no backing in the population."

"The NSDAP recently passed fifty thousand members," Joseph proudly objected.

"You already joined, I reckon?" His father had just told him, but he wanted to hear it from his brother-in-law personally. It would be true to his character to jump at this new party, both an admirable and reprehensible trait. Julius himself much preferred to wait and see, but this sometimes meant he wasn't quick enough to reach a decision.

"Yes. Great things are coming." Joseph's face shone with eager excitement.

"No doubt. But Hitler has to stifle his rhetoric if he wants to be successful."

"And become another spineless politician stabbing our nation in the back?"

"There are quite a few nuances between being hotheaded and spineless." Julius gently drew the smoke into his mouth to absorb its flavor for several seconds before releasing it again.

Joseph, though, hastily inhaled it as if smoking a cigarette. Julius cringed at the sight: some things had to be done right or not done at all. Cigar smoking was one of them. Not a hasty pleasure, but a leisurely passing of time, absorbing the many tastes and smells a premium cigar had to offer.

"We need someone to take the reins!" Joseph exclaimed.

"I agree. We've had too many leaders in the past five years, unfortunately none lived up to the name. Although I think

Gustav von Kahr, the new Bavarian state commissioner, is willing and able to clear up the mess here that the red socialists in Berlin have created."

"He and Hitler would make great allies. Von Kahr reigns Bavaria, Hitler the rest of Germany," Joseph said, a bit too confidently.

"Is there anything I should know about?" Julius furrowed his brows, scrutinizing the other man.

Joseph's lip twitched for a split second, before he shook his head. "No. Just my two cents. Don't know nothing about the private thoughts of those two."

Julius keenly observed him, almost certain Joseph was withholding information. Whatever it was, he hoped Joseph wouldn't rush headlong into some lunatic endeavor, for his sake, but also for Edith's. She adored her eldest brother and would be heartbroken if he got himself into serious trouble.

In the improbable case, though, that von Kahr and Hitler did form an alliance, it might prove beneficial if Joseph occupied an official position in the NSDAP.

He took another slow drag on his cigar, letting the smoke settle against his palate, savoring the rich aromas of leather, fresh ground coffee and almonds, before deliberately exhaling the smoke through his nose to appreciate the full range of different smells. Apart from the enjoyment, it bought him time to think. Perhaps that was the true reason why great men engaged in cigar smoking: to give their hectic lives pauses to ponder. Not a coincidence that great statesmen like Napoleon Bonaparte, Catherine the Great or Otto von Bismarck had been cigar lovers.

"We will see what happens. It's the Berlin government's move now." Julius referred to the untenable situation that Gustav von Kahr had created by disobeying a direct order of the German defense minister, and subsequently putting the national Reichswehr units stationed in Bavaria under his command. This action constituted nothing less than treason.

As far as Julius was concerned there were only two outcomes to this calamity: either the national government marched into Bavaria, claiming back their power by force, or Bavaria seceded. Whatever happened, he had taken precautions to come out on top either way. Prepared people always floated to the top. As his father liked to remind him, the well-being of thousands of people depended on the Falkenstein bank, so failing was not an option he could consider in good faith.

He checked his golden pocket watch and added, "We better freshen up. Dinner will be served in an hour."

Then he rang the bell and moments later the maid entered his office. "How may I serve you, Herr Falkenstein?"

"Please show Herr Hesse to his quarters. I reckon his suitcase is already there?"

"Yes." She curtsied. "Frau Falkenstein advised me to unpack and iron his suits."

"Good. I'll see you later," Julius said to his brother-in-law. As he watched him follow the maid, he had an unsettling feeling in his stomach, although he couldn't say why.

In the evening, the guests arrived. Edith had once again outdone herself and organized an event that was perfect in every aspect. Julius proudly acknowledged how his business partners and local politicians admired the beautiful salon and the dining room that was decked out with finest china and silverware. He squeezed Edith's hand in a short moment of privacy and whispered into her ear, "Such a wonderful party you organized, darling."

Following supper, the men congregated in Julius' office to drink spirits and smoke cigars. Inevitably the discussion turned to politics after a while. Not everyone was pleased with recent

developments. Those with a wider perspective feared an imminent secession of Bavaria from the rest of Germany, which
would put a serious damper on their businesses and possibly
bring bedlam over the state.

"Nothing to fear!" Joseph exclaimed after several glasses of
brandy. "Once we have a new national government, things will
improve greatly."

"Well, this is the first time I've heard about a new government in Berlin," the owner of one of the big breweries said.

"It's because Munich is so far away. In the capital people
talk about nothing else," Joseph responded, bigmouth that
he was.

Julius observed him, swirling the aromatic brown liquid in
the brandy balloon with his right hand. He sensed that Joseph
knew something the others did not. But what? He hoped it
wasn't to do with any foolish action. Perhaps it was time to take
a stance, clarifying that Julius Falkenstein did not condone
disloyal behavior toward either the German or the Bavarian
government.

Since the police president was present, making his position
known was all the more important, so he said, "Personally, I
support everything our government decides, although in this
very moment my most fervent wish is that the ruling men in
Munich and Berlin could align their views for the best of our
country."

"Very wise words," the police president stated, not letting
on which way he favored.

The conversation turned away from sensitive topics and
settled on the tried and trusted: business. At least there they
had a common enemy in inflation. For once everyone, including
Joseph, agreed that the cause of hyperinflation was the Treaty
of Versailles, along with the scandalous exploitation of German
industries by the victors of the war.

After all the guests had left, Julius asked Joseph, "So you

really think Herr Hitler will be able to solve our country's problems?"

"Yes! He has so many great ideas. Under his lead, the country will flourish—with Bavaria as one of the strongest states by his side."

"What makes you think that von Kahr will support him?"

"The two men think alike. Hasn't von Kahr shown that he's had enough of the weak socialist rulers in Berlin?"

"I guess we will find out when the time comes. Although I sincerely doubt that Herr Hitler will garner many votes in the next elections. His views are too extreme." Julius saw the attraction that Hitler posed for so many floundering people looking for a savior to lift them out of their misery, yet at the same time he didn't believe that many citizens were willing to vote for a party that openly purported violence.

"Nah. What he proposes is exactly what's needed to whip the country back into shape."

"He's spewing plenty of hateful rhetoric, especially about Jews. Decent people won't like that," Julius opposed.

"That's just talk." Joseph leaned against the table. "See, there's Jews and Jews. Everyone knows that immigrants from the east cause plenty of problems. They are poor, backward, and don't speak our language. They come here to steal our jobs, exploit the welfare of the state and who knows, most of them might be criminals anyway. They are the ones we need to get rid of, not assimilated Jews like you."

"I'm not Jewish," Julius responded. "I converted to Protestantism the day I came of age, and have been a baptized Christian ever since. You were at Edith's and my wedding, the Bishop of Berlin married us."

"See? That's what I'm talking about. You and your family are assimilated, you don't pose a threat to our nation."

Julius gave a short laugh. "I surely don't. I'm the bearer of an Iron Cross, awarded for bravery during the Great War."

"Germany needs valiant men like you. Hitler knows that. When he talks about the damaging Jews, he means the immigrants from the east."

Julius could see that Joseph was incapable of taking his point. "I guess you're right."

"We should call it a night," Joseph said. "It has been a long day."

"Good night." Julius finished smoking his cigar, looking through the window into the darkness until he had convinced himself that there was nothing to worry about.

Whoever was ruling the country needed hard-working honest businessmen on his side. Julius had worked hard to have the reputation and the connections to be in demand with the government. Whether Bavaria decided to secede or not, it wouldn't affect his livelihood, or those of his employees. It might even benefit him, if the new leader managed to get this raging inflation under control.

3

"I'll be going to a beer hall, don't wait up for me," Joseph called out the following evening.

"Are you sure? It can get a bit rough there at night."

He laughed at Edith. "Don't worry about me, I can take care of myself." Then he took his hat and marched off to the *Bürgerbräukeller*, where Gustav von Kahr was going to have a rally. If his sister knew where he was going and why, she'd move heaven and earth to keep him home.

Joseph had been playing it safe for much too long already, along with the rest of the country. And where had it taken them? Right into the abyss.

Hard-working people like himself had been out of a job for much too long, and lately it seemed that the entire country consisted of nothing but ragged beggars. The ones to blame for such misery sat in Berlin, appeasing the victors from the Great War and catering to their every wish.

It was high time to take back the reins to lead Germany into a bright future with a prosperous, flourishing people's community. And Adolf Hitler just happened to have the plan of how to do it.

Joseph increased his pace, not wanting to miss the moment when history was made. After a brisk half-hour march he reached the agreed meeting point, where he got to shake the hand of his revered idol.

He'd seen him before, even talked to him, but every time Joseph was overpowered by the sheer amount of energy the charismatic man exuded. Today was no different: Adolf Hitler was surrounded by a dozen devout followers as he outlined the plan.

"I have been invited to a meeting in the *Bürgerbräukeller* together with von Kahr, Generalmajor von Lossow the commander of the Reichswehr in Bavaria, Hans von Seisser the head of the Bavarian State Police and a few ministers. Passes for each one of you have been arranged, not to the actual meeting itself, but to the beer hall, where we'll later convene and announce the overthrowing of the current government."

Herr Hitler's announcement left Joseph in awe. There was no wavering, no doubt, no vacillation in his voice. That man was absolutely sure of himself and of his divine mission to rescue Germany from the clutches of the ailments brought upon her by a corrupt government.

"Hermann Göring has his two thousand SA troops surrounding the area as we speak. They will be securing the venue against intruders from the outside."

By intruders Hitler of course meant rogue policemen or possibly the Bavarian army—a negligible threat, since both the commander of the Reichswehr and the head of police would be trapped inside the venue. Hitler fully expected them to cooperate in overthrowing the Berlin government because von Kahr had already broken with Berlin over fighting in the Ruhr area.

Generous as Hitler was, he had provided important positions in the new government, under his leadership, for all three men whose hands he planned to force.

It was a brilliant idea: nudge them to do the right thing,

aided by a threat as a last resort, and then extend a hand and give them seats in the new cabinet. Who would be able to refuse? No man who had the best interest of the country at heart.

On Hitler's command, the small group was set in motion and made to enter the huge beer hall. Hitler himself was whisked away to a room upstairs. Alongside the others, Joseph entered the main hall, taking up seats at several tables in the back, next to the exit so they could prevent people from leaving if necessary. The main hall filled up quickly with folk who'd come to hear von Kahr talk later in the evening.

A nervous giddiness took hold of Joseph, and he said to a fellow called Heinz: "Not long now and we're going to witness how history is made."

Heinz was a butcher by profession, a burly man who could swallow down a liter of beer in a single gulp. "Giving the socialists in Berlin what they deserve."

"Running for cover when we come for them, that's what those cowards will do," chimed in Edgar, a policeman.

"This is our single chance to save the country. If this doesn't work..." Joseph said.

"Getting cold feet?" Heinz asked.

"Not at all." For several minutes they kept quiet, because the waitress arrived with another round of beer. Joseph found it difficult to keep up with the drinking pace of his comrades, since he wasn't used to the humongous Bavarian mugs holding an entire liter.

"No reason to worry." It was Edgar talking after the waitress had left. "Herr Hitler is confident that Herr von Kahr will join the coup. Before you know it, we're marching toward Berlin."

Marching wasn't exactly possible; Munich to Berlin was a distance of six hundred kilometers. But who cared about details when history was made? Not Joseph, and certainly not his less intellectual comrades.

"Shush, they are coming!" someone called out, and the crowd fell silent.

Joseph looked at the exit doors that had been closed several minutes ago. Meanwhile Hermann Göring and his SA must have cordoned off the entire area around the beer hall. They wouldn't let anyone escape. The job of Joseph's group inside the venue was to escort the triumvirate to a side chamber when Hitler gave the order to do so.

Anxiety prickled his skin and he reassured himself by casting side glances at the roughnecked Heinz and the experienced policeman, Edgar. A few minutes into Gustav von Kahr's speech, Hitler appeared on the stage where—to the surprise of everyone, including Joseph—he pulled out a pistol and fired into the air.

Instantly the audience of several hundred people froze in fear, giving Hitler the opportunity for his big entry.

"Esteemed gentlemen, this is a coup. Please stay calm and don't try to escape. The venue is surrounded by SA troops. I do not wish to harm anyone who is fighting for the good of Germany, so please don't force my hand."

That was the cue. Joseph and his comrades jumped up, drew their weapons and urged von Kahr, Lossow and Seisser to precede them into an adjoining room.

There, it didn't take long until Hitler persuaded the three of them to join his patriotic cause to defend the nation, by upending the socialist government in Berlin that had brought nothing but grief to Germany.

Everything went smoothly. Joseph felt a burden fall from his shoulders, as this was the crucial point in the action. If the triumvirate hadn't joined Hitler's cause voluntarily, albeit with a little nudge of the pistols pointed at them, it would have become almost impossible to accomplish the coup.

Now, he inwardly sighed with relief. The task was done.

Germany was on its way to a bright future! And he would be an important part of it.

The four politicians, plus the hastily fetched Erich Ludendorff, the designated head of the National Army, returned to the main hall, where the audience gave a joint sigh of relief at seeing their leaders unharmed and ready to participate in something ominous.

Hitler announced that the Bavarian cabinet under Eugen von Knilling had been dissolved and designated Gustav von Kahr as the new administrator. Then he proceeded to have all ministers present arrested.

It was going on midnight and Joseph's work was done here, yet he was hesitant to leave. Such was the euphoria running through his veins that he didn't feel tired in the slightest.

Hitler outlined the new strategy, the new positions, and, most importantly, the fight against Berlin. Each of the triumvirate made their own statement, von Kahr being the first one to raise his voice:

"In the Fatherland's greatest need, I am taking charge of the affairs of state as governor of the monarchy that was so shamefully crushed five years ago today. I do this with a heavy heart and, I hope, for the blessing of our Bavarian homeland and our dear German Fatherland."

Von Lossow and von Seisser made similar declarations, though Joseph couldn't shake the impression that their words were less enthusiastic and more the result of an effort to get out of the situation. He didn't care. They'd come around in time when they saw how beneficial the new order was.

"Nice and clean," he said to Heinz.

"Sure." The man nodded, taking another huge gulp from his beer mug. "What did you expect? Whatever Herr Hitler says will be done. Did you doubt him?"

"Of course not," Joseph hurried to emphasize. For a simple-minded man like the butcher, things were either black or white.

It was decided that the three newly acquired allies didn't need to be retained any longer, and they were given permission to leave the venue.

Joseph had a bad gut feeling as the men exited the beer hall, but who was he to decide? Apparently they were to go to the barracks of the 19th Infantry regiment in Oberwiesenfeld, a borough in the north of Munich.

Without further orders, Joseph and his comrades stayed at the *Bürgerbräukeller*, ordering food and another beer. He vacillated between returning to Edith's home and telling her about the wonderful happenings of the evening or waiting until she heard it on the radio, and then march into her mansion like the victor he was. He would decide later. For now he dug his teeth into the crispy pork knuckle on his plate.

"Good stuff," Heinz, the butcher, acknowledged.

"And the sauerkraut! Not even my mother's can compare," Edgar added.

Joseph laughed good-naturedly. "Don't tell her."

About an hour later he was ready to leave, just as someone rushed into the beer hall, shouting: "They have betrayed us!"

"Who? What? How?" many voices shouted at once, until a visibly distressed aide to Hitler climbed on the stage and took the microphone.

"The devious bastards have turned their back on our cause. This is the message they just announced over all radio stations: 'State Commissioner General von Kahr, General von Lossow and Colonel von Seisser reject the Hitler coup. The statement extorted by force of arms in the *Bürgerbräuhaus* is invalid. Caution is advised against misuse of above names.'"

A miserable howl broke out among the audience, interrupted by a few sighs of relief. Up on the stage Ludendorff and Hitler conferred about the best course of action.

"We should take up our arms and storm the government," Heinz shouted.

Edgar pensively furrowed his brows, before he said, "Röhm has occupied the military district headquarters in the Ludwigstrasse. If we march there and join forces with them, we will have a real chance of overthrowing the government."

"So what are we waiting for?" Heinz seemed ready to up and run at that very instant.

"We need to wait for orders," Joseph hedged.

"They better not be cowards," Heinz grumbled.

Several minutes later Ludendorff stepped on the stage and proclaimed, "We're not defeated yet. We are working on a new plan. Therefore I suggest you get an eyeful of sleep before the next action. Effective immediately, the *Bürgerbräukeller* is our headquarters."

The loyal supporters sighed with relief. Some went to sleep on the floor while others simply dropped their foreheads onto the table. Joseph entertained the idea of returning to Edith's mansion and coming back in the morning, but discarded the idea, for fear of missing out on the action.

His sister would be worried to death when he wasn't there at breakfast, but he really couldn't be considerate of her feelings during such an important event. She'd understand once he came home victorious.

Early the next morning, finally, an order came for everyone to assemble outside for a march to the Ludwigstrasse.

Joseph smiled. From there it was a puddle jump to Edith's house. Perhaps she'd even come to watch, drawn out by the noise. In any case, he could go home from there for a nice bath and fresh clothes.

The members of the SA who had secured the building were already assembled outside. Together they were roughly two thousand, mostly armed, putschists, whipped up to take by force what wasn't given by free will.

For a second, Joseph felt a twinge of guilt, which he brushed away. The German people were behind them, it was just the government clinging to its power who didn't approve of the coup.

The march along the Rosenheimerstrasse, crossing the Isar river and onward to Isartorplatz and Tal toward the main square at Marienplatz was a thrilling experience, unlike any other he'd made before.

With Heinz and Edgar by his side he marched to the rhythm of battle songs, singing at the top of his lungs. He didn't even feel the tiredness of too little sleep combined with too much beer, such was the energy of two thousand men marching for a common goal.

With every step, the importance of his actions trickled deeper into his bones, and the pride he felt at serving the head of the NSDAP, to realize the dream of a better Germany—it was close to none.

"This is the beginning of something truly magnificent," Joseph said.

"Nothing and nobody can stop us," Edgar answered. "Just look at all the men, ready to give their everything."

"It's truly phenomenal." Joseph inhaled deeply, wanting to feel the significance deep inside.

"No need to use fancy words," Heinz teased him. "Here in Bavaria we say, *pfundig.*"

"Well, *pfundig,* if you insist." Joseph marched onward, passing the Marienplatz with its neo-Gothic town hall. Just when they reached the iconic glockenspiel, the church bell chimed eleven. The famous clockwork sounded its melody and the figurines began to dance.

"If that ain't a good omen." Edgar didn't falter in his step as he risked a glance upward. "The *Münchner Kindl* itself is blessing our plan." The Munich Child was the name of the small figure in the coat of arms, wearing a black pointed hood, holding a beer mug and a radish in its hands, blessing the city of Munich.

The atmosphere among the protesters became more heated, as they turned around the corner onto the Weinstrasse and finally the Theatinerstrasse. From here on, Joseph could already surmise their target was at the end of the long straight road leading north.

Confidence about a victorious finale coursing through his veins, he was completely unprepared when he spotted Bavarian policemen waiting for the protesters in front of the Feldherren-halle on Odeonsplatz.

"What the hell...?" he exclaimed, only seconds before the first shot sounded. More shots ensued, sending the crowd scattering in search for cover. It was absolute mayhem, and panic struck Joseph, who had never been in a shoot-out before.

He was about to run as headlessly as most of his comrades, when he heard Edgar's firm voice over the turmoil. "Duck down and stay with me!"

The decisive command cleared away Joseph's vacillation. He edged closer to Edgar, looking up to the veteran policeman, who seemed completely unfazed by the utter chaos and calmly drew his pistol.

To his other side, Heinz produced a giant butcher's knife from God only knew where, waving it in the air like a sword. Coming ill-prepared, Joseph's sole weapons were his fists, so he followed his two comrades a step behind, until they ran straight into a group of policemen.

Blind to anything that was going on left and right, he punched the nearest officer on the nose, already rejoicing at the satisfying sound of cracking bone and the sight of blood splashing. The next moment, though, a violent kick to Joseph's private parts left him reeling with pain. Barely able to breathe, he folded like a pocket knife, black and red dots dancing in front of his eyes.

The noise around him was deafening, yet it was drowned out by the rushing blood in his ears. Doubled over, he felt the crowd billowing like waves in the sea. He caught his breath, noticing the stench of gunpowder—and fear. Somehow he managed to straighten up, just when another shot pierced his ear.

Next to him, Heinz dropped to the ground like a felled tree. Joseph threw himself to his knees, staring horrified at the blood-streamed face of the butcher. The bullet had shattered the left half of his face, leaving a gaping wound where an eye had been.

A brutal retch shook Joseph's body. He couldn't stop the bile rising in his throat and vomited the contents of his stomach right next to his comrade's head.

"He's dead," someone said. That same someone—who turned out to be a policeman—then ordered Joseph, "Get up real slow with your hands above your head."

The foul taste of vomit lingering in his mouth, Joseph obeyed the command and slowly scrambled to his feet. Chancing side glances around the battle scene, he realized the police were quickly gaining the upper hand and most of his co-fighters shared his dire situation. Only Edgar had vanished from sight.

4

Helga Goldmann fed her one-year-old daughter, Amelie, with a thin porridge. Ever since her husband Heinrich, an accountant, had been let go from his company three months ago, they had barely managed to scrape by.

Heinrich spent his mornings in front of the labor office, and his afternoons walking from pillar to post, asking every business he came across for work.

But each night he came home with a more forlorn expression on his face, his shoulders slumping lower as the weeks passed, with no end to their ordeal in sight. It tore her heart apart to see her beloved husband suffering, because he couldn't provide for his family the way he used to.

It wasn't that he didn't put in enough effort or that he had no references, indeed his former employer had given him a stellar one before the company was forced out of business.

But the only jobs going these days were for workers to lug around heavy sacks. Heinrich wasn't above doing such menial jobs if it meant feeding his family, but as soon as a prospective employer examined her fine-limbed husband, his delicate fingers, the finely chiseled face framed by dark-brown short hair, coiffed into a fashionable wave across his forehead, they discarded him with a wave of their hand. The employers required burly, strong men who were used to blue-collar work.

Their savings had been used up to the last penny weeks ago. If it weren't for the odd seamstress job Helga was taking on in exchange for food, their baby daughter and four-year-old son David would have starved already.

Sadly enough, little David had—against her explicit orders —become the main breadwinner of the family. She'd caught him once sneaking out and performing little tricks in front of the restaurants for the rich, who threw him leftovers from their plates in exchange.

She'd hauled him back to their apartment, about to die of shame, even as he stood in front of her, proffering food in his outstretched hands, not understanding why she was angry at him.

But her loudly growling stomach, and Amelie's whimpering, had caused her to turn a blind eye the next time David snuck out of the apartment building and returned hours later with bread, cheese and an apple in his pockets.

It was a harrowing situation, when the world had turned upside down and her little boy felt the need to provide for his family, instead of staying home and playing with his building blocks.

After being fed the last spoonful of porridge, Amelie looked at her mother with expectant eyes.

"Sorry, sweetie, but that's it," Helga said, her heart breaking a bit more when the toddler instantly started crying, her scream increasing to a banshee-like howl, shaking the walls of the apartment, which was in a huge building in a nice middle-class borough of Berlin.

Just when Helga feared the windowpanes might shatter, the doorbell rang and Amelie stopped crying. Helga sat her on the floor and ran after David who had already raced to the door, going on his tiptoes to press down the handle.

"David, how many times have I told you not to open the door!" she scolded him.

"It's me," a female voice came from the other side and, moments later, Helga's sister Felicitas pushed through the door, hugging first David and then Helga.

"What a nice surprise. What brings you here?" Helga loved her sister dearly, and always welcomed her visits.

Felicitas, four years older than Helga, had married Ernst Ritter, a scrawny, brooding man twenty years her senior. He was the Mayor of Oranienburg, a city about twenty miles north of Berlin, where the two of them lived in a beautiful mansion.

"I had some errands to run at Kurfürstendamm and thought I'd stop by to visit my favorite sister," Felicitas greeted her with an ebullient smile.

"I'm your only sister," Helga countered.

"One more reason to visit you." Felicitas held out a huge basket. "I brought something for the children."

"Thank you so much," Helga said, as she eagerly took the basket and peeked inside. It was filled to the brim with flour, potatoes, milk, cheese and even two chocolate bars. Barely able to keep her tears of emotion at bay, she escaped to the kitchen.

Eying her sister's provisions, she felt like a child on Christmas Eve. It truly was a gift from heaven, since the contents of the basket would easily put food on the table for an entire week. After furtively wiping her misty eyes, she returned to the hallway, where Felicitas was taking off her coat. "How can I ever thank you?"

"No thanks needed. We're family and we need to stick together. By the way, my gift is not entirely unselfish. I want to play with my nephew and niece, and how could I do that if they're preoccupied with hunger?"

Helga cast a grateful gaze at her sister, who made light of

the situation. She probably had no idea how dire the situation actually was. Without her visit, there wouldn't have been supper that night.

Hearing the word "play" David dashed off to get the newest addition to his collection of sticks and rocks to present it to his aunt. "Aunt Feli. Look!" He proudly showed her a rounded pebble shimmering greenish-gray.

"That is truly beautiful. Where did you get it?" Felicitas asked him.

"Down at the pond. I walked in. Like this." He pulled his trousers up to the knees and pretended to wade into water. "And there it was. It's very precious. Don't you think?"

Felicitas put a crease into her forehead as if thinking hard. "I believe you are right. It really is a precious stone. Would you sell it to me?"

David shook his head earnestly. "No. You're my auntie, I'll give it to you for free."

"That is so nice of you." Felicitas made a show of admiring the pebble before she pushed it into her handbag and then said, "Look, what I found in here. Will you accept this as my thanks for your generous gift?"

David's eyes became wide as saucers when he recognized the lollipop in her hand. Nodding with delight, he said, "Yes. Yes."

A surge of warmth passed through Helga's body. Sweets had become such a rare treat for David, who went to bed hungry more often than she wanted to admit even to herself.

By now Amelie had crawled from the kitchen into the hallway and squealed with delight when she recognized her aunt. "Feli! Feli!"

"You've grown so much, Amelie." Felicitas bent down to pick up her niece and cuddled her tight.

"Shall I make coffee?" Helga asked. She had a stash of

coffee beans hidden away exclusively for the occasions her sister visited, who loved coffee so much.

"Yes, please."

Helga left her sister with the two children and walked into the kitchen once more to make coffee and unpack the basket. Only when she had emptied the contents onto the kitchen counter did she truly realize how much it was. Her sister's help was a godsend.

Waiting for the water to boil she remembered how much her parents had opposed Felicitas' choice of man. Ernst Ritter was not only twenty years her senior, but also a very withdrawn and strict man, the complete opposite of her ebullient sister, who was full of a zest for life.

They'd been much more pleased with Helga's choice and dearly loved Heinrich, her high-school sweetheart who'd gone on to become an educated accountant with impeccable manners and an endearing appearance.

Fate, though, seemed to have a different opinion. While Helga and Heinrich struggled, Ernst and Felicitas thrived. Since they weren't blessed with children of their own, Felicitas was godmother to David and Amelie. She took her responsibility seriously, visiting frequently and helping out where she could, especially since Heinrich had lost his job to join the army of millions of jobless men throughout the country.

The whistle of the water kettle distracted Helga from her pondering. She brewed the coffee, pouring it into two cups, cutting small pieces from the loaf of bread Felicitas had brought to serve it together.

"Here you go," Helga said as she entered the living room, where David was explaining something to his aunt, who had Amelie sitting on her lap.

"Oh, thank you. I really needed a cuppa." After taking a few sips Felicitas put down the coffee and took a tiny bite from her bread, before she divided the rest into halves and gave them to the children. "Has Heinrich found a job yet?"

Helga's face fell. "No. He walks the streets from morning till night, but nothing. I've been taking on needlework to keep us afloat."

"It's such a shame, since Heinrich is a wonderful man." Felicitas jokingly added, "If you hadn't snatched him away, I might have married him myself."

"You were already engaged to Ernst back then," Helga reminded her.

"I know. I would never leave Ernst, he takes such good care of me, but I did have a slight crush on Heinrich when we were still at school," Felicitas admitted.

"It was very obvious." Helga had known it all along, although this was the first time her sister had admitted it. She'd never once felt a twinge of jealousy, because she knew that Heinrich loved her with all his heart—and only her. The same way she loved him with every cell of her body and would never so much as look at another man. From the first day he'd asked her out to the moving pictures neither of them had desired another person in their lives. If it weren't for these harsh economic realities, they would be the happiest couple under the sun.

"I nudged Ernst to put out his feelers. There might be an opportunity for an accountant, but it's in Neuruppin." That was a town about sixty miles northwest of Berlin, which meant Heinrich wouldn't be able to sleep at home during the week.

Despite the distance, Helga didn't hesitate for a second. "He'll take any job he can get, even if it means he'll have to find a boarding room over there."

"That shouldn't be a problem, as long as he brings his own bedding. The town hall has several extra rooms."

"Shall I have Heinrich call you tonight for details?" Helga

hated the idea of seeing her husband only on the weekends, but any job was better than their current situation.

"It's not official yet. Let me talk to Ernst first, he might want to be the one to inform Heinrich." Felicitas emptied her coffee cup and said, "I'm so sorry, I need to get going or I won't make it back home in time. You know how Ernst is, he hates it when I'm late."

"I certainly do." Helga smiled at her sister, remembering the first years of Felicitas' marriage, when Ernst's controlling ways had been a constant grief, until Felicitas had learned to adapt to his demands.

They hugged each other goodbye, then Helga left the children to play while she returned to the kitchen to prepare a decent dinner for the first time in weeks.

When Heinrich came home, he walked straight into the kitchen to greet her with a kiss. His eyes became big when he noticed the amount of food on the stove. Sniffing into the air, he said, "Hmm, that smells delicious. Did you rob a bank?"

Helga broke out into a giggle. "I was tempted, but thanks to Felicitas I didn't have to resort to such drastic measures. She visited this afternoon with a basket full of groceries."

"How can we ever thank your sister for all she's doing for us?"

"We're family, we'd do the same for her."

"That much is true. Can I help you with something?"

Helga shook her head. "No, you go and keep the children occupied, I'm almost done here." Since she could barely wait to see his face when she told him about the possibility of work for him, she couldn't resist the temptation to tease him. "I have more good news."

"More food? Dessert, maybe?" He swept his eyes across her person, leaving it open what kind of dessert he had in mind.

Despite having been married for such a long time, she felt

tingles racing down her skin. "You'll have to wait until after dinner to find out."

"So long?" His face was a mock grimace of indignation. "I could die of the tension."

She swatted him with the kitchen towel and uttered the same words he always used when taunting her with a surprise. "Anticipation is half the pleasure."

"Oh, you utterly cruel wife!"

After the children were asleep, she and Heinrich settled on the sofa in the living room, a beloved nightly custom. Before the depression had hit the country, they'd cuddle and talk over a glass of wine, but these days an infusion had to suffice.

Leaning against her husband, Helga said, "Feli has mentioned a job opening with one of Ernst's colleagues. She'll ask Ernst to recommend you if you want."

His face lit up with hope. "That would be wonderful." Then it fell, as he seemed to work through the implications. "Oranienburg is such a long commute, I would arrive home way after the children are asleep."

"It's not..." A lump in her throat impeded her from finishing her sentence.

"Yes, it is. And they are running less services than they used to."

"I meant to say, it's not in Oranienburg."

She must have made a miserable face, because he frowned. "Then... where exactly is the job offer?"

"In Neuruppin," she spat out.

Heinrich stayed silent for a while, his accountant brain calculating the distance and the needed travel time. Then he took a sip from his infusion, before he said, "It's impossible to commute."

She gave a wretched nod. "Feli said they have spare rooms in the town hall that you could rent cheaply."

After a long silence Heinrich said, "It won't have to be forever. Just until I find something else."

"I know. And it's not a sure thing. You first have to pass the job interview." She half hoped he would fail and not be employed.

"Are you insinuating that I'm not going to impress them with my spectacular accounting expertise?"

Giggling, she leaned into him. "I would never."

"I love you, sweetheart. Admittedly, it's not ideal, but right now any job is better than none. And..." he continued, taking her hands into his, "see it in a positive light: you'll miss me so much the entire week, that our weekends together will be ever more passionate."

She couldn't help but laugh. "Well, if you put it that way, I might just take a shine to your absence."

Now it was his time to laugh. "What if we take this conversation into our bedroom instead?"

Helga nodded. She couldn't have wished for a better husband, companion, friend, and father to her children. Heinrich was like her second half; in his presence she felt whole and happy, no matter the circumstances.

5

Edith had been sitting on pins and needles since dawn because Joseph had yet to arrive home.

"Do you think something happened to him?" she asked her husband over breakfast.

"He probably got drunk and is sleeping it off." Julius looked impeccable as always in his three-piece tweed suit, complete with a white shirt and a subdued beige tie with dark-brown rhombuses.

"It's too cold outside, he'll have frozen to death."

Julius looked up from his newspaper, giving her an austere look over his spectacles. "I bet he's nice and warm in the arms of a woman."

"How can you say that? He's a married man."

"To a wife who's fled his house to live with her parents. Don't you think he deserves a bit of joy?" Julius emptied his coffee cup and waved his hand to let the servant know he wanted a refill. "Sandra doesn't seem to have remembered her vows: In good times and bad. The very moment hardship hits them, she's running away. What kind of woman is that?"

Edith knew how traditional Julius was and that he believed a wife had to obey, serve and dote on her husband, catering to his every wish. It was a characteristic she'd come to dislike in him over the years. In the beginning of their marriage, it had been convenient, comforting even, to have him make all decisions, especially because she had been so much out of her depth being the new Frau Falkenstein.

He meant well, too, since he always considered her best interests along with his, the family's and the bank's. But the more she'd grown into her new role, the more she wished he'd at least ask for her opinion once in a while. For example, about their move to Munich. He'd planned it as a surprise for her, no doubt expecting her to be elated to get away from the—sometimes oppressive—presence of his mother.

Which she was, really. But she would have been so much happier if he'd involved her in his decision-making, asking for her opinion about the mansion, or the new servants he employed.

She gave a sigh. True to his conservative upbringing, he'd relegated her to reigning over the house: interior decoration, managing the staff, planning and organizing events. It was something she immensely enjoyed, and Julius often complimented her for her talent. Just... she felt she wanted more from their marriage.

Although there was no reason to think she was right in her aspirations. Her own mother had no say in any decisions outside the house, not even about the education of her children. And neither had Frau Falkenstein senior. Worse, she set an example of putting duty first and living a life without passion. Edith had never once seen her express an emotion or caress her husband and children. Even in the presence of her newborn grandchildren she didn't let herself get carried away to more than a measured stroke over their heads.

Edith shook her head. She still loved her husband, but being trapped inside a golden cage was getting to her, especially because she still hadn't been able to birth the heir he desired so much. With a child to care for, she would no longer suffer from loneliness and boredom.

Julius had not waited for an answer to his rhetorical question and continued to study the newspaper, until he exclaimed, "Can you believe this? There was an attempted coup last night!"

"A coup? Against our government?" Edith couldn't fathom what he was saying.

"So it seems. The article is inconclusive, but, apparently, Herr Hitler and Herr Ludendorff coerced the Generals von Kahr, Lossow and Seisser to join forces with them and depose the Bavarian government, planning to march jointly to Berlin to disempower the socialists there."

"How can they even do that?" Edith whispered.

"A pistol held to your forehead is very convincing."

"Did these men really hold our politicians at gunpoint?"

"So it seems." Julius seemed not overly shocked at this news. "Never in my life would I have believed Hitler would commit such a bold crime. I always pegged him for much talk, little action."

"What will happen now?" Panic rose in Edith's chest, making her breathing labored. They were probably safe in the confines of their mansion with the gardens and the huge wall around it, but Joseph...

"It seems the triumvirate retracted on their agreement at the first opportunity and sent a warning message to all radio stations throughout the nation. So, the coup fell flat."

"Thank God." Edith leaned back in her chair, grasping her cup of coffee like a lifebelt. A violent coup, in her own city. She didn't even want to think about the repercussions on daily life this could have had.

"Yes. As much as I think some of Hitler's ideas have merit, he has to reach them via peaceful negotiations and not by force of arms."

The ringing telephone relieved her of an answer. The butler answered it in the hallway and then entered the dining room. "Please excuse me, *gnädiger Herr*, Frau Falkenstein's brother has been arrested."

"What? Joseph?" Edith jumped up in shock, which earned her a scolding stare from her husband for losing her aplomb. "I'm sorry," she muttered.

"I'll take the call in my office," Julius decided, leaving her utterly shaken in the dining room.

A few minutes later, he returned to the dining room, with a steep frown on his forehead, and sat down to continue his breakfast. Edith knew better than to pester him for information when he was so visibly upset, so she kept silent, despite her anxiousness to find out more about her brother.

Julius tore at his scrambled egg with an unusual force, until he put down his knife and fork, gave her a frustrated glance and said, "It seems your brother participated in the unspeakable coup."

"Oh no!" Once again Edith couldn't contain her gasp of horrified surprise.

"Yes. He was arrested early this morning on Odeonsplatz, in the midst of a shooting, where a total of fifteen protesters, four policemen and one innocent bystander all perished."

"Oh my God." Edith didn't know what else to say. Joseph had always been hotheaded, but not in her wildest dreams would she have pegged him as an active participant in a violent coup against the government. "Is there anything you can do?"

In an unusual demonstration of emotion, Julius put a hand on hers. "The phone call came from Munich's chief of police. He remembered Joseph from the get-together at our place two days ago. That's why he separated him from the other protesters and called me immediately. So, it seems you already helped your brother."

Edith closed her eyes in relief, and took a moment to compose herself. "That was indeed a serendipity. Did the chief of police suggest what to do?"

"He said it was Joseph's saving grace that no weapon was found on him, which cannot be said of the dead comrade he was kneeling next to." Julius rubbed a thumb across his chin, a sure sign of his nervousness. "I'll need to go to the police station and bail out your brother."

"May I accompany you?" Her brother could sometimes be rash. In such a distressing situation, she feared the two men might engage in a quarrel they'd both regret later.

Julius looked at her for a few seconds, before he nodded. "It might prove useful. But you'll have to change into a more modest dress, I don't want to make it onto a newspaper headline as the 'complicit couple bailing out one of the protesters'."

"I certainly will." Edith looked down at her rather flamboyant red dress, which she had chosen to take her brother out for lunch to her favorite restaurant. Jokingly she said, "Perhaps my mourning dress would best serve the purpose?"

Julius looked at her with surprise, until the shimmer of love appeared in his eyes. "It definitely would, since this coup is truly a source of grief for our nation."

Less than an hour later, they walked into the police station and asked to speak to the officer in charge, who'd been advised by the chief to release the prisoner Joseph Hesse against the payment of a bail.

Once again, Edith was struck with admiration at how flawlessly Julius handled the situation, as if his day-to-day task were to liberate prisoners and not to run a bank.

When they sat in the Mercedes, heading home, Julius dropped the pleasant mask and launched a stern reproof at his brother-in-law. "How could you be so reckless and participate in a coup?"

Joseph, who never took orders or advice well, bit on his lip, before he stubbornly replied, "It was the right thing to do."

"The right thing? You don't have the slightest idea what you're talking about! Have you even thought about the repercussions... the damage this would have done to our nation had it succeeded?"

Edith wisely kept her mouth shut as she listened to the two men arguing.

Julius got more worked up, raising his voice, despite the presence of the driver in the car. "Trying to overthrow the government isn't some joke! This is a serious offense!"

"Haven't you agreed yourself that Adolf Hitler has some great ideas for Germany?" Joseph wouldn't back down.

"For God's sake. Are you really this daft? The man's ideas may be beneficial, but implementing them with violence? He didn't even flinch from using force of arms to extort surrender from the Bavarian ministers."

"It was necessary." Joseph rubbed his arm, where his suit jacket was ripped open, revealing a smeared shirt.

"Extortion is never necessary. We are a civilized people, not some primitive tribe living in trees. Common ground must be reached by peaceful means." Despite being raised very conservative, Julius often had astonishingly modern opinions, one of them being that power wasn't bestowed upon a small part of society by God himself, but that intelligent and diligent people gained it. And, thus, the government should be comprised of intelligent people, in contrast to monarchs inherited over centuries from degenerated royal bloodlines.

"Well, we've been in this mess for four years and nobody

has done a damned thing!" Joseph shouted loud enough for the driver in the front seat to flinch.

"Apart from the fact that a coup is always a poor decision, its execution was utterly incompetent." Julius was about to launch into one of his overly didactic monologues.

"What do you know?" Joseph retorted.

"A lot, actually. There was no conclusive strategy. No set rules in place, no fallback plan, nothing. The entire undertaking was a mess. Participants were given neither clear instructions nor weapons. Decisions were made on the spur of the moment, which led to freshly acquired allies betraying the cause at the first occasion. Didn't Hitler know that the police were going to show up and arrest everyone?"

"The police were supposed to be on our side." Joseph had crouched deeper and deeper into the seat, reminding Edith of the dressing-downs he'd received from their father, the school-teacher.

"Well, they weren't. If Hitler had read the room, he'd have known it wasn't the time to act."

"Not everyone is rich like you and can sit back and wait. Every day people are dying, either by starvation or because they are taking their lives out of sheer desperation."

"And you think this is somehow my fault?" Julius' voice reverberated in the confines of the car.

Edith pondered whether it was time for her to intervene, since this discussion seemed to be getting out of hand. Julius prided himself in giving a lot of money to charity and detested being called a selfish rich heir. So, she tried to deescalate the situation by changing the topic. "You must be hungry, Joseph."

Her brother stared at her with flaring nostrils. "Is that all you can think about in the wake of game-changing events? Food? What kind of heartless monster have you become?"

"Sorry," she muttered, distressed that her intervention had backfired.

"I forbid you to speak to my wife like that!" Julius was fizzing with rage.

"She was my sister long before she became your wife!"

"Please, we're all upset by the course of events. Perhaps a cup of coffee and a nap will calm us down." Edith wasn't giving up yet. She caught the driver's eyes in the back mirror and mouthed him a silent plea for help.

He promptly said, "Herr Falkenstein, would you like me to drive you to the office after dropping off Frau Falkenstein and her brother?"

Being reminded of the presence of a servant calmed Julius down enough to answer in the most casual voice, "Yes, please. I'm running late as it is."

As soon as the driver had dropped them off, Edith told her brother, "You really should be more grateful. Julius had to call in more than one favor to get you out of jail."

Joseph muttered something beneath his breath, before he admitted, "I am grateful. It's just that he can talk easily, living like a bee in clover. He doesn't seem to realize that most people are suffering."

"He does. And he feels for them." Edith didn't see the need to explain that apart from having set up trust funds for widows and orphans of former employees at the Falkenstein bank, Julius also gave vast amounts of money to the *Arbeiterwohlfahrt*, a recently founded charity organization to help the jobless poor.

"I guess sympathy alone is not enough." Joseph took long strides up the stairs to the main entrance, leaving Edith hustling to keep up with him. "By the way, I thought Julius supported Hitler's ideas."

"He does a little, I think. But he hates violence. A change must be realized by peaceful means," Edith repeated the words she had heard so often from her husband.

"Sometimes the time for negotiations has run its course and more severe measures must be taken," Joseph said, unrepentant.

Just as he reached the door, he put his hand on the knob and gazed at Edith. "I'm grateful that Julius bailed me out, I really am. He and I have similar convictions, we just don't see eye to eye on how to reach our goals."

She smiled. "That is a start, isn't it?"

6

A few days later Joseph boarded a train to Berlin, desolate over the unsuccessful coup. This had been the chance of a lifetime to alter course for the Fatherland and come out in a position of power at the same time.

It irked him that his brother-in-law had once again kept the upper hand—by inertia no less—while Joseph had been forced to eat humble pie. Julius was a decent man, a good and caring husband to Edith, but arrogant to the bone. That offspring of a wealthy merchant family simply had no idea about the hardships the rest of the population faced day to day.

To add insult to injury, Hitler had been arrested in Ernst Hanfstaengl's villa in Uffing am Staffelsee, about seventy kilometers south of Munich, two days after the attempted coup. The police arrived there mere hours before he was about to be ushered to safety across the border into Austria.

The entire planned coup had turned out to be a catastrophe, all prospects for a better future shattered. The traitor Gustav von Kahr had reinstalled the Bavarian government and even made peace with the socialists in Berlin.

"The world will go to hell in a handbasket," Joseph

muttered under his breath, attracting a few curious glances from his fellow travelers.

The next weekend he visited his parents' place for lunch. His two youngest siblings, Carsta and Knut, were still living with them, because neither could afford an apartment on their own.

"How was your trip?" his mother asked, going on her tiptoes to squeeze his cheek.

"Uneventful, really." There was no need for them to know about his involvement in the failed coup.

"Your mother was very worried about you when we heard the news," his father chimed in.

"There was no need to worry. Edith lives far enough away from where the demonstration happened, we were never in danger." He hid his scowl. The Falkenstein mansion was guarded from the public like a prison. Even if the putschists had marched by it, the inmates wouldn't have noticed a thing. Physically and mentally, his sister and her husband lived as far removed from the general public as the deluded and corrupt politicians.

"Well. It's good the coup failed." His father had never liked Hitler's ideas. "God only knows the death spiral our nation would have taken if he'd come to power."

"Yes, Father." Joseph was wise enough not to argue with him. A schoolteacher close to retirement, he had decades of practice holding lectures and easily out-debated anyone daring to enter a discussion with him. Furthermore he did not appreciate his children—no matter how grown-up—contradicting him.

"How is Edith?" his mother asked.

"She is well and happy." Joseph couldn't help the slight trace of bitterness in his voice, since his sister lived in an ivory tower, unafflicted from the chaos going on in the rest of the country.

"Is she finally expecting?" his mother asked.

"Not that I know of." Joseph knew how eagerly his mother awaited more grandchildren in addition to the two he and Sandra had given her.

"Such a shame. I don't know what's taking her so long. When your father and I married, I got pregnant within the week." His mother beamed with pride, failing to mention the three stillborn babies causing the four-year gap between Joseph and Edith. Her four children were the purpose of her life—apart from caring for her husband, of course.

"Did you bring us gifts?" Carsta, two years younger than Edith, asked.

"Yes. Edith has sent an entire bag." He pointed at the extra suitcase the Falkenstein's maid had packed, because the presents didn't fit into his own.

"How wonderful!" Carsta shouted.

"First we will have lunch, then you can unpack the presents," Father said sternly.

Despite Carsta's pout, the family gathered around the kitchen table.

"Let us give thanks to God for the food on our table," their father, a devout Christian, prayed.

Joseph folded his hands and bowed his head, saying "Amen" to the prayer, even though he believed God had nothing to do with feeding their family. Moreover, if God was as benevolent as the church pretended him to be, he wouldn't let half the country starve to death.

"Knut is joining the Reichswehr," his mother announced after a while.

"Why on earth would you do that?" Joseph looked at his younger brother, barely of age at twenty-two years old.

Knut shrugged. "It pays and gets me free food."

"Well, I guess, any job is better than none." Perhaps he

should join the army as well, although it was doubtful they would take him, aged thirty, with a family to support.

After lunch they retreated into the living room to unpack the many gifts Edith had sent for her family, mostly practical things including food, but also silk scarves for Carsta and Mother, woolen tunics for the men and many more trifles.

The time passed like a whirlwind until a doorbell interrupted their lively chatter.

"Are you expecting a visitor?" Joseph asked, even as he observed his sister blushing furiously.

"That would be Rudolf Sauer, Carsta's suitor. He's coming to pay us his respects," Father answered.

Carsta jumped up and rushed to the door, no doubt to make best use of the unobserved time to kiss her boyfriend.

"Is she going to marry him?" Joseph asked, since his traditional parents had not invited any friend of their daughters' to their house, not since Julius.

"We'll see. First I have to check him out. Then he may ask for Carsta's hand," Father said, while Mother beckoned Knut to follow her into the kitchen. "Give me a hand setting the coffee table, will you?"

"Why can't Carsta do that?" Knut complained.

"She needs to sit with Herr Sauer while Father puts him through his paces."

"This is woman's work. I shouldn't be forced to do it," Knut protested.

"Will you at least carry the cake into the living room, please? I'll do the rest."

For a moment Joseph pondered offering his mother some help, but then decided if his little brother wouldn't do women's work, neither should he. In any case it was a lot more interesting to sit by and listen to how his father engaged Rudolf Sauer into a discussion the poor lad had no chance to win. It would be quite refreshing—albeit not for Herr Sauer.

"Please have a seat, Herr Sauer." Father offered a chair to the blond, burly man with the tan of someone who worked outside.

"It is such an honor to finally meet the parents of the lovely Carsta. Please call me Rudolf."

Joseph rolled his eyes, impatiently waiting for the reaction to such a bold statement. He didn't know what his father disliked more, the admission that this man had been going out with Carsta for some time, or that he unbecomingly offered to be called by his first name.

"How long have you been seeing my daughter, Herr Sauer?" Father's voice dripped with ice and Joseph began to feel sorry for the lad, who seemed to be a decent man.

"A few weeks now."

Oh the poor fool was digging his own grave! As had been expected, Father pursed his lips. "I see. And what are your intentions toward her?"

"My intentions?" The lad seemed dumbfounded.

"Do you wish to marry her?"

Rudolf smiled. "Yes, I do. Just not yet. I'm waiting to save up some money first."

"You do realize that it's completely improper to dally around with a decent girl like my daughter behind her parents' back?"

Joseph observed how Carsta flushed in the deepest red tones, but Rudolf seemed not to be fazed. "That is why I am here."

"Can you provide for my daughter?"

"I certainly can, Herr Hesse. I'm a carpenter by trade. Currently I'm working for a company that does a lot of construction work for the government. We have no shortage of orders."

Finally, Joseph's father lost a bit of his strictness. Ever since Joseph had lost his job as a tram driver for the Berliner Strassenbahn, and Knut couldn't find anything but odd daily jobs, his father had been extremely worried. At least his prospective son-in-law seemed to be able to weather the economic depression.

"Coffee is ready," Mother called out. In contrast to his childhood, when she'd outdone herself baking cream cakes, today she had managed to buy the ingredients for nothing but a dry marble cake. Nevertheless, they enjoyed the rare treat and the conversation got flowing.

Joseph soon decided that he liked Carsta's boyfriend. Rudolf might be more agile using his hands than his brains, but he shared Joseph's political opinions.

7

BERLIN, SUMMER 1925

Helga was sewing a strip of cloth into the waist of David's trousers. The boy seemed to shoot up faster than the weeds in Berlin's parks, outgrowing his clothes at a frightening pace.

"Here, try it on." She handed the trousers to her son, who responded with a grimace.

"Why do I need to try it? It'll fit alright."

"David!"

Wrinkling his nose, he finally did her bidding. The extra piece of material was just enough to let him close the waist button, but the pant leg ended about mid-calf. At least it was summer, so she wouldn't have to worry about her son getting cold for at least another couple of months.

If she couldn't afford a new set of clothes for David by then, she'd have to think of an alternative solution. Woolen knee-length socks maybe, knitted from an unraveled sweater little Amelie had grown out of.

Thanks to Ernst Ritter's recommendation, Heinrich had garnered work with the mayor of Neuruppin. Unfortunately, he needed to pay for room and board, so he brought home only a meager sum, which wasn't close to covering the requirements of two growing children. At least they were much better off than two years ago, when Helga hadn't known how to put food on the table on most days, but their economic situation was by no means rosy.

And the currency reform more than a year ago had improved their dire situation considerably. Helga had been able to save up instead of rushing out to spend whatever money she got her hands on the minute she received it.

David dashed off at the sound of the doorbell. All her efforts to teach her son that he wasn't allowed to open the door had been in vain.

"Aunt Feli is here!" he shouted back into the apartment, jumping up and down with loud, excited steps.

"David, you have grown so much," Felicitas greeted him, wrapping him into her arms.

Helga put away her needlework and hurried to meet her sister at the door. "You haven't visited in quite a while. Are you alright?"

"I'm fine. We just have so much to do these days, I barely have a minute to myself."

"Come in then. Coffee?" On her last visit, Felicitas had brought an entire pound of coffee beans, and, as always, Helga had hidden a secret stash for when her sister visited.

"Yes, please."

"I'm afraid I don't have buns or cookies, but I can offer you a piece of bread."

"No need." Felicitas waved her off, instead handing her a basket full of goods. "I'm here for the company, not for the food."

"You can't imagine how grateful we are to have you." Helga walked into the kitchen, leaving her sister to play with the children. When she returned to the sitting room, Feli and David were building a brick tower together, which Amelie gleefully smashed as soon as she deemed it high enough.

"I see you're having fun," Helga commented.

"Will you play on your own for a while, so I can chat with your mother?" Felicitas stood up and settled at the table. "How is Heinrich?"

"He's fine. Still working in Neuruppin. The mayor is very happy with him." Helga thought it better not to tell her sister how little money was left after the room and board; she didn't want to appear needy.

"What about you? What is it that keeps you so incredibly busy?" Helga poured coffee into two cups and handed one to her sister.

Feli beamed. "Did you hear that Herr Hitler was released from prison?"

"It was all over the news. I was quite surprised, actually. Wasn't he supposed to serve much longer?"

"He was released early for good conduct." Felicitas took a sip from her coffee. "Ahh, nothing better than a hot cuppa in the afternoon. Right after his release Herr Hitler re-founded the NSDAP."

That part hadn't been in the news, so Helga asked, "Really? Didn't the authorities forbid this party?"

"Pah." Feli waved the objection away. "Fact is, the NSDAP is here to stay and..." she made a face as if expecting a drumroll "... Ernst and I were among the first ones to join."

Helga set down her coffee cup with a thud, totally aghast. "You did what?"

"Come on, don't act so surprised. Herr Hitler convinced us with his new program to progress Germany. He also repented for his injudicious coup and swore to work always within legal means in the future."

"You can't be serious." Helga shook her head. "He's a dangerous man."

"Not at all. If you'd been to one of his speeches in person, you'd be as enthusiastic as Ernst and I are. Would you like to accompany me to one of his rallies the next time he's in Berlin?"

Helga leaned back to study her sister, who featured the same pale skin, shining black hair and brown eyes she did, with the difference that Helga's hair was bound into a ponytail, while Feli's had recently been cut into a fashionable bob, modeling the unparalleled actress Louise Brooks.

The same was true about their clothing: Helga's own frumpy frock couldn't measure up to her sister's fancy outfit. "What about his anti-Semitism? You do remember that Heinrich is Jewish, don't you?"

Again, Felicitas waved the objection away with her carefully manicured hand. "Heinrich is a Jew in name only."

"A Jew nonetheless, and it seems Herr Hitler blames them for all of Germany's problems." Helga hadn't read the pamphlet called *Mein Kampf*, which Hitler had written during his prison time, but she'd heard Heinrich talk about it, since the Mayor of Neuruppin was a big fan of Hitler—seemingly a characteristic many mayors, including her brother-in-law, shared.

"Helga, there is no need for you to worry. The talk against Jews is little more than empty rhetoric. Anyway, Herr Hitler is referring to the Eastern Jews who have refused to assimilate. Unlike your Heinrich."

"I'm not so sure about that," Helga muttered. Having married a Jew, she knew from first-hand experience that some people took Hitler's words at face value, although neither Heinrich nor her entire family had directly suffered harassment, probably because they attended the synagogue only on the highest holidays, and didn't observe Sabbath, so not many people knew he and the children were Jewish.

Some of Heinrich's friends, though, observed the religious traditions and wore the kippa. They had different experiences, none of them pleasant.

"You worry too much." Feli emptied her cup of coffee, clapping her hands. "Now, who wants to go to the playground with me?"

Despite her elegant appearance, Feli had stayed a child at heart and loved to play with her niece and nephew.

"Take your time." Helga smiled, since the unexpected offer allowed her time to give the apartment a good clean as well as prepare dinner. She had no doubt that her sister loved all of them, including Heinrich, dearly. Nevertheless, she couldn't put a nagging worry out of her mind.

When even the kind and goodhearted Felicitas fell for Hitler, what about all the other people who had less qualms of blaming a scapegoat for their own misery? If history was anything to go by, Jews had proven to be an excellent scapegoat on many occasions throughout the centuries.

About an hour later, Feli returned with the children and announced, "Why don't you come to visit us in Oranienburg? Ernst has just bought us a new home, which was previously the mansion of some important person who emigrated. I'd love to show it to you."

"I'll ask Heinrich, but I'm sure he will be delighted. Shall I give you a phone call?" Helga normally used the public phone at the corner to call her sister's private line.

"I'm expecting you on the weekend, then." She kissed Helga on the cheek, waved goodbye and walked through the door. Helga stood frozen in place, staring at the closed door, a nauseous feeling creeping up her spine.

David, who was very perceptive for his six years, leaned against her legs and asked, "What's wrong, Mutti?"

"Nothing, sweetheart."

"Then why are you so sad?"

"I'm just sad because your auntie left." She rumpled his hair.

"I love her very much."

"So do I. And she loves us very much as well." *She would never mean us harm.*

8

A horrible tragedy struck the Falkenstein family. Toward the end of summer, Ferdinand Falkenstein suddenly died from a stroke. When the news reached Julius in Munich, he was devastated. Despite having moved out of his parents' home twenty years prior, his father had continued to be his mentor, business adviser and confidante.

As the only son, the task to steer the family empire through the next decades now fell heavy upon Julius. That night, he locked himself in his office, a glass of bourbon in his hand, reminiscing about the time he'd spent with his deceased father. He already missed him dearly.

By morning he toasted, "Thank you for everything you have taught me. My sincerest wish is to make you proud by continuing the legacy you have created." Then he got up and walked to the dining room with shaky legs, where Edith was already waiting for her husband, a crease on her forehead.

"Are you alright?" she asked him.

"As much as can be expected." Julius settled in his chair, biting his lip, so as not to show his deep grief. After eating in silence for a few minutes, he said, "We have to move to Berlin, so I can take over the headquarters of the bank."

Edith didn't look overly surprised. "I assumed as much."

He gazed at her, feeling sorry for everything that had gone wrong between them. They had been so much in love and then... Neither he nor Edith seemed to know how or when it had happened. Perhaps the beginning had been her miscarriage, the first of several more to follow, which had been a horrible disappointment not only for him but for his entire family.

Edith had taken it much worse than expected and had fallen into a depression afterward, shrinking away from him and shutting him out. After his futile attempts to console her, he had finally given up.

He couldn't quite say what hurt him more, her horrible grief, or that she kept him at a distance when he knew she needed consolation. Back then—and he regretted that now—he'd found comfort in the arms of frequently changing mistresses, which had caused even more grief for Edith. She had given him the cold shoulder, a behavior that had propelled him deeper into the arms of other women.

In hindsight he accepted how foolish they both had been to let their shared grief over the miscarriages escalate into their marriage's death spiral. With sudden clarity, he decided to put his hurt pride aside and attempt to mend their relationship.

"I'm sorry. When we moved here, I thought we could have a fresh start, away from everyone. But somehow it didn't work out."

She gave him a delighted smile. "I always thought you moved us here because of your business."

Julius shook his head. "Not really, that was only a pretext. I could have stayed in the headquarters in Berlin and traveled to Munich every couple of weeks. But I was worried about you and thought a change of location might help you to find new joy in your life."

"That... is... thank you." Her eyes filled with moisture. "I miss my friends and family so much. The Munich society is hard to get into."

"Yes, I realize that you became even more withdrawn after we moved here." Julius sighed. "Admittedly, I'm much better at business dealings than with personal matters. I never knew what I had done wrong and how I could make you happy again."

"Nobody understood me. Everyone just told me to move on, to forget the babies..." She visibly struggled to keep her composure. "It made everything worse, because I felt so inadequate. I never wanted to let you down and yet, I did. All these years."

For a moment he was transported back in time to their period of betrothal, and he remembered why he'd fallen so much in love with her. It wasn't only her beauty, but the way she so effortlessly made him smile. He wanted that back again.

"You never let me down, Edith." He put a hand on hers, but quickly pulled it away, when he saw that she was about to lose her self-control. He didn't want her to be embarrassed by crying in front of him. Leaning back, he skillfully skinned his *Weisswurst*, a Bavarian specialty veal sausage, and slathered it with sweet mustard. After musing for a few silent minutes, he decided it was probably best to distract her from her grief. "We're leaving for Berlin this afternoon."

"So quick?" Edith put down her knife and fork.

"Mutter insisted we follow the Jewish tradition to have the funeral as soon as possible." Since Julius had converted to Christianity before meeting her, Edith wasn't well-versed in the many religious customs of Judaism, so he explained for her benefit. "When someone dies, many rituals have to be followed. One of them is to hold vigil, to protect the dead from demons and dark forces, but also to prevent the deceased from taking another person with him."

"I see."

Julius thought for a minute. "Since we have to travel for the funeral anyway, it would be more convenient to stay there."

"But... where will we live?"

He gazed at her over his spectacles, surprised that she would ask the obvious. "With my mother, in my parents' villa."

"Are you serious? It's such a depressing place." Edith seemed unreasonably reluctant. The mansion might not be the most modern place, with its Victorian furniture imported from England decades ago, but it was still his home.

"You can redecorate our bedrooms in time."

She looked crestfallen.

"I thought you'd be happy. Haven't you wanted to live nearer to your family again?"

"Well, I am happy," she answered, very unconvincingly. "It's just, living with your mother is rather... exhausting."

He remembered how often she'd been crying under his mother's tutelage. He'd chalked it up to nerves before the wedding, but perhaps there had been more to it. "Things have changed, you're now my wife, you can talk with her eye to eye."

"I guess," she said, although she still looked unconvinced.

———

Edith retreated to her room, a whirlwind of emotions fighting for supremacy. She'd yearned to return to Berlin for such a long time, yet now she could only think of the depressing mansion Julius' parents owned, on the prestigious Schwanenwerder Island, where she apparently was going to live for the rest of her life.

During their betrothal she had suffered there under his strict mother's tutelage, with Julius having been sent away most of the time, and taking care of the business.

Frau Falkenstein, as Edith had called Julius' mother until the day of her wedding, when she'd been requested to address her as "Mutter", had made it her mission to polish Edith into an appropriate wife for her only son, despite never fully forgiving him for falling in love with a woman from an inferior social class.

A shudder went down her spine as Edith remembered the long and tedious sessions of correctly addressing any and all acquaintances of the Falkenstein family, eating a twelve-course dinner of previously never heard of delicacies with a multitude of unknown different kinds of silverware, glasses and plates.

Those hadn't been the most odious lessons by far. Proper curtsying, as if the Falkensteins were royalty, modulation of her voice, making conversation, proper dress code, menu planning, arranging flowers and flawless organizing of big and small events alike had been subjects on her crammed schedule. Organizing of events had been the only lecture to bring her joy and even Frau Falkenstein had admitted that Edith was a natural at it.

Also, her wardrobe had gotten a complete overhaul. Under Frau Falkenstein's supervision a considerable amount of money was spent, without ever asking Edith about her opinion. Henceforth she owned nothing but incredibly old-fashioned, uncomfortable dresses that were befitting of a princess from the last century. There had been nothing remotely practical or even fashionable among her clothing.

At least she had been able to remedy this and buy chic, modern dresses after Julius had brought her to Munich, far away from "Mutter's" strict supervision.

The mansion in Berlin held so many awful memories, of nights spent crying with despair, that she loathed the idea of ever setting foot in there again. Especially as she already envisioned her mother-in-law's pursed lips of disapproval every step of the way. It would be years of apprenticeship all over again.

Unfortunately, there was no way around it. Julius had decided to move into his parental home and that was that. She consoled herself with the fact that she would at least be close to her family. On an impulse she picked up the telephone and called her parents, who had proudly installed a private line the day her father had been promoted to principal of the primary school.

"Oswald Hesse," her father answered.

"It's me, Edith."

"Edith. What has happened?" It was a rare occurrence for her to call him.

"You may have heard that Julius' father died."

"My condolences. When is the funeral?"

Edith wrinkled her forehead. "Tomorrow, though we don't know the exact time yet. In any case Julius has decided to move to Berlin, to run the bank headquarters."

"A good decision." Her father seemed unfazed by the news, which was understandable, since her parents and the Falkensteins had met only on a handful of occasions. His indifference stabbed her heart for a different reason: she'd hoped he would mention how happy he was to have her nearby again.

Sadly, her father had never been affectionate. "I'll tell your mother the news, she'll want us to attend the funeral. I imagine you will have your hands full, so why don't you and Julius visit us for coffee, once you've got your bearings?"

"That would be nice. I'll talk to Mother tomorrow."

"Do that. She'll be so pleased."

At least someone will be. Sometimes Edith felt like a shadow. Or like a person that existed, but nobody actually took notice of.

Her father harrumphed. "If that's all, I need to continue with my work."

"Yes, Vati, please give my regards to the rest of the family." After the phone call she retreated to her room, feeling bereft. It wasn't that she considered Munich her home, but at least the mansion here looked the way she wanted it, since Julius had given her free range on the interior decoration.

Three days later, a second tragedy struck. Julius' mother died, presumably of a broken heart. Or perhaps the superstitions were true after all, and Ferdinand Falkenstein had taken another person with him into death?

9

BERLIN, 1926

For the past two years Joseph hadn't been able to hold down a steady job. With every passing day, his mood deteriorated, despite the fact that his wife had finally decided to return to him, probably because her parents couldn't support her and the children any longer.

It was both good and bad. Finally the natural order of things was restored and he had returned to being the unfettered head of the family. On the other hand, Sandra complained frequently that he drank too much and put too little effort into looking for a job.

He'd had to threaten her with a good beating if she didn't stop her unfounded accusations about him. That woman had no idea how dire the economic situation was. Matters were aggravated further when prospective employers found out that he supported Hitler.

Thanks to Julius he hadn't served prison time after his participation in the failed beer hall coup, so his criminal record was squeaky clean. Still, many employers were biased against anyone who had joined the newly founded NSDAP, with their ideas of using violence to achieve one's goals.

Joseph was not. For the last months he'd taken part in more pub brawls than he cared to remember, up to the point that Edith, who'd recently returned to Berlin, took him aside and told him in no uncertain words that he was on the quickest path to self-destruction if he continued on like this.

Little did his sister know about real life! Perhaps in her ivory tower it was all sunshine and roses, but down in the bowels of reality, where he roamed, violence was the only language people understood.

He placed his beer glass with a loud thud onto the counter and called, "Another one!"

The barkeeper, a like-minded Hitler supporter, looked at him with squinted eyes, as he delivered the order. "You should put your anger to better use."

"What use? We were defeated and it seems the world has forgotten about Hitler and his noble ideals." Joseph took a big gulp from the fresh beer.

"Haven't you heard? He is out of prison for good conduct and is assembling a group of loyal followers, his personal Saal-Schutz to protect him during public events."

Instantly Joseph was all ears. That was the job for him. Being a bodyguard to his idol, with the permission to beat up any naysayers who came to protest at the rallies. "How and where?"

"It seems you have to visit this address in Munich." The barkeeper gave him a vaguely familiar street name in Schwabing, before he added: "The work itself entails following Hitler across Germany on his election campaign. I'd do it myself, but the wife has put her foot down, saying I can't risk my work at the bar, since that is what feeds the family."

Joseph cocked his head. He didn't have a steady job and Sandra had no say in the matter anyway. If she hadn't run off to her parents' place at the first sign of hardship, maybe he would have considered her wishes. He scrunched his nose. No, she had forfeited the right to have an opinion in his matters. She should count herself fortunate if he'd send her money on a regular basis and visit every time he could. "Thanks for the tip. I'll buy a train ticket right away."

On his way to the station, he made a detour to visit his sister. Edith had often given him money for the rent when he was short at the end of the month. Paying for the train ticket was petty cash for her.

The maid opened the door. "Herr Hesse, what can I do for you?"

"Is my sister home?"

"I'm afraid Frau Falkenstein has not yet returned."

That was unusual. It was already past seven p.m., when she usually ate dinner.

"Shall I give her a message?" the maid asked, even as he turned on his heel and walked down the stairs.

"No need." Damn! His only hope to afford the ticket to Munich had been dashed.

Just as he started to walk down the driveway, the iron gate swung open and a vehicle rolled toward him. When it came to his side, the back passenger window rolled down and Edith peered out. "Joseph! Did you come to visit me?"

"Indeed, I did."

"Hop in." She opened the door and moved aside to make room for him. "I haven't seen you in a while. What brings you here?"

"It looks like I finally found a steady job," he said as he climbed into the back seat next to her.

"How wonderful! Where?"

"Well, that is the issue: I have to travel to Munich." He tactfully avoided telling her that in reality he had nothing but the *prospect* of getting work, since he was certain she'd try to talk him out of it if she knew.

"To Munich? Couldn't you find anything nearby?"

"You know how hard I've been trying, but there's simply no work to be had in or around Berlin." He gave a dramatic sigh.

"When do you have to leave?"

By then they had reached the mansion. The driver switched off the motor, got out and opened Edith's door. Joseph exited the vehicle on the other side, before he answered her question. "The earlier the better. But..." He paused and looked at her. "I need to buy a train ticket to get there."

Edith knew him too well. She didn't even flinch as she said, "And you came to me, because you don't have the money."

He shrugged. "I'll pay it back with my first salary." Both of them knew that he never paid back the money he borrowed from her. And why should he? The Falkensteins, rich beyond imagination, didn't need it, whereas Joseph had to turn every penny several times before spending it.

"Come inside." As they stepped into the huge reception hall, the maid came rushing toward them. "*Gnädige Frau*, may I take your coat?"

"Yes, and please serve coffee for me and Herr Hesse in the library."

Joseph inwardly grinned. He knew that Edith kept a stash of bills in her elegant writing bureau, where she wrote whatever important letters she needed to write.

As soon as the maid left them alone, Edith got up and walked toward the desk, asking, "How much do you need?"

He mentioned the sum for a second-class ticket plus a small allowance for himself to last about a week. She didn't as much as raise an eyebrow. For him it was an outrageous amount, for her it was probably less than what she spent on a single dinner in one of Berlin's fancy restaurants.

Edith opened the bureau and reached into one of the secret drawers. Then she handed him a bunch of bills. "Don't tell Julius. He thinks I'm indulging you too much."

Joseph gave a sour grin. "Easy for him to say. He swims in money."

"He works very hard for it."

"I'm sure he does. But if he weren't part of the international *Finanzjudentum*, the Jewish financial elite, he wouldn't have got the leg up he has to arrive where he is."

"Now you're talking nonsense. Julius is a Christian," Edith protested.

"He's still a Jew and his connections and business partners are Jews as well. They consider him one of theirs or they wouldn't let him participate in their profitable line of business. Julius himself might mean well, but the rest of the Jewish financial elite is getting rich on the backs of the common people. This is a problem not only in Germany, but worldwide." He repeated the phrases drummed into him. If Joseph was truthful, he didn't really comprehend what it meant, but since the assertions came from Hitler himself, he had no reason to doubt them. That man was so much more intelligent and far-sighted than everyone else.

Whether he understood the exact workings or not, it didn't matter to Joseph. He used the rhetoric all the same, just like he didn't have to understand how the engine of a tram worked to be able to drive one.

"You shouldn't rehash these conspiracy theories. One day it'll get you into serious trouble," Edith said.

"Nothing conspiratorial about it. Even Hitler says—"

"You're not falling for this man again? He went to prison for his attempted coup, for God's sake! If you care to remember, your comrade got shot and you would have ended up in prison if it hadn't been for Julius," Edith said, exasperated.

"Don't worry," Joseph lied. His sister would never understand him. She lived so far removed from reality, she didn't realize what the common people had to endure day in, day out.

After some chit-chat he bid her goodbye and returned home

to inform Sandra about his imminent departure, so she could pack his suitcase while he checked at the station for the next train to Munich.

Less than twenty-four hours later he found himself at the address the bartender had given him, in front of a secluded house. For an instant he feared it might be the wrong place; it looked eerily quiet and deserted. Then the door swung open and a man walked out whom he recognized from the beer hall coup two years ago.

"Edgar?" Joseph called out. "It's me, Joseph Hesse."

The other man's face instantly broke into a huge grin. He approached Joseph, shaking his hand with an iron grip. "Good to see you, old warrior. You've come to join us?"

"Sure. As soon as I heard about the Saal-Schutz protection group I hopped on a train."

"We need any man we can get. Our Führer has great plans. Come in and let me present you to everyone."

Joseph couldn't be more pleased, since this had been much easier than expected. "I've been hanging low and waiting for Adolf Hitler's return," he explained, lugging his suitcase inside, where about a dozen men were sitting around several tables, playing cards.

"We call him 'our Führer'," Edgar remarked.

"Our Führer. That's a befitting moniker. He certainly is our leader. His vision for a better Germany is second to none, and I for my part will follow him wherever he needs me."

"That's the spirit." Edgar stopped in the middle of the room, clapped his hands and then announced, "Hey, everyone, this is Joseph Hesse from Berlin. He traveled all the way here to join our cause."

"Can we trust him?" a young man with dark hair and a full beard asked.

"Sure can. He's one of the old warriors who participated in the beer hall coup," Edgar explained.

The dark-haired man immediately sat straighter and stretched out his hand. "Welcome, then. I'm Joachim. That must have been quite the excitement."

"It was. We did not succeed the first time around, but we'll never give up. I'm here to serve our Führer however he sees fit," Joseph answered, not mentioning that he'd vomited when a comrade was shot dead next to him, and that only thanks to his brother-in-law's influence had he not served prison time.

"If that isn't the truth," Joachim said, and then added, "Our Führer doesn't live here. He shows up every morning to let us know his schedule."

"We have invented a special greeting just for him," Edgar said. "We call it the *Hitlergruss*. You should start to practice it, because our Führer loves it so much." Edgar proceeded to show Joseph the greeting: Click the heels, stand in a straight posture, eyes ahead. Raise the right arm at an exact forty-five-degree angle just above the height of the eyebrows, elbow straight, fingers closed and pointing their tips forward.

"Now it's your turn."

Under the scrutiny of his new comrades, Joseph practiced the greeting for a full ten minutes until everyone was satisfied with his execution.

"Beer to celebrate!" Joachim filled several mugs from a barrel standing in the corner that Joseph hadn't yet noticed.

Much later, when he hunkered down on a mattress on the floor, he was elated. Finally he was part of something important. He'd protect the man whose God-chosen destiny it was to lead Germany to greatness!

10

BERLIN, SPRING 1932

During the last six years the economic situation in Germany had improved considerably. Gone were the long lines of job seekers in front of the labor offices, gone were the beggars on the streets.

Helga prepared dinner, waiting for Heinrich to return home from his new job in the accounting department of Berlin's administrative court. A job he'd been able to secure thanks to the recommendation of Neuruppin's mayor, who had been delighted with Heinrich's work performance.

Things had ameliorated so much Helga allowed herself to look hopefully into a brighter future. They were by no means rich, but the times when she'd depended on the food gifts from her sister Felicitas were definitely over.

The door opened and Heinrich entered, twelve-year-old David and nine-year-old Amelie in tow.

"Mutti, what's for dinner," David shouted by way of a greeting.

"Take off your shoes and wash your hands, you nosy boy," she scolded him, while inwardly smiling. Her son had grown into a big boy, almost her own height. Growing the way he did, he was always hungry and she thanked God every day for Heinrich's well-paying job in the Berlin administration, which meant she could put as much food on the table as her children required.

"Good evening, my love." Heinrich came into the kitchen, wrapped his arms around her shoulders and gave her a long kiss.

"How was your day?" she asked him.

"The usual. The administration seems to think the courts can exist with no expenses at all, while the judges believe the opposite and claim expenses like madmen." Heinrich sniffed appreciatively, while sneaking a peek into the pan. "Do I smell stuffed cabbage rolls?"

She laughed, swatting away his hand. "The same rules apply for you, mister. Wash your hands first."

"I already did. And put on my slippers as well," he protested, showing her his clean palms. "Can I now get a taste of my favorite meal from my favorite cook?"

His puppy eyes made her laugh. Yet, she swung her cooking spoon at him, pretending to be upset. "No. You'll wait until it's ready."

"What if I starve before that happens?" Heinrich pressed another kiss on her lips, using her distraction to snatch the wooden spoon from her hand.

"Hey... you... naughty man!" she scolded him between laughs.

"Not naughty at all, just very, very hungry." He dipped the spoon into the pan, deeply inhaled the scent and savored a sip of the sauce. "Delicious." Then he looked at her with so much love in his eyes. "But now that you should mention it, what about dessert later when the children are asleep?"

Her heart beat faster at his suggestion. She didn't get the chance to answer him, because David stomped into the kitchen once more. "Hmm. That smells like stuffed cabbage rolls. Can I taste?"

"No, you can't!" Laughing, she shooed her men out of the kitchen. A plop caused her to rush back and switch off the gas stove. "Dinner is ready. Set the table, please," she called out to her children, who immediately started arguing whose turn it was to do so.

After dinner, while David and Amelie were getting ready for bed, Helga and Heinrich settled on the sofa in the living room with a glass of wine each.

"So, tell me, how was your day?" Heinrich asked.

"Frau Theissen from the second floor threw a fit again, because someone left muddy footprints on the stairs. She swore to high heaven it was David, but judging by the size of the footprint it must have been our neighbor to the left. Anyhow, to appease her I wiped them away. There you have it: my biggest adventure of the day."

Heinrich laughed, pressing her tighter against him. "Would you like to switch roles one day? I'd gladly arm myself with a dust mop and challenge Frau Theissen to a duel, while you drill into the judges that every expense needs a receipt."

"I guess, I'll have to refuse your kind offer," she giggled, already imagining herself wearing a tight neck bun, receipt book and pen in her hands, chasing after the men who begged her to make an exception from the bookkeeping rules just this one time...

Having Heinrich around every day instead of only on the weekends was maybe the biggest improvement that had come with his new job, more important even than their economic stability. Being by his side made her happy. Always.

Even during the hard times they'd fallen upon in the early twenties, their love for each other had made everything less daunting. In his arms she felt as if the outside world didn't exist.

With him by her side nothing and nobody could take away her happiness.

Helga leaned into her beloved husband for a few silent minutes of enjoyment, before she raised her voice once more. "David's teacher called me on the phone."

Heinrich raised an eyebrow, accustomed to grief about his son's performance at school. "What did he want?"

"It's about the transition to secondary school. While David's grades don't show it, he actually believes our son is intelligent enough to attend a state gymnasium. He thinks if David is challenged, he'll find classes more interesting and his petulant behavior will stop."

A sigh escaped Heinrich's throat. "I really hope David understands that his behavior is only damaging himself. He's always been quite the rebel."

"He does have a rather strong mind and doesn't easily adapt to circumstances he considers boring or unjust. I'm not sure whether sending him to an academic secondary school as opposed to an apprenticeship is the best for him." Helga took another sip of her red wine, a small luxury she and Heinrich indulged in every night after dinner.

"He'll come around," her husband reassured her. "If the teacher thinks he's intelligent enough, then we shouldn't take this chance away from him."

"I know... but what if it makes him unhappy? There's nothing ignoble about learning a trade."

"Don't worry so much. If David doesn't cope at the new school, he can leave after ninth grade with a secondary school leaving certificate."

"I guess you're right. We'll have to sign the application and return it to the teacher by next week."

Heinrich stretched his arms over his head. "Not now, let's go to bed." Then he got up, grabbed her hands and pulled her from the sofa.

Warmth spread through Helga's body, evoking a smile. Almost fifteen years after marrying this man she was still as much in love with him as on the day she'd met him, perhaps more since they had weathered so many storms together.

"I love you," she said, snuggling against him.

"I love you, too, my darling."

11

Edith wallowed in self-pity. Initially she had been happy to return to Berlin, being close to her family again. But ever since Joseph had joined the SS, all he talked about—on the rare occasions he graced Berlin with his presence—was Hitler's greatness and what a paradise Germany would be under his leadership. The SS had recently changed its official name from Saal-Schutz to Schutzstaffel, while equipping its members with proper uniforms.

Joseph's martial demeanor had put quite a damper on their relations, especially with Julius, who feared another war. He'd witnessed first-hand the devastating effects of the last one, crippling not only men, but also the economy for years to come.

Unfortunately, her parents, along with Carsta and her husband Rudolf, had unquestioningly adopted the same patriotic phrases, blaming the World Jewry for any and all misery befalling Germany. If only they could see how ridiculous their opinions were, and that Hitler was playing to their lesser selves. Hate seemed to go further these days than rational thinking. Only her younger brother Knut seemed immune to Hitler's allure, despite the rest of the family singing his praises.

Jolted from her musings by the waiter asking her if she was ready to order, she looked at her wristwatch. Julius should have joined her in the restaurant half an hour ago.

"I'll take another glass of wine," she said, just as a man entered the restaurant, looking around as if searching for someone. When he saw her, he steered toward her. Her stomach lurched, since she had never seen the man before.

"Are you Frau Falkenstein?" he asked respectfully as he reached her.

Not knowing what to expect, she answered, "Yes."

"Herr Falkenstein has sent me to inform you that he won't be able to make your appointment, as he's tied up in work at the office."

"Thank you for your trouble." She gave him a kind smile and removed a few coins from her wallet to pay him for his services.

"No, thank you. Herr Falkenstein has already taken care of that. He also asked I tell you not to wait for him for dinner tonight, since he might have to work very late."

For a second she felt the urge to invite this stranger to have lunch with her, just so that she didn't have to eat alone. But she thought better of it, since Julius would be furious if someone were to tell him—and it was guaranteed that such scandalous behavior would be gossiped about—that she'd shared a meal with a stranger.

Staring at the back of the retreating messenger, her eye twitched with scorn. It wasn't the first time Julius had stood her up, and it surely wouldn't be the last. After their move to Berlin six years ago, things between them had improved considerably.

She smiled to herself remembering how she'd insisted on redecorating the Berlin mansion after his mother's death. At first he'd been resistant, coming up with excuse after excuse, until she'd reminded him that she was the lady of the manor now and thus it was her prerogative to choose the interior furnishing.

Once he relented, he hadn't skimped, but had given her a rather generous allowance to use as she saw fit. Within a year, she transformed the rather depressing mansion into a light and welcoming *home*. It had been a joyous day when she'd organized a party to present their refurbished house to friends and family, but her biggest gift had been Julius' approval.

In front of everyone, he'd thanked her for nudging him to do away with old shibboleths. He'd praised her for the dazzling results of her effort. And he'd promised to spend more time together, just the two of them. One of their new habits was to venture out to discover hidden gems among the restaurants.

But every so often work made him show up late—or not at all, as was the case today apparently. She hated sitting in a restaurant all on her own, like a goldfish in a bowl for everyone to stare at.

Once she'd confided in Julius, but he had only chuckled and said, "You take yourself much too seriously. The other patrons have more important things to do than worry themselves over you."

Still, she could feel the curious gazes boring into her back, all but hearing their thoughts. *What is Frau Falkenstein doing here all alone? Why isn't her husband with her? She should be at home rather than dallying about on her own.*

Tattle ran fast in her circles, where everyone knew everyone else. Struck by a wave of defiance, she squared her shoulders and walked to the bathroom to freshen up her make-up before ordering her lunch. If Julius didn't come, she'd still enjoy her meal.

On the way back, as she passed by the outside part of the restaurant that was reserved for the less well-to-do, she bumped into a woman in a frumpy dress.

"Excuse me," Edith apologized, and then paused, examining

the somehow familiar woman from head to toe. She had the most beautiful shining black shoulder-length hair.

"I'm so very sorry," the other woman answered.

Her voice finally clicked in Edith's head and she asked, "Aren't you Helga Raabe?" she asked.

The other woman raised her head, squinting her eyes at Edith. "I used to be. My married name is Helga Goldmann. Do I know you?"

It was no wonder Helga couldn't remember her. Edith had changed so much from the shy girl to the elegant lady she now was. "I'm Edith Falkenstein, née Hesse," she introduced herself.

"You are Edith?" Helga exclaimed, before she put a hand across her mouth. "Excuse me, I mean Frau Falkenstein."

"No need for formalities, we used to be classmates."

Helga gave a small smile. "Life certainly has treated you well."

Not as well as it appears from the outside. Edith didn't voice that thought, since Helga wouldn't understand anyway. Outsiders never appreciated how someone like her could suffer —nobody knew about the ups and downs in her marriage and the constant disagreements with her family that aggrieved her.

Following a sudden need to rebel, Edith asked, "Would you like to join me for lunch?"

"I couldn't possibly." Helga stared down at her less than appropriate attire.

Edith, though, had made up her mind. In her company none of the waiters would dare utter a critical word toward Helga. "Please, it would be such a pleasure to catch up on old times. My treat."

"I guess, then..."

On second glance Helga looked much too old for her thirty-five years of age. Her beautiful hair had some gray streaks, and the skin around her eyes mirrored the wrinkles of a dress that had seen better days.

A wave of empathy hit Edith, since she'd always considered her classmate to be a beautiful, ebullient girl. Life must have thrown hardships at Helga, after they had graduated from school.

"How wonderful! I'll advise the waiter that I have a guest. Please come with me." As Edith had predicted, the maître d' merely raised an eyebrow at Helga's appearance. Upon Edith introducing her as an old acquaintance, he treated Helga with the same respect as everyone else.

Almost immediately hors d'oeuvres appeared on their table. Helga dug into them with the healthy appetite of a person who never enjoys such delicacies.

"So, you already know much about me from the newspaper, but what about your life?" Edith asked her.

"Do you remember Heinrich Goldmann?"

"Of course I do, he was two years above us at school. All the girls had a crush on him," Edith reminisced.

"I married him right after graduation." A dreamy smile appeared on Helga's face, dispelling the hard lines and giving her a youthful appearance.

A pang of jealousy hit Edith at Helga's obvious happiness with her husband. She might be poor, and had clearly endured her share of hardships, but she and Heinrich still seemed to be utterly happy in their marriage.

"Congratulations! You seem to be much in love with him." Edith itched to ask her classmate about children, but she bit her lip, aware of how much she herself dreaded this question.

"I truly am blessed with him. And we have the two most adorable children: David, twelve, and Amelie, nine. They are a joy, at least most of the time." Helga laughed. "David can be quite the handful, whereas Amelie is the calm and rational one."

"Where does Heinrich work? I remember him having a liking for numbers."

"He's an accountant and currently works for the Berlin administrative court. We've had some challenging times, when he was laid off during the depression."

Edith nodded. It was an experience Helga's husband shared with so many compatriots.

Helga continued. "Do you remember our old housecraft teacher? I was grateful for her every day in those years. Because of her strictness I became quite a good seamstress and could support my family taking on sewing jobs."

"It must have been so hard..." Edith could only imagine. She herself had never wanted for anything, even during the worst of the depression.

"It was." It was like a dam had broken and Helga couldn't stop talking. "It's a miracle we survived that time. If it hadn't been for my sister Felicitas, you remember her?"

Edith nodded, not wanting to interrupt her classmate.

"She brought us food almost every week, I don't know how we would have managed without her. Anyhow, Heinrich finally found a steady job with the help of my sister's husband and life has been getting better. Just last year he began working for the Berlin administration court. The new position is a godsend, since it's nearby and he doesn't have to pay for room and board, except...." Helga sighed. "Except his boss recently joined the NSDAP and, ever since, Heinrich has had to deal with harassment."

Surprised, Edith asked, "Is he a communist or something?"

"You don't know, do you?" Helga retorted, before she lowered her voice to a conspiratorial whisper. "He's a Jew."

"I had no idea that—" Edith stopped talking mid-sentence, because several patrons passed by their table. It wasn't illegal to be Jewish, yet it wasn't something a person usually announced, because of all the negative sentiment against them.

"He doesn't flaunt his religion, but yes. Both our children belong to the Jewish community, too, which these days makes me a bit nervous." Suddenly Helga looked old beyond her years again.

Edith couldn't help the wave of empathy washing over her, so she laid her finely manicured fingers on Helga's calloused hand. "Is there anything I can do to help?"

Helga gave a bitter laugh. "Other than make Adolf Hitler stop his anti-Semitic rhetoric? I'm afraid there's not much else you could do."

"Well, I'm not exactly on speaking terms with him." Edith pursed her lips. "My husband used to like many of Hitler's policies in the beginning. As of late he believes Hitler should stop the hateful speeches."

"Most powerful men these days seem to be fond of Hitler."

The waiter came to bring their main course, cutting their conversation short. Despite the rather bleak topic, Edith felt a lightness taking hold of her. Reconnecting with Helga was balm to her lonely soul. After spending a delightful hour reminiscing about the good old times, they exchanged addresses and promised to keep in touch.

Their lives might have taken different turns, but deep inside they had remained schoolgirls who still enjoyed each other's company.

12

BERLIN, JANUARY 1933

The New Year replaced the old one, but the problems stayed the same. Julius had thrown himself into work, banishing the guilt he felt for not spending more time with Edith. Somehow through the years, despite their efforts to patch the rifts, their marriage had become lackluster. That initial love was gone, though they still liked and respected each other.

Her brother Joseph seemed to have found a vocation by traveling the country with Adolf Hitler, as his personal body-guard. Hitler's party, the NSDAP, had won close to forty percent of the vote during the *Reichstagswahl* last July, which had been a surprise.

Julius didn't like the hateful rhetoric though, especially not against the Jewish people, since his sisters and many friends were Jewish, but he dismissed it as what it was: just words. Nothing to be worried about.

Politicians promised everything under the sun to win the next elections, only to never remember their campaign pledges the very next day. Evidence that Julius' opinion was widespread was demonstrated in the next elections, only four months later in November. The NSDAP, while still the strongest party, had lost a considerable number of voters.

For the past two months the political situation had been unstable to say the least, since the positions of the parties were too diametrically opposed to form the coalition needed to run the country.

He shook his head. Nobody knew what was going to happen next. Perhaps another election, just two months after the last one? Or an appointed chancellor? Rumors abounded; nothing was certain.

Julius was confident the Falkenstein bank could weather any political turmoil, as parties of every political color needed money to make the economy go round. If Hitler—God forbid— actually became chancellor, Julius wanted to be prepared, not just for his family, but also for the several thousand people the bank employed all over Germany.

To do this he decided to capitalize on his family connection to Joseph, who was on the way up the hierarchy in Hitler's SS, and picked up the telephone.

"Falkenstein residence," the butler answered.

"This is Herr Falkenstein. Please get my wife on the phone."

"Of course, Herr Falkenstein. I'll get her right away."

Julius used the waiting time to ponder the current political situation. A week prior, President Hindenburg had passed the Enabling Act, the *Ermächtigungsgesetz*, which granted the Cabinet, and most notably the Chancellor, the authority to make and implement legislation independently of the Reichstag and President.

It had been received with both relief and dread. On the one hand it would finally put an end to the untenable situation of a splintered government that was unable to govern the nation; on the other hand, the wrong person at the helm could abuse it.

Julius had discussed this at length with his close friend

Reginald Grafenfels, one of Germany's biggest publishers, but they hadn't reached a common conclusion. While Reginald feared the power given to the Cabinet, enabling it to make and implement legislation with the authority to sidestep the checks and balances that were in place within the government, Julius saw the issue in a more positive light. If Germany could find a responsible leader, he would use the power given to the benefit of the country. Once they were out of the woods, the usual checks and balances could be reestablished by abolishing the Enabling Act.

Edith's voice on the line interrupted his thoughts. "You wanted to talk to me, Julius?"

"Yes. I thought we should have a family dinner. Why don't you invite your family and mine to come over?"

Pliant as ever, she instantly agreed. "That is a great idea. Did you have a date in mind already?"

Julius gazed at the planner on his desk. "What about next weekend?"

"I will go to work with the organization right away. Anything special I should keep in mind?"

"No, I'll leave it to you. Just make sure everyone feels welcome. In these times it's important to strengthen the familial bonds. We might need them." He hung up, ruminating that a phone call with Edith felt more like talking to his secretary than to the woman who used to give him butterflies in his stomach. He missed that feeling.

His secretary came into his office. "Is there anything else you need, Herr Falkenstein?"

He shook his head. "No, thank you. I'll see you in the morning."

Once she was gone, he stood up and stored the important papers in the safe, before he picked up his coat and fedora to go to the nearby club.

The prestigious location was members-only inside, mostly

men in powerful positions like himself. Once he arrived there, he proceeded to a table with several of his business partners, including Reginald, several bankers and Hermann Göring, an up-and-coming politician who'd recently been elected to President of the Reichstag. Göring also was a fervent supporter of Hitler.

Julius didn't like the fat man on a personal level, but that didn't deter him from being friendly with him, since Göring was a stellar contact into the highest echelons of politics.

Göring was grinning like the fat cat he was, announcing gayly, "*Meine Herren*, it is a pleasure to dine with you." After a while he advised the waiter, "Could you please turn on the radio, there will soon be an important announcement."

It was absolutely unusual to disturb the patrons with the blaring of the radio, but the waiter could not refuse Göring's request. Minutes later a folk melody filled the room. The men present turned their heads, most with a thinly veiled expression of displeasure on their faces. Nobody wanted to actually intervene after word had gotten around that this had been done on Göring's explicit request.

After several songs, the radio speaker announced that President Hindenburg would talk to the citizens of Germany. It had been rumored for over a week that ominous things were about to happen, so Julius wasn't surprised—although still shocked—when the announcement came, that Adolf Hitler had been sworn in as Chancellor of Germany and Hermann Göring was the nominated Minister Without Portfolio. If it weren't such a sinister move, Julius would have laughed out loud. The fat man as minister without any actual duties was exactly what he was useful for.

Hitler's appointment to Chancellor reminded Julius of his argument with Reginald, and he pondered whether his friend might be right in his worries. Later that evening, after Göring had left their party, a man from old Prussian nobility bent forward and said, "He won't stay in power for more than a few months."

Most men around the table nodded in agreement, except for Reginald, who opposed. "His ideas are simple, yet excessively radical. This will come to a miserable end."

The Prussian squinted at him. "You're an alarmist. He still has to rule with a coalition including the DNVP, the German National People's Party and the Stahlhelm League of Frontline Soldiers. They will keep him on a leash."

Reginald shook his head. "That's easy for you to say, you're not Jewish."

Another banker furrowed his brows. "You don't take Hitler's words seriously, do you?"

"In fact, I do. Very much so. Repressions and harassment at the hands of the brownshirts have increased over the past decade, and I'm afraid of what will happen if they are allowed to act unfettered."

Now it was Julius' turn to object. "Surely Hitler won't allow them to completely run wild?"

Reginald steepled his hands on the table, his face a grimace of worry. "That, I don't know."

"He won't because the people won't stand for it," the Prussian said. "We are the land of poets and thinkers, not uncivilized barbarians. People are righteously angry at the hardships brought upon them by the Victorious Powers of the Great War, but they would never condone brutality against common folks."

"From your lips to God's ears!" Reginald answered. "I for my part will be watching and taking appropriate actions if necessary."

Julius looked at his friend of many years, with whom he'd fought side by side in the Great War and attended university, wondering when Reginald had become so fearful.

"The other parties in the coalition will control Hitler's moves," Julius said, "making him an excellent puppet. Let him annul the harmful Versailles Treaty and then get rid of him. There's nothing for an upright German citizen to be afraid of."

13

Edith anxiously waited for the guests to arrive. It wasn't the first time she had organized a family reunion, yet she always dreaded it. Her family and Julius' didn't mesh well, even though that had improved after his parents died, because his siblings weren't half as stiff and formal.

Still, she hoped that everyone, especially Joseph, would be on their best behavior. Since Joseph joined Hitler's SS, there was no way to have a sensible political discussion with him. Perhaps she should warn Julius not to engage in political topics. After giving it some more thought, she dropped the idea, because Julius hated being told what to do and would only be tempted to spite her.

Carsta and her husband Rudolf Sauer, a carpenter, were the first to arrive. They had recently moved to Stralsund, a harbor at the Baltic Sea.

"Edith, what a joy to see you!" Carsta exclaimed, hugging her sister.

"Where are your children?" Edith asked. She and her sister had grown apart since Carsta had borne five children in the past seven years. It seemed there was only one topic for Carsta to talk about—one that Edith couldn't participate in.

"We left them with Rudolf's mother, since I didn't want them to endure the strenuous trip."

"That is perhaps a good idea." Edith would have liked to see her nieces and nephews, but there was no arguing with Carsta when she had made up her mind, especially not about the topic of parenting.

"Would you like a refreshment?" Edith offered her guests.

"A cold beer," Rudolf burst out. "That train trip was godawful."

Edith managed to keep a straight face, even as she envisioned her husband's flinch at the inappropriate request, though he thankfully hadn't arrived yet. His family and hers would never see eye to eye; the differences in social class were too big.

At her sign the maid hurried away to bring Rudolf what he'd asked for. The second she handed a full mug of beer over, Rudolf gulped it down entirely and said, "This one was against the thirst, another for the pleasure, please!"

Carsta sent him a dark stare, which he ignored. Then he asked, "Are we the first ones?"

"Yes—" Edith hadn't even finished her sentence as the doorbell rang. Since the maid had rushed off to the kitchen for more beer, she said, "Please excuse me, I'll get the door."

Outside, her parents were waiting together with her brother Knut, who still lived with them, and Joseph.

"Good evening, please come in," she greeted them. "Where is Sandra?" she inquired about Joseph's wife.

"At home, watching the children."

Before Edith could say anything else, an automobile drove up the driveway. As soon as it stopped Julius' youngest sister Silvana stepped out, together with her husband Markus and their adult twin sons, Jeremias and Jonas.

"Glad you could make it on such short notice," Edith

greeted her in-laws. Markus was a professor of literature and celebrated author, who constantly traveled around Europe for guest lectures, research and readings.

"We returned from Paris just yesterday. It's such a joyful place to visit," Silvana answered. She had been a high-school teacher before marrying Markus and giving up her profession to exclusively care for him and her sons.

"Where is Julius?" Markus asked. The two men enjoyed arguing about philosophical topics, often in the company of the publisher Reginald Grafenfels.

"He should arrive shortly. He was held up at the bank."

"Like always," Markus said good-naturedly.

"Please come in. Can I get you a refreshment?" Edith took her role as hostess seriously. Despite having organized hundreds of social events, formal and informal, she still felt anxious that every detail was perfect, especially with Julius' family. While her mother-in-law had still been alive, Edith had always felt compelled to demonstrate that she was a suitable wife for "Mutter's" only son. Even after her death, she sensed the strict stare on her back and instinctively stood taller.

After her redecoration of the mansion, every visitor had complimented her on the elegant, yet cozy and welcoming interior design, but still Edith felt Frau Falkenstein's shadow linger, and feared not measuring up to the revered old lady.

As soon as everyone was equipped with a beverage of their choice, she ushered them into the dining room, when she heard another vehicle coming up the driveway.

Shortly after Julius showed up, still looking handsome with his fifty years, although the long working hours had etched wrinkles into his face and gray streaks into his dark hair. As always he was impeccably dressed in a dark tailored three-piece suit with a patterned blue tie and a red-and-white kerchief in the breast pocket.

He approached Edith and kissed the air by her cheek, before he said, "I see the guests have already arrived."

"Except for your sister Adriana and her husband." Adriana was the middle child, known to be notoriously late.

"That was to be expected." Julius turned his attention toward the guests.

Eating the proffered hors d'oeuvres, everyone engaged in a lively discussion until the doorbell rang again, just before the main course was about to be served.

"That'll be Adriana," Edith said.

An ebullient brunette entered the room, with her husband Florian, a blond giant, in tow. In contrast to his huge appearance, he was a soft-spoken man who owned a rubber factory.

"Sorry to be late," he said. "We had to go to the airport and drop off our daughter."

"She's starting her post-graduate studies in Oxford next week," Adriana added. "I'm so excited for her."

"You're letting her go all on her own?" Carsta asked unbelieving.

"She's twenty-four and will live in a girls' dormitory. She'll be fine," Florian said.

"Isn't a post-graduate a waste of time, since she'll hopefully marry soon?" It was Joseph who asked the question.

"Education is never a waste of time," answered Silvana in her sister's stead.

Before the two of them could get into a fight about the usefulness of higher education for women, Edith quickly intervened, "Please take your seats, everyone. The maid is about to serve the main course."

After dinner, the topic inevitably turned toward the political situation and Hitler's recent nomination to Chancellor.

"I think it was a mistake," Markus said.

"Hitler is the right man at the right time," Joseph answered.

"He does have some good ideas, but his positions are too radical," Julius tried to reconcile.

"He's been to jail for inciting a coup, for God's sake! Who's going to trust him?" It was Silvana's clear voice that made the argument and suddenly all eyes were on her.

Edith steeled herself for the inevitable dressing-down, since Julius hated it when women got involved in politics. She waited in vain. Her husband had a soft spot for his youngest sister and once again indulged her antics.

It was Joseph who raised his voice first. "He is our chosen leader and every one of you better pay respect to him!"

Or else? Edith bit her tongue, since she didn't want to cause a ruckus.

"He's not respectful toward my kind, so why should I be respectful to him?" Silvana asked.

"If you don't like it in Germany, you can always leave," Joseph said.

"And I might do just that," Silvana quipped.

Edith cast a look searching for help at Julius, who had turned his head to engage in a discussion with Markus, unaware of the ongoing quarrel. Finally she caught her mother's eye, who hadn't said a single word until now and she silently mouthed, "Please."

Her mother intervened. "The food is absolutely delicious, Edith. You must give me the recipe."

Grateful for the diversion Edith jumped onto the topic, helped by Adriana who knew how hotheaded her younger sister was. Soon the conversation turned to food and the flowers in the garden, though Edith noticed that Joseph kept glaring daggers at Silvana.

14

Helga was sitting next to the crackling fireplace in her sister's elegant living room. Through the windows she observed David and Amelie engaged in a fierce snowball fight in the garden. Directly after cake and coffee, the two of them had taken off into the freshly fallen snow, wrapped up in their winter jackets, woolen caps, scarves and mittens—Christmas presents from Felicitas and Ernst.

The adults had preferred to stay inside. They had left the dining room, where the maid was clearing the table, and settled into comfortable armchairs next to the fire.

In Oranienburg the snow was a joy to watch, whereas in Berlin it turned into a dirty mud almost the instant it hit the ground.

"Would you like a liqueur?" Ernst offered his guests.

"Yes, please, an amaretto if you have one," Helga answered.

"A brandy for me," Heinrich said.

"Good choice." Ernst got up from his armchair with some difficulty and walked toward the cabinet, where he stored a vast array of liqueur bottles. About halfway across the room, a violent cough forced him to pause until he caught his breath.

Helga didn't miss Feli's worried look at her husband's condition. Ernst had just turned fifty-seven a month ago, but was not able to celebrate, because he'd had to spend two weeks in bed due to pneumonia.

"That doesn't sound good," Helga whispered at her sister.

"No. The doctor says he should take it easy, but Ernst insisted on returning to his office just after New Year's. There's always too much work to do." A furrow creased Feli's forehead, betraying her concern.

"Here you go." Ernst proffered a liqueur glass to Helga, before he dropped into his armchair, panting like a locomotive.

After a while, the discussion inevitably turned to politics in general and Hitler's recent coming to power in particular. Ernst and Felicitas had been among the first ones to join the NSDAP after its restoration several years ago. While Feli was a party member in name only, Ernst had been bestowed with many administrative positions and proudly wore his party badge at all times.

After another coughing fit, Ernst lectured his in-laws. "Hitler is good for the country, the economy and the people. You'll see, there's no reason to worry."

Helga didn't see a point in arguing with him, since he was a staunch follower of the Führer, and never saw the slightest fault with his idol.

Heinrich, though, wasn't as pliable as she was and objected. "With all due respect, Ernst, there's a lot of reason to worry. For one, the unfettered violence of the brownshirts against anyone considered undesirable is increasing every day—"

Ernst interrupted him. "That is an unfortunate side effect, which our Führer is already working on. The SA will soon be disciplined to adhere strictly to law and order."

"An unfortunate side effect?" Heinrich hissed angrily. "I've seen men on the street beaten to a pulp in plain sight by the SA henchmen, nobody daring to interfere."

"Well, you can't blame our Führer for the cowardice of passers-by, now can you?" Ernst retorted, before another violent cough shook his body.

"But I can well blame him for not reining in the thugs working for him. They beat up people because they aren't punished for their behavior."

"I can assure you, this is going to change. Admittedly the SA has been running a bit loose, but with the SS countering their actions, everything will turn for the better," Ernst said.

Helga didn't believe this was true, because with not one but two different branches of para-military troops, a normal citizen could only hope not to get caught between them.

Apparently concerned about the stress this discussion was putting on her husband's health, Feli jumped in to say, "No reason to be pessimistic, it's been less than two weeks since Hitler became chancellor. You can't expect him to work miracles."

But Heinrich wasn't ready to let the topic go yet. "He could at least find soothing words, but all I hear is his hateful rhetoric. 'The communists are vile, the opposition is dishonest and the Jews are the world's fundamental evil.'"

"You can't honestly disagree with the fact, that the Eastern Jews, poor and backward immigrants, have put a strain on the German economy. There are arguably quite a few vile elements among them," Ernst replied.

"So you'd rather have us all disappear from the face of the earth?" Heinrich spat out.

"Of course not all Jews are bad," Feli chimed in. "You obviously belong to the good ones. You are family and whatever happens, we'll stand by you, won't we, Ernst?"

Ernst nodded. "She's right. There's no need for you to be concerned."

Helga gave her husband a sign to drop the topic. It wouldn't do any good to antagonize Ernst and Felicitas. They weren't the bad ones here. They might be deluded by some of Hitler's claims, but they would never turn against their own family.

It was getting dark outside, so Helga got up to say, "I'll call the children inside."

"Yes, please. We'll have dinner soon," Feli answered.

At the dinner table, with David and Amelie present, the adults steered their discussion toward more palatable topics, forgetting about their argument.

It was already late in the evening when they bid their good-byes. Helga embraced her sister, saying, "Thanks for the lovely meal."

"You can count on me, always, you know that!"

"I do."

15

Joseph went to meet with Marinus van der Lubbe, a known communist agitator. Personally, he very much disliked the twenty-something, not only for his misguided political convictions but also for his personality.

Befriending the man, though, hadn't been his wish. He'd been tasked by his SS group leader to infiltrate the local communist underground organization, which van der Lubbe was part of.

Joseph spat on the street. Spending his free time with this kind of filth was a rotten thing to do. Yet, his group leader had stressed that this small sacrifice was needed for the well-being of the Fatherland and one day, soon, Hitler personally would thank him for it.

Knowing there was a greater cause behind his task, Joseph, who worshipped the Führer with heart and soul, swallowed down his disgust, disguised himself as an ardent communist, and befriended Marinus van der Lubbe.

A pub crawl had been the plan for the night and the amount of beer they drank had loosened Marinus' lips. As they staggered along to the next pub, he suddenly stammered, "You know. I have a plan."

"A plan for what?" Joseph asked, wondering whether his new friend had another drinking hole in mind.

"A good one. To get rid of Hitler once and for all."

Joseph gasped. Somehow the revelation reached his muzzy brain, reminding him of the task to sound out Marinus about the communist underground organization. This was his chance to come up with results. "Now that sounds promising. How you gonna do that?"

"By setting fire to the Reichstag and blaming it on him!" Marinus answered in his drunken stupor.

It was a hilarious plan, sure to fail miserably. Joseph, though, didn't voice his doubts. Perhaps he'd learn something that could be used against the communists at a later date. "Great plan! How and when?"

"It's easy as pie. A few barrels of gasoline and—whoosh— the entire thing is burning like a bonfire. Then the population will see how wrong Hitler is and they'll join our movement against him. It'll be huge! Millions marching for justice!" Marinus lost his footing, staggered upright, panting until he began walking again. "We win, the communists take back our seats in the parliament and start the Bolshevik revolution. Then the workers will be free! What you say?"

Marinus' prattling made no sense at all, yet Joseph agreed wholeheartedly. "Count me in. It's the perfect plan."

His companion stumbled and fell flat on his face. Joseph helped him up. Eager to get rid of the drunken man, he added, "I'd better get you home. When you're sober we can discuss your plan some more."

The very next morning Joseph rushed to talk to his group leader.

"Well done," the leader said.

"We need to prevent this horrible attack!" Joseph was out of his mind with righteous anger.

"Not at all, I think it's a fantastic opportunity."

"Opportunity for what?" Joseph asked flabbergasted. He'd expected his leader to be equally worried about the possible arson of such an iconic building as the Reichstag.

"To solve all our problems." The sturdy man rubbed his chin. "I'll talk to our Führer about it. If van der Lubbe contacts you again, inform me immediately. Meanwhile you keep your feet still and not a word to anyone. Understood?"

"Yes, sir." To show his dedication Joseph gave the perfectly executed *Hitlergruss*, a gesture he had polished to perfection through countless hours of practice together with his comrades.

Several days later, his group leader gathered a group of his most loyal SS men and instructed them:

"Our Führer has a vision for Germany that includes a complete renewal, implementing long needed reforms for a paradisaic future. Our nation will shed its shackles and rise like a phoenix from the ashes." He gave a short bark. "In this case literal ashes. Our Führer in his unparalleled wisdom has decided to go along with Marinus van der Lubbe's plan to torch the Reichstag."

A simultaneous gasp erupted from almost a dozen throats.

"It is a sacrifice we must make to reforge our Fatherland." Then he explained how Joseph was to become van der Lubbe's confidante in the plan and tell the rest of them about the details, including date and time of the attack, so they could set their own, more elaborate, fire at the same time, making sure the Reichstag building would be thoroughly ablaze. Obviously van der Lubbe would be seized by the police and publicly tried for his crime.

"But how does this help our cause?" someone asked.

Their leader gave a stern glare. "You should never question our Führer's wisdom."

"I'm sorry. I would never..." the man stammered.

16

Edith was getting dressed for a formal invitation by Reginald Grafenfels. She loved attending the events at his mansion; his circle of friends was such an eclectic group. She especially enjoyed the many writers, poets and artists among his acquaintances.

Therefore, she took even greater care than usual in dressing her best, choosing a dove-blue full-length dress that mirrored the blue of her eyes. The simple cut with a bow on her décolleté and a finely chiseled belt emphasized her slim waist.

She turned a circle in front of the full-length mirror, content with the image of discreet elegance she saw, unlike some of the artists frequenting Reginald's parties who liked to wear flamboyant dresses in bold colors with outrageous necklines.

A knock on the door cut her reflections short. "Come in."

"Are you ready? The driver is waiting outside," Julius asked. He looked absolutely gorgeous in his tuxedo, despite having gained several pounds in the past years and his age starting to show.

"I was about to come down."

He stepped into her bedroom, closed the door behind

himself and, in a rare expression of affection, stroked her cheek. "You look marvelous, darling."

"Thank you." She leaned into his touch, hoping for an embrace, but he had already retreated, pulling out a long, slim velvet-covered box from his pocket and proffering it to her.

When she opened the box it revealed a most precious diamond necklace. Under the electric lightbulb it sparkled in all the colors of the rainbow.

"Isn't this the necklace your mother wore to our wedding?"

He beamed with delight. "I want you to have it."

She'd assumed one of his sisters had inherited the valuable family heirloom, since Julius hadn't mentioned it in all these years. Seeing the necklace now, it reminded her fondly of their wedding day, and a time of courtship, when she'd dreamed of a marriage filled with love, laughter—and children.

His willingness to give his beloved mother's favorite necklace to her almost moved her to tears. Despite all their differences, he still had feelings for her. "Thank you. I will treasure it."

Julius put the box on the dressing table, took out the necklace and fastened it around her neck. Then, standing behind her, he rested his hands on her shoulders, scrutinizing both of them in the mirror. A delicious prickle ran down her spine, as she stood completely still.

After a while he said, "We should have been so happy."

The admission hit her deep in her soul, since she'd assumed that he was happy, just not with her. "We still can be."

"There's so much more at stake than just us."

She thought it best not to respond and instead leaned into his touch, soaking up his comforting presence. Even after years of cold distance, she still loved this man.

After another minute, he took away his hands and said, "We should leave or we'll be late."

Since she knew how much he hated to be late, she nodded. "I'm ready to go. Would you hand me my coat, please?"

Reginald's beautiful mansion was only a few minutes' drive away on the other side of the prestigious Schwanenwerder Island, where all the rich and famous resided. It was lit up brightly, the garden swarmed with guests decked out in evening gowns and sparkling jewelry.

"Here you are," Reginald greeted them, his arms wide open.

"I hope we aren't late," Julius answered, seeing that the party was already in full swing.

"Not at all. We're going to serve the first course in half an hour. Champagne?"

"Yes, please."

Reginald waved at the waiter, who held a tray full of champagne glasses. As they toasted each other, Reginald's wife Malinda, a petite brunette, joined them. "Welcome, Edith and Julius. I'm so glad you could make it."

"We wouldn't let you go without saying goodbye," Edith answered. Despite Malinda not being a close friend of hers, she would miss her.

"It won't be forever, just until things get better," Malinda said.

"I think you're overreacting." Julius returned his empty glass to the attentive waiter's tray, shaking his head at the offering of a second champagne. "This will blow over in no time at all. Hitler is too extreme to stay in power for long."

Edith pressed her lips into a thin line, since she couldn't hear that line anymore. Why did everyone seem to believe the harassment, especially of Jews, would blow over if they all simply ignored it? Wasn't there anyone among these intellectuals who intended to do anything?

"You're much too optimistic, my friend," Reginald disagreed. "The writing is on the wall. For the Jewish among us it will get a lot worse before it gets better. I, for my part, would prefer to sit it out in the comfort of the Hamptons in America."

Although Edith secretly felt that Reginald, with all his power to influence public opinion, should do something other than resign and emigrate, his opinion was a refreshing change.

"Who is going to take care of your business?" Julius asked.

"I have a very capable manager running the day to day. Also, I'm not out of the world. There are telephones and phototelegraphy for urgent documents."

"It will only be for a few years, perhaps less," Malinda added to her husband's explanation with a nostalgic look in her eyes. She had grown up in Berlin, as the sixth child of eight. As far as Edith knew, none of her siblings were leaving Germany. "You can always come to visit. We would be delighted to host you in our new house for a few weeks. According to the locals, it is especially refreshing during summer."

"If Julius' schedule allows, we would certainly like to visit." In contrast to her husband, Edith did not deny the increasingly oppressive atmosphere, and would have loved to escape for a few weeks.

"Who will take care of your house?" Julius asked, always more interested in practicalities than in emotions.

"The staff will stay on, and Reginald's cousin will live here on and off while doing business in Berlin. So there's no need to worry." Malinda looked as if she might burst into tears, so Edith gave her an encouraging smile.

Julius, oblivious to her heartbreak at having to leave her homeland, offered, "I'll keep an eye on it, too, and let you know of any trouble that should arise. Empty houses tend to attract shady subjects."

"Shady subjects? Perhaps in the rest of Berlin, but here on Schwanenwerder Island? Nobody who doesn't live or work here even sets foot on the bridge before getting caught." Reginald laughed the worry away.

Edith inwardly shook her head at the men. The mansion was the least of their problems. The island had been the residence of the very rich long enough to have been converted into a veritable fortress. What was at stake here were the friendships, family ties and a feeling of belonging, a loss Edith herself had experienced when making a much smaller move from Berlin to Munich many years ago.

More guests arrived, among them Julius' sisters Adriana and Silvana with their husbands. Malinda, patron of the arts and lover of literature, immediately engaged in a discussion with the revered author Markus.

Silvana greeted Edith cordially. "What a beautiful gown you're wearing. And isn't that my mother's diamond necklace?"

Edith blushed, hoping Silvana wasn't jealous. "Yes. Julius gave it to me today. All these years I thought you or Adriana had inherited it."

"No. We both received a trust fund. Everything else was given to Julius. The necklace looks great on you, take good care of it, won't you?"

"I assume Julius puts it into the safe at his bank whenever I'm not wearing it."

Silvana gave her a strange look, furrowing her brows. "It might be safer in your home."

That was a rather strange thing to say; it sent a shiver down Edith's spine. Their mansion featured several safes hidden in different rooms, but the vault at the bank was so much better protected against intruders. Before Edith could inquire further, Silvana was whisked away by some friend of hers.

Despite the morose occasion, the gathering was a lively event. After dinner the crowd returned to the glass-clad terrace that kept out the chilly February air, while allowing a view across the magnificent gardens onto the lake. The reflections of the colorful lights sprinkled throughout the gardens danced merrily on the surface of the Wannsee lake.

The serene scenery deeply impressed Edith in a way she couldn't quite explain. It almost felt as if this was a sanctuary of peace in a world that had become belligerent. Acting upon an impulse, she asked for her coat and stepped outside. Walking down to the beach, she came upon a group of women who'd had the same idea, standing in the crisp air, gazing out onto the water, reflecting the light of the houses nearby.

"Berlin definitely is the best place to live," said a blonde woman with braids around her head, whose husband owned a paper factory.

"It's a shame Malinda and Reginald are leaving," a familiar voice answered. Edith turned around and recognized her sister-in-law Adriana.

The blonde woman shrugged. "I have nothing against the Grafenfels family personally, but our country is better off without the Jews."

A violent shiver took hold of Edith, similar to the one she'd felt earlier in response to Silvana's cryptic remark, yet so much more fierce, and it had nothing to do with the cold air. How could this woman come as a guest to the Grafenfels' party and then make such a hateful remark?

"What is that?" someone suddenly asked.

Edith craned her head until she noticed the slight orange shimmer on the horizon. "Very strange. It's much too early for sunrise."

"Especially because the sun rises in the east, and we're looking westward." A man with a huge mustache had sidled up to them, putting his arm around the waist of the blonde-braided woman. "I was looking for you, darling. You should come back inside, it's much too cold out here."

After the couple left, Edith said to Adriana, "Perhaps a house is on fire. Let's go inside, my feet are getting chilly."

Adriana nodded. "Yes, probably nothing of importance."

17

Julius woke up as usual at six in the morning, dressed and walked downstairs to his office. Not even the horrible headache from staying too late at Reginald's party could deter him from his duty.

A lifelong habit of putting the Falkenstein bank above his personal pleasure did not dissipate just because his best friend had decided to emigrate from the country they both loved so much. He understood Reginald on an emotional level, because he, too, felt the aggressive undertones in the current atmosphere, stoked by Hitler's incessant hateful patter against communists, dissenters and especially Jews.

From earliest boyhood he'd been drilled not to show emotions and certainly never let his judgment be clouded by them. Logical thinking told him that Reginald was overreacting. Probably at the insistence of Malinda, he put family before duty, which was a notion Julius could not entertain, even if he wished to. Too deeply had the need to foster the family business been ingrained in him. The Falkenstein bank was so much more than a business, it was the livelihood of his family, and that of close to five thousand families who worked for him.

His father had considered himself not only an employer, but also a benevolent patriarch, considering his employees as extended family. Julius had stepped right into his shoes when taking over the business. If he upped and left, what would happen to the workers? Who would take care of them and their families? Shelter them during the storm that was sure to come? Help them to weather the bad times? Provide a well-paying job to feed their children?

No. He did not have the luxury of leaving this country for his own convenience. Hitler would come and go like other chancellors had. This crisis would pass, just like the Great War and the depression had passed, too. Thanks to vigilance and prudence, the Falkenstein bank had come out stronger after every crisis, and this time would be no different.

"Good morning, Herr Falkenstein, the newspaper is already on your desk," greeted the butler.

"Would you please get me a strong coffee and an aspirin?"

"Certainly, sir. The headlines are not good."

Julius instantly stood straighter. If his trusted butler made such a remark, something serious must have happened. He wondered whether it had anything to do with the fire somewhere in Berlin Edith had mentioned on their ride home.

As he settled in his armchair and took up the newspaper, his headache increased. On the title page was an image of the Reichstag building in flames, the headline shouting in bold letters: THE REICHSTAG ABLAZE! SET ON FIRE BY COMMUNISTS.

He asked himself how they had found the culprit this fast, since fewer than nine hours had passed since the first fire alarm. According to the news article, not much else was known at the time of printing.

"Herr Falkenstein, your coffee and the aspirin. Do you require anything else?" The butler had silently entered Julius' office, interrupting his perusal of the news.

"Have you read the article?" Under normal circumstances Julius wouldn't discuss politics with the butler, a perfectly trained man who'd been working for the family for close to forty years.

"I did, *gnädiger Herr*. It doesn't say much, though."

The butler was a man with many connections, so Julius asked, "Do you know anything else?"

"With all due respect, *gnädiger Herr*, at the moment everything is hearsay." Encouraged by Julius' nod, the butler recounted what he knew. "The driver has a cousin who works for the fire brigade. According to him, there were several fire sources distributed across the building. It took less than an hour from the first spark for the flames to spread out, resulting in the fire workers needing more than three hours until they finally managed to contain the flames. It seems they arrested the culprit, some communist."

"I wonder how he could pull off such a huge arson without help."

"He must have prepared this with a lot of thought." The butler bowed slightly, indicating that he didn't have any further information.

"Please, switch on the radio, will you?"

"Certainly." After leaving the radio on the news channel, the butler vanished as silently as he had appeared, leaving Julius to his thoughts.

According to the radio news the police arrested the Dutch refugee Marinus van der Lubbe, a known communist rabble-rouser who gleefully confessed to the heinous deed, claiming it was his way to alert the German public to the threat Hitler's authoritarian government posed, hoping to reunite them in a revolution against him. Van der Lubbe claimed to have been the sole perpetrator, which Julius doubted severely. Even with plenty of preparation, a single person wouldn't be able to pull this off, especially not if there had been fire sources spread across the entire building—if that was true.

In any case, it would explain the orange hue Edith had seen the night before. Since the Reichstag was located close to the headquarters of the Falkenstein bank as well as their city apartment, where Julius often slept after a long working day, he mused about going downtown to have a look for himself.

Then he shook his head. It was a foolish notion, led by emotions rather than reason. The police and fire workers were more than equipped to deal not only with the fire and its ramifications, but also with shady subjects trying to pilfer the rubble. It was best to stay away and work from home for the day.

Around noon an announcement from Chancellor Hitler personally came through the radio:

"There will be no more mercy; anyone who stands in our way will be slaughtered. The German people will have no sympathy for clemency. Trample down communism! Crush the social democracy!"

It sounded like a declaration of war and, while Julius harbored no love lost for the communists, he felt empathy for them. They would be hunted like rabbits.

About fifteen minutes later, Hermann Göring, who had also been nominated Minister President of Prussia, clarified who had to be afraid of the government's wrath. "This is the beginning of the communist uprising, they will strike now! Not a minute must be missed!"

Julius put down his newspaper. He loathed all kinds of upheaval. An image formed in his mind of long queues of customers in front of the bank branches, wanting to withdraw their savings. Swift action was needed.

He took up the telephone to call the branch manager and alert him to deliver a sufficient number of banknotes to all subsidiaries. An upcoming panic was best countered by blighting it; catering to any and all wishes to retrieve cash was primordial to calm the mood and demonstrate that the situation was under control.

It turned out the extra cash was not needed, because the National Socialists diligently arrested hundreds, maybe thousands, of government critics. Apparently, it didn't matter whether the offender was indeed a communist, since plenty of social democrats and trade unionists were among those arrested. Even left-leaning intellectuals as well as novelists, journalists and editors felt the ramifications.

At three in the afternoon Julius left his office to join Edith for afternoon coffee. She looked as beautiful as ever, yet he didn't fail to notice a worried crease on her forehead.

"Will the Reichstag fire have repercussions?" she asked.

He chewed on his piece of walnut cream cake, before he reassured her. "There's no need for you to worry. The culprit has been arrested. After a few days of agitation everything will be back to business as usual."

"I hope you are right." Edith impaled a piece of cake with her fork, putting it into her mouth. The gesture looked so much like his mother's, he had to blink.

"Everything will be fine." From his point of view, that was the end of the discussion. It wouldn't do any good to get all worked up on speculation as to what might happen. He'd taken the necessary precautions to keep the bank afloat; their personal safety had never been at risk.

"The party last night was very beautiful, don't you think?" Edith changed the topic. "Markus told me about his new book, which will be released by the end of the year. He hopes to have it translated into English, now that Reginald is moving to America."

"Yes," Julius said absent-mindedly. Even though he had spoken soothing words to Edith, he wasn't as sure in his opinion as he made everyone believe. On the contrary, a nagging concern in the back of his head kept him alert.

"Do you agree?" Edith asked after a while.

He looked up, realizing that she'd continued talking while he had tried to identify the source of his misgivings. "I'm sorry, dear. I was deep in thought."

If she was angry at him for not listening, she didn't show it and repeated, "I was wondering whether we should have the gardener plant new rose bushes. And perhaps get some of the colorful outside lights Reginald has in his garden. What do you think?"

For the second time, she didn't get an answer, because the butler entered the dining room with a grave expression. "Please excuse my interruption, Herr Falkenstein, Frau Falkenstein. There will be an important announcement in five minutes. Shall I carry the radio in here?"

Julius hated to listen to news during a meal, which the butler knew quite well. But on a day like this one, Julius was inclined to make an exception, so he gave a nod. Almost immediately the door opened again. The maid wheeled the radio inside on a rolling table and plugged it into the wall socket.

At the full hour the news speaker announced that the cabinet had declared a national emergency. An emergency decree for the Protection of People and State, also known as the *Reichstagsbrandverordnung*, was issued by German President Paul von Hindenburg on the advice of Chancellor Adolf Hitler, in immediate response to the fire that occurred in the Reichstag.

After the news report ended, Edith asked, "What does this mean for us?"

Julius wasn't so sure himself. The decree abolished a significant number of the fundamental civil liberties enjoyed by German citizens and gave the government the legal basis to imprison any critic without due process, as well as the means to suppress the right of free speech.

With frightening clarity he realized that in the hands of the wrong person the emergency decree could be a dangerous precedent, yet he decided not to tell Edith this thought, so as not to cause her undue anxiety.

"It does make it easier to arrest subjects working against our government. As law-abiding citizens we won't have to fear a thing."

She wrinkled her nose. "I hope you're right."

"Edith, I know you are worried, which is understandable. But as long as you stay within the law nothing will change for you and there's no need to fear possible repercussions. The criminals, though, should be very afraid." He leaned back, looking out of the window into the gardens that were still barren from winter.

The mayhem would pass once the arsonist was tried and convicted. Then everything would return to normal and the emergency decree could be revoked. That was the way things worked in politics.

No one was less likely than this little Austrian with his funny mustache to become some sort of almighty dictator.

18

BERLIN, APRIL 1933

Helga was at home ironing the laundry when the door unexpectedly swung open. Startled, she looked up, the iron in her hand like a shield, to find Heinrich standing in the door frame.

"What happened? Why are you here? It's not even noon yet."

His shoulders slumped as he scuffled without a response to the sofa and crashed onto it.

Alarmed by his behavior, Helga put the heavy iron onto the stove, filled a glass with water and settled next to her husband, offering it to him to drink.

"Thanks," he croaked, still not giving an explanation, the corners of his mouth drooping.

Looking at his defeated expression, a horrible dread crept up her spine. Heinrich was the most optimistic, happy and energetic man she knew. Even after being married so many years, he made her laugh every single day. All throughout the awful depression years he'd never been this low. This face of utter desolation was new.

"What's wrong, darling?" she insisted, kneeling in front of him and putting a hand on his arm.

"I've been fired."

"But... why?" Her voice failed her.

"There's a new law," he croaked, making a long pause before he managed to continue. "It's called the Law for the Restoration of the Professional Civil Service and allows only Aryans to be employed by government institutions."

Helga's eyes opened wide, feeling righteous indignation on her husband's behalf. "How dare they! They fired you because you are a Jew! That's just so... wrong!"

Heinrich's eyelids twitched as he slumped further into the sofa cushions as if he wanted to disappear into the crack between them. He closed his eyes, his voice but a whisper. "Wrong or not. That is the law. They assured me that I could continue to work for the private sector, just not for the government."

"I'll talk to Felicitas!" Helga said, even knowing that despite Ernst's position her sister couldn't go up against the law either. She crawled onto the sofa, snuggling up to Heinrich and leaning her head on his shoulder. For several minutes they remained silent, his desperation encroaching on her until it felt as if she'd been the one fired by this new and unjust law. How much she hated the Nazis and their constant harassment of Jews!

The speed with which the situation for Jews had deteriorated after Hitler's coming to power was astonishing, and if it weren't so awful, she'd have to give him credit for being utterly efficient in keeping his election promises. Promises not many had believed he would act upon.

"What will we do?" Heinrich whispered after a while.

"You'll find a position in the private sector and I know just who to ask." It was time to call upon her former classmate

Edith, who had graciously offered to help if the need should arise.

"Who?" Heinrich seemed to recover some of his spirits.

"Do you remember Edith Hesse, my former classmate?"

He furrowed his brows in thought. "Wasn't she the shy blonde girl who never spoke a word?"

Helga laughed. "Exactly. You wouldn't recognize her today. She married Julius Falkenstein and has become a veritable society lady."

"She married the owner of the Falkenstein bank?"

"Yes, and she offered to help if I ever needed it."

Heinrich shook his head. "I hate to depend on the charity of other people. It's bad enough that your sister's connections brought me back into work. What kind of man am I if I have to rely on your female friends to be able to care for my family?"

"You're the man I love." Helga whisked away his concern, snuggling tighter against him. "You lost your current job through no fault of your own, just because our government issued this outrageous and absurd law!" She was getting so agitated that Heinrich kissed her temple and ran his hand down her back, as if she was a child he needed to calm down.

"Don't get upset on my behalf, sweetheart."

"I'll talk to Edith right away, God knows we need the money you earn." She shivered at the memory of the hard times during the depression, when she'd often forgone her own meal to be able to feed the children. If it hadn't been for Felicitas, the children would surely have starved. Infused with new energy, she got up from the sofa, took off her apron, walked into the kitchen and removed the iron from the stove to cool down. Then she told Heinrich, "I'll go to Edith's right now."

When she reached the bridge to Schwanenwerder Island, the guards told her she couldn't pass without invitation from one of the residents. In her hurry to talk to Edith as fast as possible, she hadn't thought about this detail. Resigned, she walked back to the tram station. There, her gaze fell on the red public phone booth and her mood brightened.

She entered it, dug in her purse for her notebook and dialed Edith's number.

"Falkenstein Residence," a male voice answered.

"Helga Goldmann. May I talk to Frau Falkenstein, please?"

"On what account?"

"I'm a former classmate of hers."

"I'll see if she can pick up the call. Please wait on the line."

Helga searched frantically for another coin in her purse in case the waiting time got too long. Thankfully, it wasn't needed, because within a minute she heard Edith's modulated voice over the line. "Helga. What a joy to hear from you."

Pressed by the expense of a phone call during peak hours, Helga cut right to the chase. "I'm sorry to spring this on you in such a manner, but you offered to help when we first met."

"I did." Edith's voice suddenly sounded wary, or was that just Helga's imagination?

"It's just... Heinrich was fired today due to some new law which allows only Aryans to work for the government." Helga gathered all her courage before she continued. "Perhaps... I mean, they told him he can still work in the private sector..."

"... and now you want me to ask my husband if he has a position for him?" Edith completed her sentence.

"That would be wonderful."

"Wasn't your husband an accountant?" Edith asked.

"Yes. And a very good one, I must say," Helga answered with pride.

"I'll ask Julius and let you know, but I can't make any promises. Can I call you tomorrow?"

"Thank you so much!"

"Don't thank me yet. So far nothing has come out of it."

"Just your willingness to ask on Heinrich's behalf is more

than can be said of many others. So, I thank you from the bottom of my heart."

Once Edith hung up, Helga stared at the black apparatus in front of her, a shimmer of hope warming her soul. Herr Falkenstein simply had to employ Heinrich. He couldn't refuse.

Turning the coin she held in her hand several times, she decided to call her sister without Heinrich's prying ears nearby. They didn't have secrets from each other, but she knew how much his pride was hurt by being laid off. He didn't need the additional aggravation of her begging Felicitas for help.

"Felicitas Ritter."

"It's me, Helga. I'm on a public phone. Can you call me back, please?"

"Sure."

Helga told her the number written on the apparatus. She didn't have to wait long until it rang.

"What's so important for you to call me on a weekday afternoon?" Feli asked, since Helga usually shied away from the expense and preferred to wait until the cheaper nighttime rate for a chat with her.

"Heinrich has been laid off."

"How awful! What happened? I've heard only raving recommendations from everyone." Oranienburg was an independent city from Berlin, which didn't impede Ernst and Feli in having social connections with almost everyone in Berlin's administration.

"He was fired because he's a Jew!" Helga said with indignation in her voice.

"Are you sure? That sounds a bit far-fetched to me."

"It's not. Apparently, the government issued a new law that prohibits Jews from working for them."

"Oh... that. I totally forgot about it. Ernst says it's been done to keep shady subjects from harming the German public."

"My Heinrich is not a shady subject!"

"Of course not. He's a very unfortunate casualty in the government's quest to weed out the criminals wanting to undermine our administrative structures. Hitler is doing all he can to have them arrested, but the Jews especially are cunning and always seem to find ways to act against the best interests of our nation."

"You don't really believe this, do you?" A pricking pain took hold in the back of Helga's head. Even her kind-hearted sister was falling for these lies.

"That's what Ernst says."

"How does your husband know? All the Jews I'm aware of are patriotic Germans who want our country to flourish. Look at Heinrich! Look at his parents. The people from his synagogue. When has a single one of them conspired against our government?" Helga's agitated voice was ricocheting off the glass panes, filling the phone booth with rage.

"Calm down, sister. There obviously are good people among the Jews, like your Heinrich, but it remains a fact that the World Jewry has their stooges everywhere. They are plotting to bankrupt our country so they can steal the means of production and enslave the rest of us. Do you want this?"

"That's not true," Helga feebly protested, since she had no rational argument against such an outrageous claim.

"Sadly, it is. Hitler said so, and he has the clear vision we normal people don't have. Everything he does is for the benefit of our nation."

"Just not for the benefit of my family?" Helga rested her forehead against the telephone, uncomprehending how and why the world was unraveling around her. What had she done to deserve this? What had Heinrich done?

"Unfortunately, even the best intentions sometimes harm the wrong people. I'll talk to Ernst to see if he can get an exemption for Heinrich. Since he's married to you, you could vouch for him."

Helga didn't know whether she should be flattered to be considered a trustworthy citizen or disgusted by the notion that her husband needed vouching for. Since neither emotion made a difference to her situation, she gave a resigned shrug and said, "Please do that."

"Why don't you come to visit us on the weekend? Then Ernst and Heinrich can discuss possible solutions in person."

19

Edith waited for Julius to come home for dinner, hoping he wouldn't sleep in their city apartment as he often did. After all, she had promised Helga an answer for the following day.

Julius might be unfazed by the whirlwind of changes after Hitler had become chancellor, but her heart broke for everyone who suddenly saw himself ostracized by the *reign of hate* as she liked to call it. Helga's husband, though, was the first of her acquaintances to suffer tangible consequences.

It rattled her sense of justice, perhaps because she knew him from back when he'd been one of the popular boys at school whom everyone liked. A thoroughly kind and friendly person who never meant to harm anyone. If someone like him could be caught in the Nazis' net, supposedly cast for catching criminals, then who was safe from them?

When she heard the automobile rolling up the driveway, she walked down to the entrance hall to greet her husband. "Good evening, Julius. How was your day?"

He looked up at her, seemingly confused, before he answered. "Exhausting, but let's not dwell on business. Have you heard from Silvana?"

Markus, her husband, had taken on a guest professorship in Rome and the two of them had recently moved there to stay for six months.

"No. Were you expecting a call?"

When he shook his head, she could see how tired her husband was, and Edith pondered whether it was a good time to ask him a favor on Heinrich's behalf. She'd wait and see how his mood evolved when he found out that she'd instructed the cook to serve his favorite dish. "When would you like your dinner? The cook has prepared roast pork."

"With bread dumplings?" His face showed a dreamy look. He'd come to love this side dish during their time in Munich. It had taken Edith a good deal of effort to find a cook who knew how to prepare them in the original way Julius loved so much.

"Yes."

He cast her a suspicious glance. "Roast pork and bread dumplings on a normal weekday, what are you up to?"

She knew he'd found her out and it wouldn't make sense to delay, so she admitted her plan. "I wanted to talk to you about something."

He shook his head. "I had a hard day at the office, can't it wait?"

"I'm afraid not." She tried in vain to keep the hard edge out of her voice.

He must have noticed it, because he relented. "If it's so important, go ahead, but make it short." When she paused, his impatience got the better of him. "Are you going to tell me your important news or not?"

"A while ago I met an old classmate of mine. Today she called, because her husband, an experienced accountant, has been let go, and is in dire need of a new position. So, I told her I would ask if you might need someone."

His face immediately closed up. "We will talk about this over dinner. I'll see you in half an hour in the dining room."

Edith bit her lip to keep herself from uttering a quippy remark. At least he hadn't refused her request outright. There was still hope that the pork roast would soften his mood.

Later, halfway through dinner, she gently reminded him about her issue. "Julius, what shall I tell my friend?"

"You are insisting on this, aren't you?" he said between two bites.

"What is so bad about it? You always complain how hard it is to find good accountants. And here's someone who wants to work for you."

"Whom I don't know and, given that he's been laid off, probably isn't the good catch your friend wants you to believe."

"Please. Will you at least have a look at his resumé?"

He glared at her. "You know that I don't condone nepotism."

Edith took a deep breath, trying not to show her annoyance with him. "Nobody expects you to. I only ask that you give him a chance."

"Alright. Tell your friend that I'll interview her husband, let's say this coming Friday at nine o'clock in my office. What's his name?"

"Heinrich Goldmann."

His face fell. "He's a Jew?"

"Yes, does that matter?"

"Edith, you need to keep out of other people's business."

"He cannot work for the government anymore because of some new law, but they told him that he's still allowed to work in the private sector."

"Your intervention puts me into a tough position. While private companies aren't explicitly forbidden to employ Jews, we're encouraged to follow the government's example and hire only Aryans."

"That's rich coming from you." Edith was close to tears of anger.

"If you care to remember I'm a baptized Protestant. Those people and I have nothing in common."

"Will you still see him? Please?" she begged.

"If you insist. Just don't make any promises on my behalf. Whether Herr Goldmann gets a position in my company or not depends solely on his professional qualifications."

"Thank you, Julius. Shall I ring the maid for dessert?" When he nodded, she took up the bell sitting on the table and shook it. Moments later the maid appeared and asked on a curtsy, "Do you want anything else, *gnädige Frau?*"

"Please, serve the dessert."

Just then the doorbell rang. Edith and Julius looked at each other, since neither of them expected guests. It was rather unusual for a visitor to show up without an appointment.

"I hope this isn't your classmate," Julius hissed.

Seconds later, the butler walked into the dining room, announcing, "Alexander Lobe has asked to see you, Herr Falkenstein. What answer shall I give him?" Alex was a good friend of Julius, an intellectual who made no secret about his disdain for the Nazis.

"Show him into the library, and ask him whether he would like coffee and cake. If he does, we'll have our dessert with him there."

Edith knew for sure that Alex would not be able to resist the offer, since he had a very distinct sweet tooth. Julius seemed to have come to the same conclusion, because he threw the napkin onto the table and beckoned her to follow him into the entrance hall.

"Good evening, Alex, what brings you—" The rest of the sentence got stuck in Julius' throat as he noticed his friend's terrible appearance. "Whatever happened to you?"

"I was arrested."

"What? And you're telling me this just now?"

Alex noticed Edith coming into the hall behind her

husband and made a bow that contorted his chiseled face into a grimace of pain. Despite his discomfort, Alex was all manners. "Please apologize for intruding on your evening like this, dear Edith."

"We're always happy to see you." Somehow she managed to keep her voice even, although Alex's mangled appearance stabbed her heart. He looked like he'd been run over by a bulldozer, blood oozing from several wounds on his face, a nasty bruise around his eye, his lips swollen thick.

"Let's talk in the library, shall we?" Julius ushered them into the room, where cake and coffee were being served for them. Once he'd closed the door to keep the staff from listening in on their conversation, he asked, "Tell me what happened?"

"Three nights ago they came for me. Dragged me out of my bed and took me to one of their clandestine prisons. Supposedly I betrayed the country by criticizing the Nazis." Alex's voice was hoarse and he formed the words with much difficulty. "They beat me day and night, forcing a confession out of me. When I finally signed their shameful document full of lies, admitting to heinous crimes I never admitted to, they graciously allowed me to go free in exchange for the payment of an outrageous 'penalty'."

"You shouldn't have voiced your criticism so freely." Julius' well-meant advice caused Alex to flinch.

"You think they were right doing this to me?"

"Of course not, but you know how nervous everyone is after the Reichstag fire. Laying low for a while could have prevented this," Julius insisted.

"I will not be silenced!" Alex said with all the drama of a veritable actor.

Edith admired his verve but didn't dare to tell him, for fear of angering Julius, who was convinced that staying within the law guaranteed a person wasn't unjustly treated by the government.

Julius got up to fetch two cigars from his collection, offering one to his friend. "You know that this attitude will get you into trouble. The next time you might not get off so easy."

Judging by his bruises Edith didn't think Alex had gotten off easy. Her concern for his well-being caused her to take Julius' side. "I beg you, please be more careful in the future."

"It will please you to hear that I'm leaving the country."

"You are... what?" Edith couldn't suppress a very unladylike gasp.

"My arrest was the last straw. This country is headed for a disaster worse than anything mankind has experienced, and I don't intend to stay along for the ride." Alex took a long smoke, savoring the cigar's aroma, before he exhaled again, staring directly at Julius. "I know you think you'll be safe, but you might consider leaving too, at least for a while."

"Me leaving Germany? Never! I was born and raised here. I fought for the Fatherland in the Great War. Only over my dead body will I be leaving my homeland!"

"You just might," Alex said dryly.

Edith noticed the vein on Julius' temple pulsating and wanted to calm the mood, but Alex cut her off with a swift hand motion. "Don't, Edith. I know Julius doesn't want to hear the truth." He gave a barking laugh. "Look at me and what Hitler's cronies did to me. Nobody is safe in this country."

"You shouldn't have criticized the government. Then nothing would have happened to you," Julius said through gritted teeth.

"Old friend, you're a fool, burying your head in the sand. A nation that doesn't allow its citizens to criticize the government isn't worth fighting for. Moreover, you are..." Alex deadpanned his friend "...a Jew."

Julius was silent, but looked like he might explode.

Alex shrugged. "Keep deluding yourself, but don't say I didn't warn you." Then he took a step toward Edith, taking her hand and blowing a kiss on its back. "This is my goodbye. Thank you for the many happy hours I was allowed to spend in your home. If you or Julius ever need my help, please don't hesitate to contact me. I'll be sending my address as soon as I am settled in England."

A wave of horrific foreboding caused Edith to become nauseous. Before her inner eye she saw a Berlin covered in a sea of blood filled with bruised corpses. It took her a few seconds to recover. Hoping neither of the men had noticed her discomfort, she answered, "Thank you so much. We wish you all the best in your new endeavors and are looking forward to hearing from you."

Then Julius shook hands with Alex, grumbling, "You're overreacting, old friend, you'll see."

"Then I'll return and you can rub it in my face for the rest of our lives that you were right." Alex didn't seem in the slightest fazed that he might throw away his entire livelihood in Germany without reason.

"Please give my regards to your wife," Edith added.

Once Alex was gone, Julius said, "He's an intellectual, always overly dramatic. There's no reason to flee the country, just because of one unpleasant experience."

Edith had appreciated Alex as a thorough thinker, so she didn't believe he would make such a far-reaching decision on a whim. Secretly, she applauded him for his foresight, wishing Julius would be more open-minded toward the looming dangers. Yet, she would never contradict her husband. "I'm sure he'll return a few months from now, admitting it was a mistake to leave."

Julius wasn't done yet with grumbling. "Does he assume everyone can just up and leave? Even if I shared his fears, I have a business to run. My employees depend on me. The customers depend on me. The entire nation depends on a functioning economy and banks are the backbone of that economy. If we just leave at the first stumbling block, our country would go to hell. What kind of man would I be? A coward!" He was talking himself into a veritable rage.

"Please, Julius. Nobody said you should emigrate. Try to understand Alex, though. Have you seen his awful bruises? He is scared; I would be too."

"You have nothing to fear, because you are my wife and I will always protect you."

"I know." Edith didn't fear for her personal safety, since she never engaged in politics and didn't deal with the government at all; it was Julius in his exposed position she was worried about. Alex's visit had thrust a nagging doubt into her mind; he wasn't some lowlife criminal. He was an honorable man, who mingled in the highest circles. If they could arrest and beat him up, they could do the same to Julius. "It is late, I should retire," she said, not wanting to show him how much she was scared.

"I still have work to do. Please tell the maid to brew a strong coffee and serve it in my office."

"I will. Good night." Edith retired to her room, but the shock of Alex's visit kept her awake until the early hours.

20

The end of 1933 was approaching fast. It had brought a flurry of new laws and regulations, restricting the rights of citizens in one way or another.

Julius cursed under his breath as he pored over last month's numbers. It was high time for the government to stop pushing out new laws faster than businesses could react to them.

Almost every day there was something new. Most regulations didn't impact the Falkenstein bank, yet he had to stay on top of the legislation and evaluate whether it meant having to change the way he ran his business. It was tiresome to say the least.

Reluctantly he had to admit it was mostly thanks to Heinrich Goldmann, who had deeply impressed him during the interview, that he could keep up with the additional accounting work. Starting out in the smallest Berlin branch of the Falkenstein bank, Herr Goldmann had soon proven himself to be a quick-witted, fast-learning and diligent man.

Julius' initial qualms of employing a Jew in the current political climate had evaporated at Herr Goldmann's performance and he'd promoted him to chief accountant in the bank headquarters. He'd even thanked Edith for her intervention, albeit reminding her this case had been an exception.

A knock on his office door drew him from his musings. "Come in," he said, wondering who the visitor could be, since his secretary hadn't mentioned any appointments.

"Silvana! What brings you here?" he asked, delighted to see his youngest sister. He'd missed her while she and Markus had been in Rome, and was thrilled to have her back near him.

"Good morning, Julius. I came to see you as a prospective customer." She cast him an excited smile.

He loved his youngest sister with all his heart. She was so full of life and happiness, making everyone around her feel lighter. The only disagreement between them had been her choice of husband. Markus was a good man, intelligent, well-to-do, and, unfortunately, a devout Jew. To cap it all, Silvana had embraced Judaism and even started to learn Hebrew after marrying him. For Julius it had felt like a betrayal of their family's efforts to be as German as anyone else.

"Now I'm intrigued. Please sit."

Never one to beat around the bush, she said, "I need a line of credit to open a school."

"You, open a school? What are you talking about?" This must be another folly of hers.

"Oh, Julius! Don't you follow the news?"

"I do meticulously, since my business wouldn't flourish if it didn't adhere to all the rules and regulations in place." He gave her an indulgent look. "There was nothing in the newspapers about you opening up a school."

Another woman would have been cowed or at least shocked into silence; Silvana merely rolled her eyes. "Very funny. Shall I ask Theodore for credit then?" Theodore had been a friend of their father, and also the fiercest rival for owning the biggest bank in Germany.

"Don't you dare!"

Silvana gave him a smug smile. "So, you're going to stop being condescending and will hear me out?"

He grumbled something akin to an agreement. Six years younger than him, she'd always been able to twist him around her little finger.

"You probably know that the *government*," she spat out the word as if it was poisonous, "installed a quota for Jewish students."

"Yes, I heard. A maximum of five percent of the students at any institution can be of Jewish descent. That should be more than sufficient, especially since offspring of war veterans are exempt."

"Do you believe everything the government tells you?" Silvana quipped.

He didn't want to get into an argument with his quick-witted sister, so he answered, "You want to open your own school?"

Her eyes lit up bright. "Yes, an institution of higher education for Jewish students only. To give them a secure place to learn, sheltered from the harassment they have to endure in the normal schools."

"You must be out of your mind. A Jewish school? Is that even allowed?"

She ignored his insult. "It is. As long as I make sure that none of the teachers, staff or students are Aryans. Can't you see how much better this will be for the children? We can teach them not only the usual subjects, but also Jewish religion and culture, both of which aren't allowed anymore at public schools. We will prepare them to stand their ground after they graduate and are released into the world. I'm planning to form alliances with businesses that are friendly to Jews, who will take on my graduates as apprentices." She apparently had spent a considerable time planning this folly.

"Does Markus know about your project?" Julius asked.

Silvana's face fell, letting him know he'd asked the right question. Apparently, her husband hadn't approved of her crazy plan, or she hadn't asked him yet.

"Look, you know I can't go against your husband's wishes—"

She interrupted him with a wave of her hand. "That's not a problem. In fact, he's furious at the government for its constant harassment and wishes to help his brothers in faith." Julius raised an eyebrow without interrupting her. "The university fired him. They *kindly allowed* him to stay on until the end of the semester, but made it clear that being a Jew, he cannot return after the break."

"That's nonsense." Julius didn't believe his sister. As far as he knew, and he made it a habit to pore over all issued laws, there was no rule in place requiring the universities to fire Jewish professors.

"It's not! He's livid! I'm livid!" She jumped from her seat, pacing his office like a caged lioness. "Hence we decided to open up our own school. It was his idea as much as mine, but because you're my brother, I came to ask you for a loan."

Julius furrowed his brows when the realization hit him. "If this is a request for a business loan, I must unfortunately refuse. We cannot give loans to a man without a job or other securities."

"I have a trust fund." She stopped her pacing and planted herself in front of him.

"Your fund is under my management, so it wouldn't be proper business dealings."

Her eyes sprayed flames at him. "You're not giving me the loan?"

"Unfortunately, I can't. My hands are bound."

She hissed, "Looks like I'll have to ask Theodore after all."

Julius knew it wouldn't do any good to tell her that Theodore worked under the same rules he did. The Oppenheim bank wouldn't give her the requested loan either.

Long after Silvana left, the conversation with her kept nagging at him. He hadn't wanted to disappoint her or tell her the truth in such harsh words, yet he needed to protect her from her own dangerous ideas.

When he returned home in the evening, he entered the mansion deep in thought, surprised when the butler greeted him. "Herr Falkenstein, your sister is in the library with Frau Falkenstein."

Both sisters visiting on the same day was more than unusual. He hoped Adriana didn't have a preposterous idea like Silvana. Entering the library, he stopped dead in his tracks at the sight of Silvana animatedly chatting with Edith.

"Julius dear, look who's come to visit with us," Edith said.

"Silvana. I certainly hadn't expected to see you again so soon." If she was here it could be for only two reasons: either to rub it under his nose that Theodore had financed her foolish project, or hoping he'd be more pliable if she begged for a loan in Edith's presence.

Edith squinted her eyes at him, but neither he nor Silvana took the time to explain to her what had transpired earlier at his office in the bank.

"Dearest brother, your stance on business dealings gave me reason to think." Silvana stood up, very tall for a woman, with a lithe figure that didn't show her forty-five years. After air-kissing his cheek, she added, "You were absolutely right. Your bank is not in a position to give a loan to a Jew out of a job."

Julius knew his sister too well to feel joy or even satisfaction at her words. "You came all the way here to tell me I'm right?"

Silvana smiled sweetly. "You should know me better than that."

"What's going on here?" Edith asked, a bewildered expression on her face.

Julius usually didn't make her privy to business dealings,

but since Silvana was family, he'd make an exception. "Silvana visited me in the office this morning to request a loan."

"A loan for what? Are you somehow in trouble?" Edith sounded concerned.

"Not at all. At least no more than every other Jew in this country." Silvana cast a scathing stare at her brother. "Markus and I want to open our own school and I asked Julius to loan me the money we need."

Edith nodded wordlessly, sending a puzzled gaze toward Julius. He had no choice but to answer her unspoken question. "It seems Markus was let go from his position at the university. Sadly, I had to refuse her request, since the credit committee would never approve such a loan."

"And Julius is right. He shouldn't put his business at risk for me." Silvana returned to the armchair, crossing her slender legs before she launched her frontal attack. "So, I came here to ask him for a private loan."

Julius glared at her, livid at her cunning plan to outmaneuver him in front of his wife.

"I know you gave Adriana a private loan when her husband wanted to enlarge his factory."

"That was a completely different situation!" Julius hollered.

"What kind of school do you want to open?" Edith asked.

"A Jewish school for Jewish children. It is the foolhardiest project I've heard about in a long time," Julius answered the question.

"Someone has to give these children an education," Silvana argued.

Edith looked at him pleadingly. "I think it's a noble cause. Hasn't the government a new rule that Jews should have their own schools?"

Julius shook his head, even though he knew he wouldn't be able to resist the joined forces of these two women. "It might be legal, but it still poses a risk to Silvana."

"Don't you always say that taking risks is the foundation of business?" As he'd feared, Edith was completely on Silvana's side. He should have known his sister would attempt to trick him like this, since she and Edith had become good friends.

"Calculated business risks, not foolishly endangering oneself by opposing the government."

"I'm not opposing it, I'm doing exactly what they want. They'll be grateful for me taking those students off their plate." Silvana wasn't backing down.

"I'm just trying to protect you." Julius voiced a last argument, although he realized he had already lost the battle.

"That's honorable of you, my dearest brother. You seem to forget though, that I'm old enough to take care of myself." Silvana had never subscribed to the idea that she needed a man to shield her from the world.

"Would it be such a bad thing?" Edith came to Silvana's aid once more. "I mean, if the government gives her trouble in the future, she can always close the school again."

Defeated, Julius nodded. "I'll give you the money under one condition: you will never mention my name in connection with this school."

"Thank you so much, Julius." Silvana jumped up and embraced her brother, which was an entirely inappropriate demonstration of emotions.

Julius just knew that this concession would return to haunt him in the future.

21

BERLIN, SPRING 1934

David Goldmann had recently turned fourteen. Unlike his younger sister Amelie he had never been a good student. The only thing he enjoyed about school was hanging out with his classmates, including his best friend and bench neighbor Gerald.

On his way to school he pounced on his friend, throwing him into a half-melted snow heap.

"Hey!" Gerald protested. As soon as he recognized the attacker, the two of them engaged in a friendly fight, rolling across the muddy ground.

"You pig!" David cried out when Gerald stuffed a muddy mass into his mouth.

"Don't start a brawl when you're not strong enough to win it." Gerald laughed and reached out to help David up.

"God, I wish school was already over. I can't endure another Latin class with the 'Spitting Eagle'." The students had given their strict teacher this moniker, because he loved to come crashing down on an unsuspecting student, spraying him with spittle while asking some boring grammar question. In the past months, David had become the Spitting Eagle's preferred victim.

"Yeah, he really dislikes you. And you're not even the worst troublemaker in our class." Gerald brushed the snow off his jacket. "We better hurry up or we'll be late."

Each school day began with a roll-call: the students lined up in the yard, grouped by class. When the bell chimed, the school director raised his hand, almost like a choirmaster raised his baton, and hundreds of throats sang—more loud than beautiful —the Horst Wessel Song. It was the one thing David looked forward to. He put his heart and soul into it, roaring at the top of his lungs, feeling the energy of so many youths, eager to serve their country.

Singing the song with every other student in his school was the highlight of his day. Every time, without fail, exhilaration like none he had experienced before rushed through his veins. An all-encompassing feeling of belonging took hold of him, devoured him, sucked him in. For three minutes he wasn't David Goldmann, the bad student who hated Latin grammar. During the course of the battle song he was part of the bigger picture, a tiny piece in the grand puzzle for a greater Germany. He was proud. Alive. Jubilant.

The last note faded. Silence descended on the yard. Laden with positive energy, David and Gerald raced each other to their classroom, where they settled in their bench. Not even the prospect of having to face the Spitting Eagle could put a damper on David's elated mood.

Spitting Eagle's bald head appeared in the door frame. He had a habit of rapping his knuckles twice on the desk as a sign for everyone to stand up. It took him four long strides from the door to his desk. David, along with the rest of his classmates, sat in rapt attention, ready to shoot up at the signal.

As soon as he reached his desk, the teacher rapped his knuckles and gazed benignly down at the group of young boys standing proud and straight in front of him. Then his smile faltered, and the third rap, the one indicating to shout the obligatory Hitler greeting, didn't come.

The teacher pressed his lips into a thin line, shook his head and said, "Not you, David. From today on you'll sit in the last bench, and you will not desecrate our Führer by opening your mouth while your classmates praise him."

David's elation evaporated, leaving a dark emptiness behind. "But why..."

Spitting Eagle squinted his eyes, pushed back his shoulders and said, "You're a Jew."

"I'm not..." David wanted to scream that only his father was a Jew, while his mother wasn't. Looking around him for support, he realized that none of his classmates would stick out their necks for him.

Humiliated to the core, he bit back the tears pricking at his eyes. All of a sudden, every single child in the room seemed to dislike him, just because he was a *Mischling*. Overwhelmed by grief, rage and despair, he gathered what was left of his spirit and straightened his shoulders. He'd never give these turncoats the satisfaction of begging to belong.

Hurriedly, he packed his satchel and skulked to the empty bench in the last row that was usually reserved as a punishing bench for troublemakers. Gerald mouthed a wordless *sorry*, while the rest of his classmates, whom he'd considered friends, looked the other way.

David fell onto the chair, staring at the backs of his mates as the class began. If he'd thought that being the Spitting Eagle's favorite victim was bad, he now realized that being an outcast was so much worse.

For the rest of the day, he remained in the last row, completely invisible to teachers and students alike. He counted the minutes until he could rush home, vowing that he'd never set foot in this place again, where nobody wanted him anyway.

Gerald was the only one to chance a gaze backward, but quickly averted his eyes when the teacher called him out on it.

When classes were finally over, David hastened out of the building, racing down the street, not listening to Gerald's calls to wait for him. As soon as he turned the corner, he slowed down, furiously kicking a pebble along. He'd never return to school, ever.

At home, his mother waited with lunch for them. "Where's Amelie?" she asked, since usually the two of them returned together.

"I... she..." Mired in misery, he had completely forgotten about his sister.

His mother cast him a probing stare, before she asked, "Did the two of you fight?"

"No."

"Then what?"

"Nothing."

Shortly after, the door slammed open and Amelie came inside. "Hello, Mutti, David..." She stopped mid-sentence when she noticed him, glaring at him with anger. "Here you are! I waited for you at school, you imbecile!"

"Imbecile yourself!" he hissed at her.

Mother intervened. "None of this talk in my house. Go wash your hands and sit at the table!"

Amelie silently stuck out her tongue at him. Lunch was a somber affair, until mother asked again, "What's wrong with you, David?"

"Nothing."

"Has something happened at school?"

"No." He mumbled beneath his breath.

"A bad grade, maybe? Or did you get into trouble again?"

From experience he knew that his mother wouldn't let up, so he might as well tell her. "I'm not going back to school!"

"Oh dear! What have you done this time?" She was used to

David getting into trouble at school, so she naturally assumed it was his fault.

"I did nothing wrong!"

She sighed. "Forgot your homework again? Talked in class? Played tricks on the teacher or your classmates? Just tell me."

"Why do you always assume it was my fault?" David stubbornly pushed out his lower lip. "I didn't do a thing!"

Mutti visibly fought for composure, whereas Amelie, sitting opposite him, pricked her ears at what she suspected would turn into a good dressing-down. "So, if it wasn't something you did, why the fuss?"

"The fuss?" David couldn't sit still a second longer. He jumped up, rescuing his water glass from toppling over at the last second. "It's all their fault! Theirs and Father's!" The suffering of an entire day as outcast came rushing back, bringing angry tears to his eyes. "The teacher made me sit in the last row all day and kept me from singing with the others in the morning because I'm a Jew and I'm desecrating our nation!"

Mutti's face turned chalk-white. "Don't you ever say that again!"

"That's what the teacher said. The school doesn't want me, because I'm not a pure-blooded Aryan."

"Look, I'm sure we can find a solution. I'll talk to the headmaster first thing in the morning," Mutti tried to soothe him.

"I told you. I'm not going back. None of my classmates talked to me all day. Not even Gerald dared to."

"You can't just drop out of school. Education is important if you want to achieve something in life," his mother tried to reason with him.

He locked eyes with her, feeling the wisdom of his entire fourteen years and four months of age behind him as he said, "I'm not going to achieve anything in this country as long as Hitler is in power. Therefore, I might as well drop out and find work somewhere."

She sighed, obviously coming to the same conclusion. "You're much too young."

"I'm fourteen and big for my age, you say so yourself. I'm certainly old enough to find a job. Something I like." A smile tugged at his lips, as he realized that the events of this morning, perhaps weren't as bad as he had initially thought. He might find an apprenticeship in a profession he actually enjoyed. Electrician, maybe, or auto mechanic... automobiles were a hot thing and most owners had no idea how to fix them when the motor stopped working.

"Until you find an apprenticeship you'll continue going to school. That is my last word," Mutti said.

David grumbled, because he knew there was nothing he could do to change her mind. If he wanted to escape the humiliating situation at school, he'd better find something else quick.

22

Despite David's protests, Helga accompanied him to school the next morning, intending to complain to the headmaster about the shameful treatment her son had received.

It wasn't that she hadn't seen this coming. The writing had been on the wall for quite some time, especially after the new laws installing a quota for Jewish students at public schools. She had deliberately pushed all thoughts about the future away, taking things on a day-to-day basis. Life was difficult enough without worrying what the future might bring.

Thanks to Edith, Heinrich had secured a job at the Falkenstein bank. Thanks to his own merit he had soon been promoted and transferred to the headquarters. He was safe there—for now. But if the government issued new regulations, Herr Falkenstein might have to let him go, whether she was friends with his wife or not. She shrugged. That was a problem to deal with if and when it arose; for now she needed to make sure David could stay in school.

Whatever happened, she fully intended to use her standing as an Aryan to speak her mind to the headmaster, solving the problem once and for all. She left Amelie and David in front of their respective classrooms and continued to the headmaster's office.

"How can I help you, Frau...?" he asked upon her knock.

"Goldmann," she introduced herself.

His face fell. "Your son is a constant source of trouble. I wish he would put more effort into his studies."

She cut him off with a wave of her hand. "I'm here about another issue. May I sit, please?"

"Off course, how inconsiderate of me." He beckoned her to sit on a chair in front of his immense wooden desk and waited until she'd settled before asking, "So, what is your concern today?"

"Well..." Helga had carefully rehearsed her little speech the night before, but now her brain drew a complete blank. "It's just..." She swallowed the lump in her throat and started again. "David came home yesterday, telling me his teacher has relegated him to the last bench and he's been forbidden to sing with the others in the morning."

The headmaster's face twisted into a grimace of discomfort. "I'm so very sorry about that. Please don't believe I condone this kind of behavior."

Relief crept into her heart and she gave him a small smile. "So, David can return to his usual bench?"

He furrowed his brow. "I'm afraid it isn't that easy. I can't unilaterally override a teacher's decision."

Her eyes widened with shock. "Aren't you the headmaster?"

"I am."

"Then, what exactly is the problem?"

He engaged in a lengthy monologue about his duties as government-employed civil servant, before he ended with, "Due to your marriage to a Jew, your children are considered Jews as well. In these matters my hands are tied. It's not that I'm unsympathetic to their plight, but in the current political climate it's simply not opportune to take the side of a Jew against anyone, especially a well-respected teacher." He paused, looking at her intensely. "I hope you can understand my tenuous situation, Frau Goldmann."

Helga didn't think his situation was tenuous. After all, it was her child being ostracized. "Are you advising me to stand by and watch David suffer?"

"Certainly not, Frau Goldmann." His twitching eyelids clearly demonstrated his discomfort with the topic.

"So, what do you suggest I do?" Her voice was more scathing than she had planned on, and she noticed him crunching his jaw.

"There's no need to be aggressive, Frau Goldmann. We're both on the same side."

Helga suppressed a scoff, as it would only antagonize him further.

"If you want to hear my advice." He cast her a false smile, before he continued. "Divorce your husband."

"What?" she gasped out loud.

"Don't look so shocked. We all need to be reasonable here. Your children are in this situation because of your husband. If you divorce him and dissociate yourself from his entire family, cutting all ties, your children will be considered Aryans, especially if you also baptize them as Christians—"

She interrupted him. "What you're suggesting is outrageous. I love my husband and I vowed to stick by him through good times and bad. What kind of person would that make me if I left him at the first sign of trouble?"

The headmaster carefully avoided looking her in the eyes. "It doesn't have to be forever, just until things blow over. Then you can remarry him."

"I will not!" Her eyes were glaring daggers at him, wanting to stab him for his scandalous suggestion.

"Then, unfortunately, I cannot help you, and your children will continue to be treated as Jews."

"Harassed and humiliated, you mean?"

"If you're not happy with our school, you can always enroll them elsewhere."

"You're kicking us out?" Helga could barely keep her voice down.

"Not at all. I'm merely suggesting possible solutions. I've heard the Lembergs are going to open up a Jews-only school. It has received many recommendations and I personally know some of the teachers they have hired."

Jewish teachers whom you sacked at the government's request? She bit her lip to keep the scathing remark inside. The upcoming opening of the Lemberg school had been a topic on the Jewish grapevine. Several of Helga's better-off acquaintances had already enrolled their children there. "Thank you for your very *kind* suggestion, but that is a private school and we unfortunately can't afford the tuition." She got up to leave his office. "Have a good day."

Just as she pressed the door handle, the headmaster added, "David will finish eighth grade in a few months from now. If he decides to leave school for a workplace, I'll write a recommendation for him."

She turned around, wanting to hit the complacent man in the face, but instead she said, "That is so very kind of you. I'll gladly take you up on your offer when the time comes."

Then she rushed down the long hallway toward the exit, fighting to keep her angry tears at bay. Only when she was far enough away from the school building, did she let out her fury, shouting vicious words at the trees.

"Ma'am?" A policeman approached her, and for the first time in her life she felt deathly afraid of a member of the authority.

"I'm so sorry," she hastily declared. "A personal issue with my husband. I see now how much I overreacted. Thank you." She turned on her heels, leaving the dumbfounded man behind her as she hurried away. Right now she needed a nosy policeman like she needed a hole in the head.

The thought of emigrating crossed her mind. She wanted to sob. Visas were hard to come by and the queues in front of the foreign consulates grew longer by the day. They had neither the money to afford to emigrate nor affluent relatives in receiving countries who might issue the required affidavit.

She bit her lower lip, telling herself they would be fine. Hitler couldn't stay in power much longer, his policies were just too extreme. Soon enough the German population would realize how harmful all those new regulations were and would vote him out. Then, life would return to normal for everyone, including for Jews.

Her family just had to hang on for a little while longer.

23

Edith was putting the final touches to her outfit, a powder-blue dress hugging her ankles, when a knock sounded on the door.

"Come in," she said as she slipped on her elbow-length silk gloves, then put a fascinator in a matching color on her head.

Julius entered, scrutinizing her appearance for hidden flaws, as he always did before leaving for an important social gathering. After half a minute, he gave an approving nod. "You look perfect, my dear."

"Thank you." She had known he would appreciate the subdued color and the unostentatious design, apt for the respected wife of a businessman. Sometimes she'd love to dress more brashly, perhaps add a flamboyant scarf to her outfit.

"Are you ready?" Julius entered Edith's bedroom.

"Yes," she answered, grabbing her handbag.

"Let's go." Julius offered his arm, looking exceedingly hand-some himself in the dark three-piece suit. Although Silvana's school had been operating for a few weeks already, tonight was the official opening ceremony.

Parents, sponsors and important members of the Jewish community were invited. Silvana had offered to make them the guests of honor, which Julius had refused. Edith knew he was proud of his sister, but he still shied away from the public knowing about his financial involvement.

In the end, they had found a compromise: the Falkensteins would attend the event in their position as relatives to the school founders. Edith couldn't understand her husband's reluctance to attend the opening ceremony, since he normally jumped on every opportunity to socialize and make new business contacts.

As their Mercedes approached the school, hosted in a former administration building of the Jewish Society, Edith said, "Aren't you proud of Silvana's achievement?"

Julius paused for a moment, carefully weighing his answer. "I am. Very much, indeed. Yet, I wish she would do something less controversial."

"The school has been approved by the government. In fact, the education ministry seems to be relieved that she's taking the Jewish students off their hands."

"Which is exactly why I'm worried. What will happen if the government changes its mind and allows the students back into mixed schools?"

Edith raised her shoulder, not comprehending the problem. "Can't she simply take on other students if that happens?"

Julius cast her an indulgent gaze. "It's not that easy. Nobody in their right mind will send their children to a Jewish school, whereas all the parents who enlisted their children with Silvana, out of necessity, will transfer them back to a place that is nearer to their home, more convenient, requires less tuition... The same will probably be true for the teachers. The entire undertaking is doomed."

Her eyes opened wide, because Julius had never voiced such stark arguments on the topic before. "So, why did you agree to finance it?"

"You know my sister, she would have pestered me till kingdom come. It was the easiest way to get her off my chest."

Inwardly Edith rolled her eyes. Julius was such a successful businessman, overseeing dozens of branches of his bank, reigning over thousands of employees, dealing with hundreds of business partners, and yet he was horrified of confrontation.

Perhaps that was the reason why he so willingly obliged every ridiculous rule the government implemented on a near-daily basis. She squinted her eyes at him, reassessing his dominating stance until she realized that he always got what he wanted, for the sole reason that nobody dared to oppose him.

The instant someone did, he was putty in their hands. Silvana knew this weakness and capitalized on it for her benefit. It was both a frightening and a liberating realization. If Edith found the courage to follow in her sister-in-law's footsteps, she might lead a more fulfilled life, too. One where she decided what to do, instead of complying even to Julius' unspoken wishes, down to the dresses she wore and the food she ate.

The driver stopped and opened the back door to help them out.

"What a lovely place!" Edith was instantly overwhelmed with admiration. The beautiful mansion surrounded by gardens looked nothing like the gray and dull school building she had expected, but more like a romantic castle, sheltering its inhabitants from the world outside. Footpaths were lined by bushes that had been decorated most beautifully with ribbons.

Silvana stood on the flight of stairs leading up to the entrance door, talking to someone. As soon as she noticed her brother's car, she excused herself and walked toward them.

She looked fabulous, much younger than her years, in a swinging bright-red summer dress with flowers painted all over. Only the way her hair was coiffed into an elaborate French pleat gave credit to her position as the headmistress of the school.

"Julius! Edith! Thank you so much for coming!" Silvana

beamed from ear to ear. "Come inside. I want to introduce you to Herr Kendl from the education ministry."

"You have done a magnificent job with the school. It's so beautiful," Edith complimented her.

"It is. Most importantly, it's a safe haven for our students. They can feel at ease in here."

Edith nodded pensively. It hadn't escaped her attention that the building was surrounded not only by beautiful gardens, but also by a sturdy, ten-feet-high wall with barbed wire on the top and guards at the entrance gate.

"Congratulations. Where is Markus?" Julius asked.

"Inside, conversing with important people. He'll be glad to have your assistance. You know how much he hates talking to bureaucrats." Two dark automobiles drove up the driveway and Silvana shooed them away. "Go inside. Mingle. Have fun. I'll welcome the new arrivals."

A ping of jealousy hit Edith, since her sister-in-law had obviously found her vocation in life. She looked so happy, energetic, and incredibly beautiful, while Edith herself often felt like a useless appendage to her husband. She had no achievements to her own name, never did things out of true passion. Her entire life consisted of doing what was expected from her.

She scolded herself not to be ungrateful. Julius had never treated her badly nor was he disrespectful. Yet, she often yearned for less respect and more passion in her life.

As they entered the auditorium, she instantly spotted Markus standing next to a tall, blond man in SS uniform, who reminded her of her brother Joseph. Julius walked over to greet Markus and the blond man, who turned out to be Herr Kendl, the envoy from the education ministry. After the introductions were made, Edith stood silently by, not listening to the men's conversation, her thoughts drifting away.

She hadn't seen Joseph in several months, since he was busy traveling with Adolf Hitler across Germany on government business. Her heart ached at the thought of her brother drifting apart from her ever more—as did the rest of her family, except for Knut—because she couldn't stand their constant admiring talk of *Unser Führer*.

When exactly had Adolf Hitler turned not only into the chancellor, but into *our leader*? He certainly wasn't her leader, and not Julius' either. On the outside, her husband always defended the actions of the government, finding excuses for every new regulation they installed, yet she could tell from the way his eyelid twitched that he wasn't behind the policies, or the person imposing them. Julius still believed that someone—who exactly was a mystery to Edith—would rein Hitler in, or end his political career altogether.

It was a miracle to him that Hitler had stayed in power so long, when the twelve chancellors before him had each barely lasted a year.

"Edith? Is that you?" a voice came from behind asked.

As she turned around, Edith recognized Helga, wearing an austere, black dress reaching down to her ankles. It was the kind of dress Julius' mother had forced Edith to wear during her time of betrothal, straight from a picture book of the eighteen-hundreds. A wave of empathy hit her. Here she was, complaining about not living a life of passion, whereas Helga very obviously could not afford to renew her wardrobe according to the current fashion.

"Helga. How wonderful to meet you here. Are your children attending this school?"

Helga's bright smile evaporated, and with a side glance at the man in SS uniform she whispered, "Yes they are going to start in the new school year. It became unbearable at the public school."

"I'm so sorry." Once more Edith was reminded how privileged her position was. Edith walked a few steps away from the men, to talk to Helga without the possibility of prying ears. "Were they harassed because they are half-Jews?"

"Yes... at school they were called bastards, half-bloods, half-Jews and worse... they weren't allowed to even sing the national anthem with the other students, had to sit in the last row..."

"Wasn't there anything you could do?" Shaking her head, Edith realized there were a lot of things happening in the outside world she didn't have the slightest inkling about. The situation out there must be so much worse than she, or Julius, had acknowledged. She intended to ask Silvana about it.

"Other than divorcing my husband..." Helga pursed her lips.

"You're not seriously considering that!" Edith's voice must have conveyed her shock; a few nearby heads turned, including Julius, scowling at her for making a scene. For his benefit she put on a smile.

Helga though, seemed amused. "I reacted the same way when the headmaster came up with this solution. Anyway, he suggested I enroll my children into a Jews-only school and Frau Lemberg kindly accepted them. She even went out of her way to arrange for a stipend, because we couldn't afford the tuition for both of the children."

The existence of stipends was news to Edith. Perhaps Julius could sponsor a child, too. "Frau Lemberg is very resourceful."

"What are you doing here?" Helga asked, knowing that Edith didn't have children of her own. "You aren't going to be a teacher, are you?"

"No, not at all." Edith laughed. "My husband—" She stopped herself from saying *financed the school*, aware of Julius' insistence not to be linked to it. "We were invited because Frau Lemberg is his sister."

"Oh." Helga's mouth formed a perfect O of surprise. "I had no idea. But then... I mean..." Despite being in a supposedly safe place, Helga glanced over her shoulder. "She is Jewish."

Edith looked at the woman from her childhood, seeing nothing but a kind soul. After another glance around for prying ears, she whispered, "My husband's family are Jews, but he's not practiced the religion in years, he converted to Protestantism when he came of age."

"I had no idea." Judging by Helga's wide-open eyes, the confession had shocked her to the core.

"Not many people do. And in the current climate it is best if it stays that way."

Helga nodded eagerly. "I would never. I don't want to... you have been so kind, offering your help back when Heinrich lost his job."

"That's nothing worth mentioning."

"On the contrary, I will never be able to thank you enough. Without your intervention... I don't know how we would have coped. Not many business owners employ Jews for fear of running foul with the government. What you did, what your husband did... we'll forever be grateful."

Edith's face flushed with the praise, since it was not often that she had a true impact on someone's life.

"I know this sounds strange coming from someone without means, but if I or Heinrich can ever help you in anything at all... we'll treat you as if you were family." Helga gave her an absolutely sincere smile, letting Edith know without a shadow of a doubt that it wasn't an empty promise.

"Your offer means a lot more to me than you may imagine." Edith suddenly seemed to hover inches above the floor, feeling a strong bond of friendship she had missed for so many years in her glamorous life.

"I never believed I would say this, but these days I'm so glad I didn't convert when marrying Heinrich. His mother and grandmother would have liked me to, but since he didn't care, I chose not to. This has been a true blessing." Helga's face took on a defeated expression.

Edith who had never experienced the harassment of Jews first-hand, tried to console her with the same words Julius always used. "I'm sure this is only temporary and things will get better soon."

"I hope you are right..." Helga paused when a waiter approached them with a tray full of canapés. After taking two delicious-looking pieces and eating the first one, she continued. "Many of our friends are considering emigration."

"Some of ours are, too. But they all believe it to be a temporary choice and plan to return in a year or two when things have normalized." Then Edith scolded herself for being so insensitive and asked, "What about you? Are you planning to emigrate?"

Helga shrugged. "It's not a viable option for us, so I haven't given it much thought."

"I understand. Leaving your home, even for a short time, is a hard thing to do."

This time, Helga looked more astounded than depressed. "Germany has become so oppressive, it sure doesn't feel like home anymore. My husband regularly gets accosted on the street and my children had to switch their school. Believe me, I'd leave this place in the blink of an eye and smile while doing so. Unfortunately, we can neither present an affidavit, nor do we have the financial means to be issued a visa."

Now it was Edith's turn to form a surprised O with her mouth. None of their friends had ever mentioned the cost of obtaining a visa. According to them it had been a simple matter of going to the consulate and applying for one. "How much do they charge for a visa?"

"They don't charge, except for a very modest fee. The problem is, they require you to show proof that you own the funds to support yourself for approximately one year. Some countries waive that requirement if you have a much in-demand profession. I'm afraid, though, neither accountant nor housewife with sewing experience qualifies."

Edith's head was swimming with the information. She had never realized that getting a visa entailed so many requirements —but then, she had never thought about it in the first place. In her marriage all decisions were taken by Julius, who had both the connections and the means to get almost anything he desired. Biting on her lower lip, she wondered whether she should offer to help out with money. It was an idea she'd have to ponder.

"I'm sure people are overreacting and things will settle down soon enough," she said instead.

"I hope you're right." Helga cast her a rebellious stare. "And if not, I'm prepared to do anything to save Heinrich. Absolutely anything."

In awe of her friend's fierce resolution, Edith could only nod her head.

24

David had grudgingly accepted his mother's decision to send him to a new school, but only after she had promised that he could leave after finishing ninth grade. One more year he could handle.

In contrast to Amelie, who had been looking forward to the new school, he loathed having to go there. Most of all he hated losing his friends, although, truth be told, his classmates had long ceased to be friends.

Starting that fateful day when his teacher had forbidden him to participate in the daily singing of the Horst Wessel Song, the other boys had unleashed their worst behavior on him.

More than once, he'd skulked away to the bathroom to wipe spittle, mud or another gross substance from his face and clothing. He'd never told his mother about it, hoping his classmates would soon grow tired of their game.

Never in his life could he have imagined that this was only the beginning. Soon after the older boys had joined in, hitting him or tripping him over, and then singing gleeful rhymes about dirty Jews.

Not even Gerald had stood up for him. The boy whom he'd

considered his best friend looked away whenever David was attacked, mimicking the teachers who either pretended not to notice or watched silently without raising as much as a brow. Perhaps he should be grateful that Gerald at least didn't join the packs attacking him.

One day, David came home with a broken nose. Mutti had clasped her hands and said, "That's enough! If the headmaster is not willing to stop the abuse, you won't return to that place! I'll ask at the Lemberg school whether the two of you can start right away instead of waiting for the beginning of the new school year."

The following day, she took him and Amelie to the Lemberg school, not even bothering to excuse their absence with the current headmaster. From outside the place looked like a prison: surrounded by a high wall topped with barbed wire.

David's toenails curled up. His mother seemed to anticipate his plan to bolt and quickly put a hand around his wrist, even though they both knew she was no match for him if he really wanted to free himself from her grip.

He sighed theatrically. "Really? You're going to send me to prison?"

Amelie, walking on their mother's other side, giggled.

"It's very nice inside," Mutti assured him.

"Hmm." He didn't believe one word. How could a school be a nice place, anyway?

"What are the teachers like?" Amelie asked, giddy with anticipation. His little sister had bombarded Mutti with thousands of questions about everything and anything at the Lemberg school, apparently looking forward to attending classes there.

"You will meet Frau Lemberg, the headmistress, in just a minute," Mutti answered.

"This is so exciting!" Amelie danced along the path, whereas David itched to turn around and dash off. It was a mystery to him why Mutti insisted he continue with school. He'd be much better off finding work somewhere.

"Here we are." Mutti knocked on a door in the long hallway.

"Come in!"

"*Guten Tag*, Frau Lemberg, I'm Helga Goldmann, we talked on the telephone yesterday."

"Oh, yes. You must be David and Amelie, right? Welcome to our school! You'll find that we do things a bit differently here." Frau Lemberg gave them a warm smile, and despite his best intentions to dislike her, David had to admit that she might not be all bad.

After clarifying a few organizational details with their mother, she pressed a button and talked into some kind of loudspeaker. "The new students are here. Would someone please come and get them?" Then she turned toward them again. "Your classmates will explain everything to you. Our goal is to make you feel safe and welcome in our little community."

Less than a minute later, a girl Amelie's age and a boy David's age entered Frau Lemberg's office.

"Hello, I'm Thea Blume," the girl said. To David's eyes she was the most beautiful girl he'd ever seen. Her angelic face with its big blue eyes was framed by shining, golden curls, and she cast them the most welcoming smile.

"I'm David, and this is my younger sister Amelie," he said, totally ignoring the boy who stood beside Thea.

"You'll like it here. This school is a great place," Thea answered, before she—much to David's chagrin—turned toward Amelie, and said, "Come with me, I'll show you around."

Staring after the marvelous Thea, he barely registered that the boy stepped forward and said, "I'm Emil. You're David, right?" Following David's nod, the other boy continued, "Let's go."

As soon as they were out of earshot Emil said in a low voice, "Thea is a stunner, isn't she?"

David's ears burned hotly for being called out. "I..."

"Never mind. Every boy in the school is wild for Thea."

They walked down long corridors, while Emil explained where everything was. "At the Lemberg school there are only Jewish children, so nobody taunts us."

"I'm not really a Jew," David protested.

Emil stared at him for a moment, then he asked, "So why are you here then?"

"It's... My father is a Jew."

"Ach, a *Mischling*. I guess that's bad too, because you don't belong to either side. Best not to tell the others." Emil wrinkled his forehead. "In any case, don't you worry, the students here are cool. I don't believe they'll make you feel bad for being of mixed race."

"Thanks," David answered, and then, in a sudden burst of emotion, he declared, "I hated my old school. They beat me up every day. Some older boys broke my nose, and the teachers didn't even flinch."

Emil nodded like an old, wise man. "That won't happen here. Frau Lemberg is a very nice person, but she'll expel you for hurting another student on purpose."

David would never admit how impressed he was. Not only by Frau Lemberg, but also by his new classmate who seemed so sure of himself and so at ease—just like David had been before Hitler and his stupid hatred for Jews had ruined everything.

"So how are the teachers?"

"Most are alright, except for our English teacher. He can get rather grumpy with everyone who doesn't know his grammar. I like our religion teacher most, she always tells wonderful stories. And we learn a lot about the Jewish traditions, history, everything. She even speaks fluent Hebrew."

"Do we have to learn Hebrew?" David answered,

completely aghast. Having to study English and French was bad enough, he surely didn't need to scramble with another language.

"Don't you know any already?" Emil asked surprised.

"No. Why should I?" David didn't intend to emigrate to Palestine like many Jews aspired to.

"Didn't you ever go to the synagogue or read the Torah?"

"My father never practiced and my mother is a Christian, so we celebrated the important holidays, but that's it." David suddenly felt inadequate. The Aryans despised him because he supposedly was a Jew, yet he had no idea about Jewish culture and traditions.

Emil seemed to pick up on his mood. "Don't you worry. You'll see everything is better here than in a public school."

25

Julius looked forward to seeing his family at tonight's birthday party for Adriana, yet he felt strangely nostalgic. When his parents had still been alive, these family gatherings had been much more frequent than nowadays.

His mother had loved to have her children and grandchildren around, so she always found a reason for a family reunion. Whether it was Hanukkah or Christmas, Rosh Hashanah or New Year's—like many assimilated Jews they celebrated both—Yom Kippur, a birthday, graduation, wedding or baptism, the occasions never lacked.

After his mother's death, he'd counted on Edith stepping up and taking over the role of family matron. It wasn't that she hadn't tried, yet somehow it had not worked out. Perhaps because she was so much younger than his sisters, or that she lacked the emotional bond to his family. Whatever the reason, the cheerful reunions had become rare.

Whereas Julius missed his mother on days like this one, he missed his father every single day. He had been Julius' pillar of strength: the person he called to discuss business problems, ponder politics or philosophize. The old man had always given sound advice and, without his backing, Julius doubted he would have been able to steer first the Munich branch and later the national operations of the Falkenstein bank through the tumultuous decades behind them.

He wandered to the window in his office and looked out onto the gardens, which were exceedingly beautiful at this time of year. Edith had a gift for everything beautiful, and flowers were no exception.

After she'd finished redecorating the formerly old-fashioned and slightly oppressive mansion, she'd employed a new gardener as well. Under her supervision, he had transformed the stern-looking park-like garden. Right now, in June, the flowerbeds blossomed in diverse pink and white tones, the perennials lining the pathways glowing in the brightest yellow. It was a sight to behold, which gave him a sense of harmony that he'd come to miss so much in the world since Hitler came to power.

At first, he'd awaited developments for a better future, and Hitler had delivered: he got rid of the unjust Treaty of Versailles, managed to get Germany's men back into employment, and launched an unparalleled infrastructure plan.

The innovative idea to build fast motorways crisscrossing the country from north to south and east to west as a means to provide mobility not only for the people but also for the transport of goods, was brilliant to say the least.

Soon, the Autobahn became synonymous for prosperity and progress. No other country in the world possessed a remotely comparable road network; it was truly the epitome of a road into the future.

To populate these roads, the government demanded the production of a *Volkswagen*, a people's car. And just this week, the Reich Association of the Automotive Industry had tasked the genius engineer Ferdinand Porsche with a prototype. Soon, every family would be able to afford a Volkswagen to enjoy unknown mobility, progress and unequaled prosperity. It would be a wonderful new world.

On the other hand, Hitler was overshooting with his measures against certain parts of the population, most especially Jews. Julius didn't deny that a strict hand was necessary in forcing lazy, criminal and antisocial parasites to pull together with the rest of the population, but harassing hard-working men, like his accountant Heinrich Goldmann, wasn't beneficial for the nation.

Herr Goldmann was an exemplary German citizen, except for the fact that he was Jewish. He wasn't one of the orthodox Jews from the east who refused to adapt to the modern times, but an assimilated Jew, who was no different from every other middle-class German.

A steep crease appeared on Julius' forehead. He wasn't worried about his own position—he had assimilated so much that no one would guess his Jewish background. But he hoped the government wouldn't force him to let all his Jewish employees go. That would not only cause grief for the affected people, but also make a harsh dent in the bank's operation and thus harm all of its employees, even the customers.

Julius glanced up to his father's portrait hanging on the wall, looking down upon him as if he were actually there, and he heard his father's voice in his head. "You must always put duty first. The Falkenstein bank has to be your prime concern—because without it, nobody can prosper. Not you. Not your family. Not your employees. Not the local community. And, ultimately, not the German nation."

Rubbing his chin, Julius answered the painting. "Father, be glad you don't have to experience this. If Hitler isn't stopped soon, I'm afraid the country is headed toward a catastrophe."

"Those who are well-prepared will weather every storm," his father's portrait seemed to say. "Don't lose heart. Assess the situation with a clear mind, then take the necessary actions."

Pondering the advice for a few minutes, Julius decided it was time to be proactive. He took up the phone and called his deputy director. "Herr Dreyer, I want you to make a list of all Jews in the company."

"Yes, Herr Falkenstein, may I ask if this is for another government requirement?"

"No. It's purely precautionary. I want you to train back-ups for all Jews in critical positions in the hierarchy. Just in case the government forces us to let them go."

Herr Dreyer was silent for a while. The only thing Julius heard over the line was the scribbling of pen on paper. "I made a note, Herr Falkenstein. Anything else you'd like me to do?"

"Not at the moment. Just... don't tell anyone what we're doing. I don't want the staff to get upset with speculations, when probably nothing will come out of it." Julius hung up, thinking, *preparation is half the battle.*

For a fleeting moment Heinrich Goldmann appeared in his mind, asking what would become of him. Julius quickly shook off the image, since there was nothing he could do. If and when the government ruled that Jews weren't allowed to work at the bank, he had to obey. It was as simple as that. The thought of opposing the authorities never once crossed his mind.

Pushing away the stab of guilt, he told himself, *You must think about all of your employees and can't risk the livelihood of thousands for the benefit of a few.*

A knock came on the door and the butler entered. "Herr Falkenstein, the driver is waiting for you."

"Is Frau Falkenstein ready?"

"Yes, sir, she's in the entrance hall." The butler proffered Julius his fedora and helped him into his jacket. Edith was waiting for him in a much too bright and colorful summer dress he didn't recognize. "Is this a new dress?"

"Yes." Edith smiled brightly. "I asked Silvana for her seamstress. She tailored me a dress in the same style as the one your sister was wearing at the school opening ceremony. Do you like it?"

He pressed his lips into a thin line. What had suddenly gotten into Edith to wear a dress befitting a rebellious twenty-year-old at her age?

"It is much too flamboyant."

Edith's face fell. "You complimented Silvana when she was wearing it, so I thought..."

"It might look nice on a headmistress, but it is completely inappropriate for a woman in your position. I thought you understood how my wife is supposed to dress." He inwardly shook his head. Had she forgotten everything his mother had taught her about her role in society?

Mutter had been the epitome of correctness from birth to her deathbed. Not even Julius had ever seen her bare ankles or a trace of her neckline, since such pleasures were reserved for a husband.

"Times are changing, and I'm intending to go with it," Edith said.

He looked at her astounded. There seemed to be much more to this flamboyant dress than a mere fashion statement. It looked awfully like a declaration of independence. Something he would have expected from his non-conforming sister Silvana, but not from his sweet and pliable wife. Although he secretly found Edith's newfound gumption very attractive, he would not tell her, fearful she might use his approval to justify even bolder choices.

With a glance on the clock atop the mahogany sideboard he said, "You can't change now, or we'll be late." Taking in her striking appearance, he added, "The dress does look very beautiful on you, but perhaps you could keep this kind of fashion for family and keep dressing the traditional way when we have business events?"

"I will." She smiled at him with genuine pleasure and for a

moment he believed he saw a spark of fire in her eyes—like the one that had made him fall in love with her so many years ago and that had slowly faded away after their wedding. Perhaps her wearing a much too bright dress wasn't all that bad?

They arrived at Adriana's mansion in the villa colony, Grunewald, at the same time as Silvana and her husband. Markus got out from the driver's seat of his vehicle.

Julius shook his head. Seemingly everyone around him had decided to engage in inappropriate, yet apparently modern, behavior. Driving oneself was for motor sports men, or perhaps the common people who would soon be able to afford a Volkswagen.

"What happened to your driver?" he asked Markus after greeting him and Silvana.

"We need to save money. Since I've been expelled both from the university and the national association of German writers, I don't have a regular income."

"Shouldn't the school provide your means of living?" Julius asked.

"It does. Just not as much as we had previously." Markus laughed. "Especially because Silvana insists we give scholarships to students who cannot afford the tuition."

Julius shook his head. What Markus allowed his wife to do was business malpractice. First and foremost a business had to produce profits, and only if all your needs were covered, could you turn into a philanthropist.

"Thank you so much for coming!" Adriana swooshed down the stairs in a frisky pink dress covered with flounces and ruffles that showcased her beautiful bustline.

"Happy birthday," he greeted her with an air-kiss to her cheek. "You look wonderful."

Adriana beamed with delight. "Florian bought it for me when we were in Paris. Isn't it gorgeous?" She did a full-turn on her high heels.

"Happy birthday, sister!" Silvana pushed in to embrace her older sister. "It's been too long!"

"I wish we could have attended your grand opening. But Florian couldn't put off his business trip to Paris," Adriana answered. "How was it, by the way?"

Silvana started gushing about the event until Julius finally interrupted her. "Shall we go inside?"

It was a happy reunion with not only immediate family, but also cousins, uncles and aunts. Just before dessert, Florian clanked a spoon against his glass.

Julius raised an eyebrow, wondering what kind of announcement his brother-in-law had in store. Perhaps a new production line at his rubber factory?

As soon as everyone fell silent, Florian cleared his throat. "It may come as a surprise to some of you... After giving it much thought, Adriana and I have decided to move to London for the time being."

Instantaneously everyone was talking at once. "Why? What are you thinking? Won't you miss Berlin? When? What will you do there?"

Julius was as taken aback as the rest of the guests and it irked him that neither Adriana nor her husband had made him privy to their plans. After all, he still considered himself the family patriarch. A momentous decision like this should first be run by him, although it seemed that these days nobody gave anything for tradition anymore.

Florian clanked his glass again. "Since our daughter is studying in England, we will kill two birds with one stone. Adriana has wanted to live nearer to Alice, and at the same time we'll get away from the oppressive atmosphere in Berlin."

Everyone in the family knew that Florian loathed the Nazis, since one of his business partners, a trade union official, had died at their hands in the Dachau concentration camp mere weeks after Hitler came to power.

"You're running away from the Nazis?" one uncle asked.

Florian though, wouldn't take the bait. "Under the current circumstances you can only stay in Germany for two reasons: you're either on board with the Nazi ideology and the horrible things they do, or you lack the money to emigrate. Neither is applicable to me."

Julius pursed his lips. Florian was on his high horse. Not everyone could just up and leave. "What happens to the employees in your factory who depend on you?"

"I have employed a capable manager who will run the business. I can visit on business trips if needed, but,"—he gazed at Adriana—"it will be much safer for her over there."

Later, when everyone but the three siblings and their spouses had left, Florian said, "You should think about emigration, too. I have a friend working for the justice department, he tells me they're working on a new law that will deprive Jews of their citizenship."

"I'm not a Jew," Julius protested.

Adriana rolled her eyes. "Silvana and Marcus are. And you are too, really."

The two of them exchanged a look, before Silvana said fiercely, "We will never leave. Our work is cut out for us here. If we don't give our students a safe haven, nobody will."

Markus added. "Silvana is right. We have a mission to fulfill."

"So, your decision is final?" Julius asked Florian.

"Yes, we'll be leaving next month."

"We can always return when things have changed," Adriana reassured him.

"You might not be able to. If there's a war—" Edith said, attracting surprised gazes. It was the first time she'd added to the discussion, and she wasn't known to be a political woman.

"Oh, come on. The last war wasn't even twenty years ago.

Nobody wants another one, not even Hitler." Julius grabbed his lighter and a cigar.

Much to his surprise, Florian sided with Edith. "She might be right. All signs are pointing to increased armaments production. Why, if not for another war?"

"To be prepared, of course. We need to show other countries that we're done being pushed around," Julius said.

Florian shook his head. "That's not what I'm hearing. Between us, the armaments manufacturers are on high alert, hiring as many employees as they can."

"It would be political suicide. The wounds in the population, both physical and emotional, are running too deep. The population won't support another war." Markus always considered the human side of an issue.

Julius nodded. "Apart from the missing support in the population, Germany lacks in every military parameter, even against the weakest of countries. Admittedly, Hitler is a bit out of control, but he'll either come to his senses soon or the conservatives will rein him in."

"Well, I for my part won't be a sitting duck, waiting for disaster to happen." Adriana threw back her long dark-brown hair. She was still a beautiful woman at fifty years.

"I think you're exaggerating, but it's your life." Julius was still angry about not having been consulted in advance.

"We do understand that you dislike our decision and therefore we are all the more grateful that you're approving of it." Adriana put a hand on his arm.

Julius couldn't remember when exactly he'd approved of their folly. "Since I can't prevent you from leaving, I hope you'll at least visit frequently. My house will always be open to you."

Sometime later, Florian took him aside. "Can I talk to you alone for a moment?"

Julius wasn't surprised, because he'd already sensed there was something else. They entered Florian's office and his brother-in-law offered him a glass of brandy. "You, too, should consider emigrating."

Julius swirled the brown liquid, before he inhaled the sharp, yet sweet scent. "That's a good one."

"Armagnac. We bought it in Paris." Florian took a sip, swallowed it with pleasure and insisted, "At least think about it, will you?"

"Has Adriana asked you to pester me?"

"She did. She's quite worried."

"There's nothing to be worried about. As I keep having to tell people, I'm not a Jew, because I converted decades ago. Secondly, I'm a war veteran, bearer of the Iron Cross and thirdly I am a very well-connected man. Herrmann Göring is one of my acquaintances. You see, there's nothing to be worried about." Julius took another sip from his brandy, before receiving the cigar his brother-in-law proffered. "Why is Adriana so afraid? In contrast to Silvana, she didn't marry a Jew. Whatever happens, you can protect her."

"You know her. She can get rather worked up. In this case, though, I fully agree with her." Florian glanced over his shoulder, despite the two of them being alone in his office. "The Gestapo was here a few weeks ago, asking questions about whether I still had contact with some of my business partner's friends. They said his group was involved in some kind of treason. They left when I told them that as far as I knew all of his friends were in prison, which is the truth. But they warned me that I was under supervision. I don't want to die the way he did at Dachau."

Julius watched his brandy swirling in the glass. Florian had never admitted how much pain it must have caused him: his friend's corpse had been maimed almost to the point of not being recognizable, supposedly from an accident where he'd been run over by a tractor. But all evidence had pointed to torture.

"Look. I think she's overreacting, and it eludes me why you indulge her."

"I have my own reasons." Florian smiled, taking a smoke from his cigar. "All differences aside, I wanted to propose a deal."

Julius perked up his ears. He liked the other man and, being family, he trusted him implicitly. "Let me hear."

"I have plans to open a branch of the rubber factory in England. I've already talked to some local contacts. But I'd need financial backing."

Coming from Florian, he knew the proposal was based on a sound plan that made financial sense. "I'm always open for a good deal. Give me the business plan and I'll study it."

Florian walked around his desk to retrieve a thick manila envelope. "Take your time to read through it. I'd appreciate an honest opinion."

"You can always count on me."

Later, as they sat in the car on their way home, Edith asked, "What did Florian want?"

"To offer me a deal." Despite the shocking news, it had been a good evening. Moreover, it had made him reassess the situation. War or no war, he wanted to be prepared for every eventuality.

Julius leaned back in the seat and added, "We'll be going on a vacation soon."

"Where are we going?" Edith didn't let the surprise show in her voice, and he loved her all the more for her poise.

"Switzerland. If everyone is so worried about war, we might as well take a few precautions." One of them would be to retrieve Edith's jewelry from the bank vault and have her wear it for their journey to Switzerland.

26

Joseph had received orders to travel to Bad Wiessee near Munich on a top-secret assignment. Even his unit leader didn't know the exact reason.

Apparently, Hitler had ordered the head of SA Ernst Röhm to hold a leaders' meeting with about one hundred of his senior men, where the future strategy of the SA should be discussed. It would be the last official act for the SA before taking a month-long summer vacation in July to recover from the exertions of the struggle for power on the streets.

Joseph knew that Göring and Himmler wanted Röhm gone, along with his brownshirts, as everyone called the SA, while the Führer was reluctant to remove his old comrade-in-arms. After all, he and Röhm went back to before the unsuccessful coup in 1923.

Personally, Joseph tended to follow the Führer's opinion: together we are stronger. Yet, he also believed that the rivaling SA was a serious threat to the SS's aspirations to gain full national power. If this meeting resulted in Röhm putting his organization under SS command, he was all for it.

Sitting on the train to Bad Wiessee, wild rumors abounded:

Röhm was planning a coup against Hitler, in revenge for Hitler calling him out on his homosexuality. Joseph almost laughed. Röhm's abhorrent habits had long been known to the public and everyone, including the Führer, had turned a blind eye.

As Joseph's unit reached the beautiful Lake Tegernsee, they took residence in a simple, yet nice, hotel in town, waiting for orders that never came. Instead he and his comrades passed relaxed days swimming, fishing and sunbathing at the lake.

He began to believe that the journey might be a secret bonus for the hard-working SS men, when the order came rather surprisingly in the afternoon of the twenty-ninth of June. *Stand by tonight.*

Everyone in his unit was veteran enough to realize that the vague order meant something truly big was about to happen. It wouldn't do any good to rack his brain about details, since the Führer knew best and would advise them when the time was right. A good SS man obeyed and fought, he did not ponder, waver or make suggestions.

Stand by tonight. The order caused a thrill of anticipation to course through Joseph's veins. No doubt, there would be fighting. Every man under his command was fed up with doing nothing and yearned for action. Getting into a man-to-man fight with the SA was exactly the medicine they needed.

In the late afternoon he ordered everyone into uniform. They assembled in their hotel, readied their weapons, did a few hand-to-hand combat exercises, and then they waited.

The tension was palpable in the room. Nobody uttered an unnecessary word. Joseph was so proud of his men who sat there, fully concentrating, ready to spring into action at the Führer's command.

Just after nightfall, his leader arrived with the long-awaited instructions. The planned events were a lot more exciting than Joseph could have wished for in his wildest dreams. Adrenaline rushing through his veins, he instinctively stood taller, as he repeated his superior's words to his men.

"We will storm the hotel where the SA reside in complete silence. Once in, we kill them in their sleep." Joseph looked at his men, seeing their eager faces, but also noticing a few doubts. "If this may sound harsh to you, you must remember that you don't have the vision our Führer has." He let the words sink into his men, each one of them sworn to Hitler's person, having pledged allegiance, bravery and obedience until death. "With a heavy heart, our Führer has ruled that this is the only way left to protect our beloved Fatherland from a vicious coup the SA has planned."

His veteran men nodded with a combative spirit. Though one young man asked, "Shouldn't we at least wait until the SA actually commits a crime?"

"Not at all. A preemptive strike is the best option here. It will prevent horrible bloodshed."

"Y-yes." The youngster was pale as a ghost.

For the benefit of everyone in the room Joseph explained. "It might seem like a cruel thing to do, especially for those of you who don't have the same experience I have. A decade ago, during the beer hall coup, we would have won if we had proceeded with ruthless action." He let his gaze rove over each of his assembled men. "Our nation is in great peril! If we want to prevent a catastrophe, it has to be done tonight. Only a ruthless and bloody intervention will be able to stifle the spread of the revolt." He stared directly into the fearful eyes of the shivering youngster, as he struck with his biggest bullet. "Would you rather kill fifty traitors and mutineers or let ten thousand innocent SA and SS men bleed to death in a pointless fight?"

The panic in the youngster was palpable. For an instant, Joseph feared the boy would embarrass himself by emptying the contents of his stomach all over the floor. Thankfully, after giving him a stern glare, the boy's training took over and he stood erect, clicking his heels and shouting, "I will always do my duty! Heil Hitler!"

Joseph was immensely proud of the way his youngest team member had pulled himself together in the presence of the enemy and clicked his heels in response. "The victory is ours! Sieg Heil!"

The rest of the group fell in, their "Sieg Heil!" shouts echoing off the walls, filling the room with an exhilarating dedication to *Führer* and *Vaterland*.

Filled with anticipation, Joseph led his men to the SA's hotel. A contact man already on the inside waited for them, opening the back door and briefing them on the location of the rooms where the SA elite slept.

"Remember: The entire operation has to be conducted in absolute silence. If one of the victims realizes what's about to happen, they'll fight back and cause horrible bloodshed," the man dressed as a waiter impressed on them, as he handed Joseph the master key. "Don't touch Ernst Röhm in room seven. The Führer is on his way to deal with him personally."

Joseph noticed how the eyes of his men lit up at the mention of Hitler. The younger ones had never talked to their idol in person and were understandably excited at the prospect.

He used this knowledge to appeal one last time to their honor and loyalty. "I count on every one of you doing an outstanding job tonight. If our Führer has time in the morning, I'll personally ask him to commend each one of you for your excellent service."

The rest was pure adrenaline.

In near darkness Joseph led his unit upstairs to the second floor with the guest rooms, where he quietly opened the first door with the master key. The contours of the bed showed in the dimmest light falling through the curtains, revealing a figure covered by a white bedsheet.

Beckoning the youngster to follow him for a practical lesson, he flung out a long knife, took three long strides toward the bed and covered the traitor's mouth with one hand, while cutting his throat with the other one.

Silent. Perfect. Elegant.

Apart from the soft gurgling of blood, no sound could be heard. On his sign, a team member switched on the light.

Satisfied, Joseph examined the scene. Judging by the amount of blood soaking into the linens, his knife had slit open the victim's throat in the accurate location. He still opted to put his ear to the traitor's heart, and verify it had stopped beating, before he removed the hand clasping the man's mouth.

"See how it's done?" he whispered into the youngster's ear. Then he motioned for his men to continue to the next room, so that each of them could get the satisfaction of personally eliminating a vicious traitor and enemy of the Reich.

In less than an hour they had rid Germany of her most evil opponents and retreated to their own hotel as silently as they had arrived.

Only when they gathered in the communal room, did he allow himself to give a sigh of relief. Operation Hummingbird had gone exceedingly well; the Führer would be so proud of them. To let his men blow off steam, he produced several bottles of schnapps, which he'd learned to be a very efficient means to keep remorse or guilt far away.

Joseph offered a toast. "Our leader Adolf Hitler can always rely on his SS. We will do our duty. Heil Hitler!"

Not much later most of them were drunk enough to boast about their deeds, singing the praises of Hitler and his SS, while numbing their feelings. Unfortunately, not all of them were hardened enough yet to kill in cold blood and not feel a thing.

Joseph himself felt no remorse. He knew that the Night of the Long Knives, as the action had already been nicknamed, was a tough but necessary step to rescue Germany from evil.

Almost like a mother would slap her child to prevent him from making a dangerous mistake.

Back in Berlin, Joseph was called to Hitler, who commended him for the flawless operation and informed him that, indeed, a vicious coup had been prevented and everyone in the unit would receive a promotion.

Over the course of a week, not only had fifty SA leaders in the hotel been eliminated, but also Ernst Röhm had been arrested and shot on Hitler's order.

"Mutinous divisions have at all times been called back to order by decimation. I gave the order to shoot the chief culprits of this treachery, and I further gave the order to burn out to the raw flesh the ulcers of our internal well poisoning and the poisoning of foreign countries," Hitler told his senior SS men, in the same words he later repeated in front of the German Parliament, consisting solely of trusted NSDAP members.

All in all, about two hundred men had been killed: Inner-party opponents, associates of Vice-Chancellor von Papen, German nationalist politicians, former Vice-Chancellor von Schleicher and his wife, General von Bredow, and Gregor Strasser. Only Vice-Chancellor von Papen evaded death and was placed under house arrest.

Hitler had won on every count, and at the same time had shown his people that he was their sole leader, who would ruthlessly oppress any and all critics, no matter who they were or how much power they held.

27

About a week later, shortly before their planned trip to Switzerland, Julius received a visit from Florian in his office at the bank.

"Can I talk to you in private?" his brother-in-law said.

"Is it about the proposal you gave me? I have glanced over it, but haven't had time to study it carefully."

Florian shook his head. "It's personal and delicate."

That was new. Despite being family, they never consulted each other on personal matters. Julius didn't show his surprise. "Sure. We can talk here."

"Is it safe?" Florian looked around the room as if expecting uniform-clad men to jump out and attack him. It was a paranoid habit Julius had begun observing in his compatriots for quite some time now.

"I'll tell the secretary not to disturb us under any circumstances." Julius walked into the anteroom to inform his loyal secretary. Upon returning, he closed the door and stepped behind his desk, where he made a show to close the curtains and unplug the telephone. "Satisfied? Nobody can hear or see us."

"Don't take this lightly. What I'm going to say can get us both in trouble."

Julius inwardly groaned. Recently, the entire world seemed to have turned upside down. Even his down-to-earth brother-in-law seemed to have been infected by general paranoia. "Let's sit over there." He pointed toward the dark oak meeting table with four chairs made of the same wood. A carafe of water and several glasses stood on top. He poured them water and asked, "Or do we need something stronger?"

"This should do it for the moment." Florian settled on the chair and gulped down the entire glass, before he cleared his throat and explained. "It's about our move to England. Because Adriana is a Jew, the authorities have decided that our move is of a permanent nature and are going to treat it as emigration."

Rubbing his chin, Julius said, "Which means you'll have to pay the Reich Flight Tax of twenty-five percent of your net worth." Making a rough estimate he whistled through his teeth. "Approximately several million Reichsmark."

Florian gave him a miserable look. "Cash I don't have, since everything is tied up either in the factory or real estate."

"And if you have to sell it, the buyer will steal you blind."

"Yes. So, I thought..."

"... that I could loan you the money?" Julius finished his brother-in-law's sentence.

Pouring himself another glass of water, Florian nodded. "That... and I have some assets the state doesn't know about."

"I see." Julius had expected as much. "What is it?"

"Mostly Adriana's jewelry, but also some precious paintings, antiques, and cash."

Julius furrowed his brows. "I've been planning a trip to Switzerland with Edith for that exact reason, perhaps you'd like to join us?"

"Too dangerous. Since the authorities know we want to

emigrate, they'll search us at the border, which may also impli-
cate you."

"Hmm. That puts a new light on things. Perhaps even doing
the trip ourselves is not opportune. The authorities know
Adriana is my sister, so they might suspect something and
search our luggage. I'll have to send a messenger instead."

"I'm sorry for ruining your vacation plans." Florian seemed
honestly mortified.

"Don't worry. It's not your fault, although I still believe your
move to England is the wrong decision." Julius stood up to take
two cigars from the cabinet, offering one to Florian.

"Actually, their antics with the Reich Flight Tax reinforces
my decision to leave this country for good. I mean, taking a
quarter of everything we own? When it's their treatment of my
family that caused this decision in the first place?" Florian
chewed much too ferociously on his cigar.

"What will happen to your mansion? I'd hate to see it go to
the government."

"Adriana suggested that you could buy it, well below market
price, which will also reduce our tax burden."

Julius scratched his skin, thinking. It was an attractive deal,
for both parties involved. Yet, he shook his head. "It would
cause undue attention, but I can certainly find a buyer for you.
Someone trustworthy who'll reimburse the true value via a
Swiss bank account. We will have to use extreme caution, both
vetting the business partner and the actual transaction. There
can be no shadow of doubt from the government's side, or you'll
never receive the tax clearance certificate needed to leave the
country."

"Thanks, I knew I could count on you." Relief showed on
Florian's face.

"It might be beneficial if we opened a common account
either in Switzerland or in England with one of my partner

banks. This way we can deal more easily in the future, also in regards to the extension of your rubber factory."

"I had the same thought."

"Let me prepare everything for the official part as well as the other one." After glancing at his watch, Julius said, "I must leave for a board meeting. I'll contact you when everything is ready. And give Adriana my best regards."

"I will." Florian stood up. "If you ever need to leave the country, we'll always be there for you."

"That won't be necessary."

Several weeks later, everything was settled. Cash and valuables had been stashed with friends or been ushered across the border, and the business was put into the hands of a capable manager. The house was sold to a trusted Aryan who paid them a fraction of the real value, while at the same time transferring an additional sum from his bank account in Switzerland to Adriana's in England.

When being questioned by the tax authorities about the low purchase price, the buyer simply shrugged with a vile smile and told them, "That woman is a Jew. She should be grateful I paid anything at all!"

The Nazi bureaucrat could not object to such logic, and dutifully issued the tax clearance certificate Adriana and Florian needed to be allowed to leave the country. Adriana threw one last family gathering to say goodbye to everyone.

"I'm going to miss you so much," Silvana said, hugging her sister.

"We're not moving to another planet," Adriana responded.

"Just across the Channel, which is about the same." Silvana giggled as if she'd made a joke, but Julius knew how she felt.

Being Jewish in these times was hard. Every day new rules were issued, prohibiting one thing or the other.

If only she had converted when he did so many years ago. But no, his stubborn sisters had both insisted on staying Jewish despite not actually practicing. To add insult to injury, Silvana had then married a man who was very devout and an active member of his synagogue.

Edith shook Adriana's hand. "I'm wishing you a good start over there. Please, write often and let us know how life is treating you."

"We will. Don't worry about us," Adriana graciously responded. She was an avid letter writer, much like their mother had been, who'd never missed the opportunity to write a personal thank you note or a birthday card to their vast circle of friends and acquaintances.

Looking at the women of his family, Julius sensed they wouldn't be able to hold their tears at bay much longer, so he stepped in to avoid an embarrassing meltdown.

"My dear sister, my dear brother-in-law, I don't have to remind you, that from now on you're going to represent our family and our nation in England. Make us proud!"

"If need arises, all of you are always welcome at our house," Florian said, looking at each family member.

The next day Adriana and Florian took the plane to London. Julius hated to admit it even to himself, but he would miss them. His best hope was that they'd sooner rather than later realize the foolishness of their actions and return home, where they belonged.

28

On the 15th of September 1935 the world Helga had known ceased to exist. With one stroke of the pen, or more specifically two infamous laws, Hitler outlawed not only her marriage to Heinrich, but also made him and their two children second-class citizens.

The Law for the Protection of German Blood and German Honor supposedly protected the racial purity of the Master Race and forbade "miscegenation", or inter-breeding, between Aryans and Jews.

The Reich Citizenship Law additionally stipulated that a Jew, and to a lesser extent a half-Jew, did not belong to the German race and nation, thus was not allowed to have the Reich citizenship.

So far Heinrich had still been allowed to work for the Falkenstein bank, in contrast to so many of his friends, who had lost their jobs. Helga didn't labor under any illusion: it was only a matter of time until Heinrich was dismissed from his job, too.

Herr Falkenstein might be sympathetic to their plight; after what she knew about his heritage, she fully understood that he had to protect himself first, and cutting all ties to Jewish employees or acquaintances might be his first step.

Her eyes roamed the living room in their modest yet cozy apartment in a middle-class neighborhood of Berlin. How long would they be able to pay the rent if Heinrich lost his job?

Overwhelmed with desperation, her gaze fell on the sewing machine in the corner. Maybe it was time to brush off the dust and get back to searching for orders as a seamstress. She'd done it before; she could do it again.

Nobody, not even Hitler, would defeat her, or harm her family! With newfound energy she grabbed her coat and walked to the tailor for whom she'd done contract work during the Great Depression.

Herr Regenbogen was rather surprised at her request. "Frau Goldmann, you're not Jewish, are you?"

"No."

"So why do you want to work for a Jew then? It'll cause you plenty of problems, and me too." He gave her a miserable smile, meant to disguise the shame he must be feeling.

Not having expected this reaction, Helga was left without words. The silence between them expanded, causing the tension in the small shop to thicken, until she finally found her voice again. "My husband is a Jew."

The expression on Herr Regenbogen's face changed from ashamed to compassionate. "It certainly is a difficult situation. It doesn't change anything, though."

"So, you're refusing to employ me, because I'm Aryan?" Helga was righteously upset. She'd never expected to be discriminated by the very people who were suffering so greatly from this type of treatment.

Herr Regenbogen winced. "I'd love to contract you, but for several reasons I can't. First of all, I need to be loyal to the members of my synagogue, they need the work more than you do."

Helga wanted to protest, but he silenced her with a tired wave of his hand. "Secondly, it's for your safety—and mine. Since the Nuremberg laws took away our citizenship, no Jew is safe. The Nazis come to my shop and harass everyone working here. They stand in front of the door, menacing, shouting at customers not to do business with a Jew. You'd be caught in the middle of it. You'd be harassed the same as we are."

"I wouldn't mind..."

"I can assure you that you would. For the love of God, don't make your life harder than it has to be. Go and find employment with an Aryan business. There are plenty of them, and I hear"—he gave a sarcastic grin—"they're short of staff because they're letting go of everyone who's a Jew."

Herr Regenbogen might have a point on a logical level, but that didn't make her feel any better.

"This is so wrong," Helga murmured.

"It is. My wife and I are looking into emigration. Skilled tailors are always needed."

"Good luck." Helga left his shop, letting defeat wash over her for a full minute, before she made an effort to shrug it off. She'd never give up.

On her walk home, she mused about leaving Germany. Neither she nor Heinrich had even ever left Berlin, except for short trips into the surrounding countryside. Both of them were born and raised here, true Berliners on all accounts. Moving elsewhere had never crossed her mind. Not within Germany and certainly not to a foreign country, a place where she didn't speak the language, didn't know the culture... no, her home was here.

She was German, pure-blooded as Hitler liked to stress, and this vile monster would not expel her from her homeland. Perhaps she should thank him that he'd not given in to the demands of Reich Health Leader Gerhard Wagner, who'd supposedly pleaded for forced divorces of existing mixed marriages.

She balled her hand into a tight fist. Never! During their wedding ceremony she'd sworn an oath to stick by Heinrich through good times and bad. Apparently, another stretch of bad times had come upon them, just when things had turned for the better.

At least Amelie and David were sheltered from the increasing animosity. The Lemberg school was a safe haven, where the headmistress and her teachers took the best care possible of their charges and kept hateful propaganda outside the thick walls.

Nevertheless, Helga feared for the future. David was going to finish school next summer. Then what? The way it looked now he wouldn't be allowed to work for any company owned by Aryans.

29

Julius was livid. No, livid wasn't a strong enough word. He was fumingly, berserkly, rabidly irate.

"How dare they!" He paced the bank's meeting room until he came to a standstill in front of his deputy, Herr Dreyer, and shouted at him, "They can't do that! I'm as much a German as everyone else! I served in the Great War! My family has been here for generations!"

"I'm so sorry, Herr Falkenstein," Herr Dreyer muttered.

In his rage Julius didn't hear him. Herr Dreyer was fine. He hadn't suddenly been deprived of his citizenship by some outrageous law, defining him as a "person of inferior race". Reeling with the Nazis' audacity Julius took up his pacing again. "I'm not even a Jew. I converted decades ago. I'm a Christian. A German. A veteran of the war. I belong to the highest circles. Hermann Göring is a good acquaintance of mine." Julius flopped on an empty chair, his head bent forward with misery.

"I'm sure there will be a clarification to the Reich Citizenship Law, granting exception for cases like yours," Herr Dreyer said in a helpless attempt to soothe his boss.

"Why should I even need an exception? I'm not one of

these Eastern Jews coming here as refugees, refusing to assimilate."

"You shouldn't, Herr Falkenstein."

Julius gave a bitter chuckle. "They even outlawed my marriage. Can you imagine? I've been married to this woman for seventeen years and now the government tells me it's all been an unfortunate mistake?"

"I'm so sorry."

Hit by another bout of fury, Julius jumped up and shouted, "Don't be sorry! Do something!" Then he flopped back onto his seat, spent. Burying his head in his hands, he murmured, "This is insane. It's going too far."

"Perhaps if you talked to Herr Göring?" his deputy suggested.

Julius was close to exploding. The entire situation was absurd. He, one of the richest men in the country, had been demoted to a supplicant, begging for his very birthright of German citizenship.

He slowly shook his head. "Yes, perhaps I should do that."

After a long silence, his deputy raised his voice again. "Please forgive me, Herr Falkenstein, but perhaps you should consider taking precautions for the bank."

"The bank? They can't take its citizenship away," Julius groaned.

"It's just..." Sheens of sweat appeared on Herr Dreyer's forehead. "For safety reasons you might want to consider transferring the ownership of the bank—"

Julius jumped up, ready to strike his deputy for this affront. Once standing, his spine seemed to fall into itself, making him stagger until he found his balance again. "I'm not going to sell the Falkenstein heritage."

"I..." Herr Dreyer wrung his hands. "I... never meant to suggest such a thing. I rather... if you transferred it to someone in your family who's not a... who is Ary— I mean, someone who is not in danger of losing citizenship."

"And who should that be?" Julius didn't like the insinuation one bit. The only person in his family remotely adept in running a business was his brother-in-law Florian, who had emigrated to England.

"Your wife, perhaps?"

"Edith?" Julius could only shake his head. Edith was a woman, she had no idea whatsoever about business dealings.

"It would be in name only. It's actually not that uncommon for men to transfer property to their wives to secure it from being seized, for example if there were a lawsuit."

"I'm not a criminal!" Julius exploded. "I'm an honest, hard-working businessman. There's no reason for me to use the same tactics shady gangsters do. The Falkenstein bank is mine and it will stay mine. This is my final word on the subject."

When Julius returned home in the evening, a visibly agitated Edith was waiting for him.

"Have you heard?" she asked.

"I have. Let me take off my coat first, will you? We can talk in the library."

"Of course." Edith immediately regained her composure, slightly bowing her head. Then she rang for the maid to take his coat and fedora. "Would you like to have coffee served?"

"Yes, please, I had a rather hectic day." While walking first into his office next to the library, he considered how to approach this delicate topic with Edith, who seemed even more shaken by the new law than he was. Putting down his briefcase next to the desk, he decided on reassuring her at all costs. His wife needed the comfort of knowing nothing would change, and that he'd always be able to protect her, much more than she needed to fully understand the gravity of the situation.

A smile plastered on his face, he entered the library, sniffing the incomparable aroma of freshly ground coffee beans. "Hmm, what is better than to come home to a hot cup of coffee. Do we have some sweet buns as well?"

Edith gave him a bewildered gaze, as she dutifully called the maid to serve them buns to go with the coffee. The delay gave him time to work out how to protect Edith from heartache.

As soon as they were alone, Edith fired her first question at him. "Haven't you heard about the new Nuremberg racial laws?"

He patted her hand. "Of course I have, my dear. It's my job to be on top of all new legal developments."

"You don't seem to be worried. Don't you realize how bad this is? They have outlawed marriages like ours."

Under her subtle make-up he noticed red spots forming on her cheeks and forehead. The only other time he'd seen her in such anguish was after her first miscarriage. The fear of a relapse into those dark times of depression fortified his intention to sugarcoat the situation for her. He would not admit to the slightest trace of a problem in order to make her feel safe.

"Well, then it's fortunate that we married so many years ago." He gave a slight chuckle to emphasize his words. His light-hearted joke provoked the opposite reaction he had intended, because she glared at him.

"This is not the time for jokes. Aren't you aware how critical this situation is?"

"My dear, I understand how disturbing this must be for you, but I assure you, there's no reason to be worried. They won't outlaw existing marriages, because they don't want to anger the churches, especially the Pope and his powerful bishops. Whatever happens, I will always be here to protect you."

"Will you really?" She cast him a doubtful look.

"Naturally, I'm your husband. Have I ever let you down?"

She bit into her bun before answering. "You might not have a choice. What if they forcibly deport you?"

Her insistence annoyed him. "Look, Edith. They can't just deport a German citizen—"

"You're not a citizen anymore! At least not in their eyes." Surprised by her own outburst, she lowered her gaze, wringing her hands. "I'm sorry, I shouldn't have raised my voice."

"No, you shouldn't, but I don't blame you, we're all on edge right now." Julius remembered his own much more violent outburst in the morning. Compared to him she was a paragon of calm. "This new law is overshooting the government's competence in a big way. It violates our very constitution, therefore it will never hold up in court."

"I don't see anyone affected by the law brave enough to bring a legal challenge to this," she quipped.

Julius chalked up her response to being excessively worried about their situation, pushed his spectacles up his nose and said in a soothing tone, "I promise, there is no need to worry, for so many reasons. First of all I'm not a Jew—" He held up a hand to cut off her protest. "I know what the law says. It never defines, though, who is actually Jewish, and you must agree with me that a baptized Protestant cannot be considered Jewish. Surely, they will amend the law to clarify that just because someone was born to Jewish parents doesn't make him a Jew for his entire life. Especially not if he has fully assimilated into Christian life."

"If you think so..." Edith said, with a defeated look on her face.

"I do. People like me will be exempt from all the restrictions the Nazis have put on other Jews." He gave her an encouraging smile, and, as expected, she nodded, relief washing over her face.

"See, it's not half bad. If insult comes to injury, which I consider highly unlikely, I can as a last resort pull some strings

and call in a favor from my good friend Hermann Göring."
Göring wasn't actually a friend, more like a customer and
someone who frequented the same social circles.

"You think that would help?"

"Oh, my dear, we've been married for how long? And you
still don't understand that money makes the world go round.
The Nazis, like everyone else, need money. They need the
Falkenstein bank. They need me."

"I guess you're right."

"Let me tell you something. I do appreciate your concern
for me, and I don't want you to think I'm oblivious to the
danger. My father taught me to always be prepared for every
eventuality. So, let's entertain this idea for a bit. What could be
the worst thinkable outcome? The very, very, worst you can
think of?" He knew she wouldn't come up with anything worth
fretting over.

Edith worried her lower lip, thinking hard, before she
answered. "That they dispossess you of this house, your bank,
and then forcibly deport you."

He hid a smile. If this was the worst she could imagine, then
he would have an easy time calming her worries. "Well, then we
take up Adriana and Florian's offer to stay with them in
London, until we have found a beautiful mansion to live in,
which we will buy with the money stashed away in Switzerland. Would that be so bad?"

"I guess not," she reluctantly admitted.

"See? I told you there's no reason to be upset."

As they left the library to change clothes for their planned
visit to the opera later that night, Julius made a mental note to
transfer some more of his private money to Switzerland, and
also to Adriana's hands in London. Just in case.

Nothing would happen, but if it did, he would be prepared.

30

BERLIN, SPRING 1936

"I'm traveling to Switzerland after all next week," Julius said over dinner. "If you wanted to accompany me, we could finally enjoy the vacation we've had to delay for so long."

"I'd love to, but don't you remember that we're invited to the baptism of Carsta's youngest child?" Edith answered.

His face fell. "Isn't that the week after?"

"No." Edith picked up a piece of broccoli with her fork. "Can you postpone your trip?"

Now it was his turn to shake his head. "Sadly not, I was lucky enough to arrange a personal meeting with the Swiss minister of finance. I can absolutely not ask him to change the date for me, it was difficult enough to get an audience in the first place."

Edith was used to his business taking precedence over their personal life. "Then, I won't be able to accompany you."

"We'll split up: I visit with the finance minister and you represent the family at our niece's baptism." With that decision, he asked the maid to serve him another portion of vegetables.

"Why are you traveling to Switzerland anyway?" Edith asked.

He looked up with a surprised glance, since she rarely asked about his business. Just like he rarely asked about household matters. Then he smiled. "I'm planning to open a branch there."

"You are?" Previously, he'd been firm on the opinion that opening up dependencies in foreign countries would mean spreading the bank's resources too thin.

"I've been thinking a lot about Adriana and Florian's decision to emigrate, especially with the recent developments. Though I still don't believe there's reason to worry, you know that I always like to be prepared. All the people fleeing Germany in a haste will need access to their money throughout the trip and after. What better place to keep it than in the very country that has made neutrality its doctrine? Having a branch in Switzerland is a sound business decision."

He drank from his red wine before continuing his explanation. "It will comfort you to know that I am planning to harbor more of our private funds outside of Germany, which will be even more convenient if it's in a bank we control. This way we'll never have to want for anything, whether the Nazis stay in power or not."

Edith was amazed at his shrewd thinking, especially since he kept reassuring her that the Nazis didn't pose a threat to people like them. "That's very far-sighted of you."

"My father taught me well," he said with a content expression. "So, will you give my congratulations to Carsta and excuse my absence, please?"

"I certainly will, and I assume I'm not to mention the new branch?"

He nodded. "You are a very wise woman. Just tell them I had to attend an unpostponable business meeting and that I'm inconsolable at having to miss this beautiful occasion. Have you arranged for a gift?"

"The jeweler delivered it just yesterday. I ordered a golden necklace with a pendant forming her name. The first letter features a small diamond. Do you want to take a look? It's truly beautiful." They had given similar jewelry for the baptisms of Carsta's older children, so she expected him to say no.

"Actually, I would."

She rang the bell and asked the maid to bring the package for her niece. The necklace was lying in a box of blue velvet, the golden shimmer a promise of happy days.

"It's perfect," Julius said. After a moment's thought he added, "We should invite both your and my family for Christmas, what do think?"

"That's a lovely idea. It's been much too long since we all got together. Perhaps Adriana can travel from England?"

"Ask her. I'll leave the organization up to you."

A week later Edith stepped into Carsta's apartment in a middle-class borough of Berlin, where the immediate family gathered after the official reception at the church.

"Such a beautiful service," Edith complimented her sister.

"We've known the priest for a long time, he always finds the right words of compassion and charity," Carsta's husband Rudolf answered.

"Please, everyone come to the sitting room. There's coffee and cake." Carsta was glowing with joy and pride, holding her six-month-old daughter on her hip.

After the cake was distributed and the children had eaten, the adults stayed at the table and talked.

"What exactly is Julius doing in Switzerland?" Carsta asked.

Before Edith could answer, Joseph cut in, "What do you think the Jew is doing? Hiding money from our government."

Edith swallowed down the indignant remark on the tip of her tongue. Instead she said, "First of all, he's a Christian and, secondly, he pays more taxes than all of you combined."

That answer earned her a derisive sneer from Joseph. "Just because he converted, doesn't make him an Aryan. Once a Jew, always a Jew."

"He may be a Protestant by religion, but his bloodline is Jewish, has been for centuries," Edith's father explained.

"You can't seriously believe this? Since when is Judaism a race opposed to a religion?" A queasy feeling crept into her stomach, since this was exactly what she had feared after the issuing of the Nuremberg laws weeks prior.

"It has always been the case. The international Jewish conspiracy has lulled you into believing being a Jew is a choice and not some inherited mean streak. Something their members can shed themselves of, like the wolf putting on a sheepskin to wreak havoc among the herd," Joseph spewed.

"This is absolutely ridiculous." Edith had lost her appetite at hearing the incomprehensible prejudice, and pushed her plate away.

Carsta put a hand on her arm. "Edith, your agitation is understandable. All of us have been misled, most of all you."

"It doesn't have to stay this way," their mother added. "You can always divorce him and free yourself of his evil influence."

Edith looked at her mother absolutely aghast. In the past, whenever she had hinted at problems in her marriage, her mother had insisted that holy matrimony was indissoluble. A good wife had to take second place and strive to please her husband, no matter how difficult. "You of all people suggest this? What happened to the notion of holy matrimony?" Edith hissed.

Her mother gave a sheepish shrug. "Things have changed. And, I reckon you're not even properly churched, given that Julius gave false vows during the wedding ceremony, being a Jew and all that."

Edith gazed imploringly at Carsta, who quickly fussed over her baby, so she didn't have to pitch in.

Joseph though, had no problem voicing his opinion. "Mutti is right, you should get a divorce. It's the best for everyone involved."

"I don't remember asking any one of you for advice regarding my marriage." The rage gave her voice a sharp edge.

Her younger brother Knut tried to smooth the waters. "We all value Julius as a person, but in the current climate—"

Joseph interrupted him. "Fact is, Julius is a Jew and we don't want Jews in our midst." He looked around, his gaze resting a moment on his father, who should have spoken as the patriarch. Vati, though, was squirming with discomfort.

"You don't consider my husband part of the family anymore?" Edith had difficulty keeping her voice down. "Is that your way to thank him for all he's done for you? Joseph, have you conveniently forgotten how he bailed you out of prison after the failed beer hall coup? Vati, how he supported all of you throughout the depression? Carsta, how he loaned you the money for your house when no other bank would?" She glared at one after another of her family members. The only reaction she got were shrugs, and a very uncomfortable gaze from Knut.

"That's all water under the bridge. Times have changed and we have progressed with them, now it's your turn to adapt." Joseph cast her a challenging glare.

"Is that what you think?" Edith couldn't believe these were the people she had cherished throughout her life. The parents who had raised her. The siblings she'd grown up with. She had helped them in need, as they had helped her. Carsta had consoled her after each miscarriage and given her new hope. In turn Edith had given her sister food and money during the recession. Didn't any of this count anymore?

She decided to gamble on the wisdom that blood was thicker than water. "He's my husband. I vowed to stick with him through good times and bad. If Julius is not welcome in your midst anymore, I'm not either."

"Please, Edith, don't be so dramatic," Carsta said. "You can visit anytime you want, just not with him."

Meanwhile, Edith was shaking with fury. Slowly, she folded her napkin, put it on the table and stood up. "If this is your last word, then today is the last time we speak to each other."

"Don't do anything you might later regret, my girl," Mutti tried to intervene.

Edith shook her head. "I can't in good conscience belong to a family that hates my husband because of his Jewish heritage." Then she turned on her heel and walked out into the hallway, where she grabbed her coat and hat from the hook. Her hands were shaking so violently, it took several attempts to slip into her coat, until she felt someone holding it for her.

When she turned, she faced Knut, looking rather affected. "I'm so sorry, Edith. Please don't leave like this."

She shook her head. "You don't expect me to condone their behavior?"

He bit on his lip. "It's Joseph who has radicalized them, I'm sure they'll come around. Just give them some time."

"Oh, Knut," she sighed. "I appreciate you wanting to mediate, but I don't think you understand the severity of this. Hitler has poisoned our nation with hate. He has put half of the population at odds with the other half. Right now his rhetoric is breaking up our family. We aren't the first ones and won't be the last. Believe me, there will be so much more suffering to come, for everyone, even for the likes of Joseph on his high horse right now."

"Please don't say that." He took her hand in his.

She smiled sadly. "Each one of us has to decide where our loyalty lies. Mine is with Julius. I'm his wife. For better or worse. If my family doesn't value him anymore, that's their problem, not mine."

He nodded. "I want you to know that I will always be there for you."

"Thank you so much." Fearing she'd erupt into tears, she quickly opened the door and left.

Later that night, in the solitude of her bedroom, she was surprised at herself. Until that day she hadn't realized how much Julius still meant to her. She remembered the heartbreak of losing her babies. How the disappointment in his eyes had given her the feeling of having failed him, when all she had craved was his solace. Back then she had toyed with the idea of divorcing him many times. But in the end, she'd always known her place was by his side.

Their relationship had improved again over the years, he'd been more considerate and she'd come to depend less on him. They both had reached a state where they loved and respected each other, where they lived comfortably in the same house, albeit not in the same bedroom, shared joy and grief, supported each other.

In good times and bad.

31

When Julius returned from his trip to Switzerland, he found Edith moping around in the worst possible mood.

"What has happened?" he asked, having expected a more enthusiastic greeting.

"My family has..." Her voice was shaking. What was worse, she looked as if she'd break out in tears right there and then in the reception hall, for the entire staff to witness.

"Let's talk in my office," he said, taking her elbow. As soon as she settled into one of the armchairs in the corner, she lost the battle with her emotions and began to weep as if she were attending a funeral. Impatience rose in his chest. "By God, woman, will you please tell me what has happened?"

"They hate you!" she spat out, looking at him like a petulant child.

"Who hates me?"

"My family, every one of them. They basically disowned you."

Edith's words made no sense. Since she was behaving completely out of character, he suspected a graver cause behind it than just her family saying something disrespectful.

Therefore, he walked over to the cabinet and poured two glasses of brandy, handing her one. "Drink this, take a few deep breaths and then start from the beginning."

She kept sobbing, barely able to drink the brandy. It was a most unsettling experience, comparable only to when she'd lost their first child.

He yearned to console her, to make her stop crying, and took a clumsy step forward. Then he stopped mid-step since he had no idea what might comfort the blubbering mess in front of him. His mother had taught him many things; dealing with emotions, especially negative ones, had not been among them.

For lack of a better idea, he poured another glass for both of them. Edith looked up, determination slowly crowding out the pain and fear in her expression, and finally her tears petered out.

"I'm sorry," she whispered. "Could I have your kerchief, please?"

He gave her the crisp, white linen he always had in his breast pocket, glad that there was at least something, however small, he could do.

"Feeling better?" he asked, while watching her dry the traces of tears from her face.

Her answer was more sniveling, this time into his handkerchief. Several minutes later she finally found her voice to explain. "I went to the baptism of Carsta's daughter. When the other guests were gone, it was just the family eating cake in her house. They told me, in no uncertain terms, that you are not welcome in our family anymore."

"But... why?" He pensively raised an eyebrow, since her family wasn't prone to rash decisions.

"Because you're a Jew." She looked at him, the pain pooling in her eyes.

"I'm not..." He didn't bother finishing his sentence. Mere days ago, the government had finally issued the first decree of the Nuremberg racial law, clarifying who exactly was considered a Jew. The Nazis had decided that a person with two Jewish parents, which included himself and his sisters, were considered *Volljuden*, or full Jews; those with one Jewish parent as *Mischling ersten Grades*, or half-breeds, like Adriana and Florian's children.

The law included several more gradations of "Jewishness" as if it were a mere mathematical problem, ranging from full Jew to one-eighths of a Jew, which was considered German-blooded, because apparently the poisoned blood coursing the veins was too little to cause lasting harm on the Master Race.

Julius groaned. It truly was high time somebody reined Hitler in. The man had achieved many good things for Germany, but his insistence on labeling Jews as a vile race was a clear path into a catastrophe—not only for those affected, but for the entire nation. Apart from the personal pain it inflicted, ostracizing an—admittedly small, yet economically active—part of the population, it simply wasn't a sound strategy for the well-being of the country.

"The law says you are a Jew. Therefore, my family made it clear they never want to exchange another word with you."

Up till now he'd considered most of Edith's family to be fairly educated and reasonable people. Her father was an advocate of solid schooling, being the headmaster of a primary school.

Many times, Oswald Hesse and Julius had discussed how education was the key to a modern society, where everyone had the opportunity to live well. Both agreed that the dark times of illiterate peasants, deliberately held in stupidity so as not to endanger their master's superior role, had outlived its usefulness.

The world depended on independent-thinking, well-educated men, and, to a lesser extent, women, to progress into a future with less social injustice and more wealth for everyone.

There would always be differences, since not everyone was cut out to be an astute businessman, but even the lowest worker would have a life worth living, unlike the medieval peasants or the exploited English proletarians with their dark Satanic mills.

Caught in his thoughts he shook his head. He'd never believed Oswald would fall for Hitler's hateful propaganda. Did he not see through the damaging rhetoric that ran foul of everything they had argued about so many times?

"Do you even care?" Edith raised her voice, trying to get his attention.

"I'm sorry, my dear. I was just thinking about the many conversations I've had with your father. Are you quite sure this isn't just one of Joseph's follies?"

"It certainly originated with him, but Carsta and Mutti are fully behind it. My father barely said a word to stop them from spewing their hate."

"That's not like him. He always jumps in to correct everyone else."

Edith deadpanned him. "Clearly he's of the same opinion. Knut was the only one to come after me when I rushed off, promising never to return."

Trying to cheer her up, he said lightheartedly, "It'll make the organization for our Christmas party much easier for you, at least."

His remark didn't have the intended effect, on the contrary, she visibly struggled to retain her composure, squeezing his kerchief in her fist as if she wanted to obliterate it.

Her voice was still coarse, when she spoke up again. "They suggested I divorce you."

"They... did what? But why?" It was outrageous advice. Apart from treating the indissolubility of holy matrimony with contempt, they must not have considered the more practical issues. Who would provide for Edith if she left him? Who would give her a roof over her head, clothe her, feed her? Was her family equipped to support a woman with Edith's standards?

Edith's face turned into a grimace of misery. "So that I won't suffer because of you. They say anyone associated with a Jew will have to bear the consequences. Whatever those are."

"Your family is deluded." His voice came out a lot angrier than he'd intended, because the words had hit a sore spot. His worst fear was that he couldn't protect Edith. Whatever might happen, he would not allow her to become a victim because of him.

"I want to leave the country, Julius! Can't we move in with Adriana and Florian in London, at least for a while?"

"Nothing will happen to you or me. I promise. I'm not some random run-of-the-mill worker, one of the biggest banks in Germany belongs to me. All the Nazi bigwigs know and respect me."

"Do you really think this will save you?" Edith looked at him with such a pained expression, he couldn't help but feel moved by her worries.

"Of course I do. But if you feel safer, why don't you plan an extended visit to London? Stay with Adriana a month or two, and return home when you are more relaxed?"

"Oh, Julius, you don't understand. I'm not worried about me, but about you. I'll leave this country only if you come with me. It doesn't have to be forever." She looked at him expectantly.

He emptied his glass of brandy before answering. Even if he agreed with her, there were more things to consider than just his own well-being. "It's not as easy as you might think. Who's going to run the bank?"

"Florian has a manager for his business, couldn't you as well?"

"I could." He had no intention of explaining to her how difficult it was to find talented, trustworthy employees. His deputy director Herr Dreyer was both, yet he lacked that certain something to run the bank in his stead. As far as Julius was concerned, Florian was committing a grave mistake by handing the factory over to a manager, which would return to bite him in his backside before he knew it. "It will take time, though."

Looking at her grave expression he added, "I'm sure your family will come to their senses. Everyone is a bit jumpy after hearing about the Nuremberg laws, but this will pass. Such nonsensical notions never last long. It'll be a matter of a few months before everything is back to normal. There's no reason to be worried."

"I hope you're right," she said with a thin voice. "I told my family in no uncertain terms that I'm not going to visit them as long as you aren't welcome to join me."

Despite the foolish notion, it warmed his heart. He realized he'd never expected his soft-spoken wife to fervently take his side. He stepped nearer and tenderly stroked her hair, while she leaned her head against his hip. "Thank you, my dear, but you shouldn't have to stop seeing your family, just because of me."

"Yes, I must. After everything you have done for them, it's repugnant of them to disown you. They have liked you for years and suddenly, when it's not convenient to associate with you, they want me to dispose of you like a piece of trash?" She was talking herself into a rage, standing up and waving her hands about. "I will not stand for such behavior."

"And you don't have to. Everything will work out in due time." He kept stroking her hair, feeling a sudden tenderness, an emotion he'd neglected for such a long time. He pulled her up by her wrists, embracing her for many long minutes, before he led her over to the sofa and made love to her there.

32

BERLIN, SUMMER 1936

Helga returned home from grocery shopping, her hands full with two heavy bags. As she walked up the stairs, the landlady shot out of her apartment, stepping firmly into Helga's way.

Helga shrunk in fear at the sight of the robust woman, dressed in a flower-sprinkled apron tied over her dress. Wrinkling her forehead, she tried to remember today's date. It was way too early for the landlady to collect the monthly rent, due within the first three days of the month.

David should have given her last month's payment and for a second she feared that he'd missed the errand. No, he might be a rebellious boy, but he'd never forget such a vital thing.

"I've been hoping to see you," the landlady said, giving her a fake smile.

"What is it about, Frau Bohlen?"

"Here's the termination of your lease," Frau Bohlen said with a sheepish expression as she waved an envelope in the air.

"Why? We've lived here almost ten years and have never once missed a payment," Helga answered, even though she anticipated the answer.

"I've been kind enough to let you stay in my house for as long as possible."

"You've doubled our rent to make up for the favor," Helga spat at her, not caring about the distinct clicking of doors further up to listen in on what was sure to become a very humiliating conversation for her.

"Instead of thanking me for my generosity, you're attacking me! If anything, you've given me yet another reason to kick you Jewish vermin out of my house." Spittle flew from Frau Bohlen's mouth as she made her accusations.

"I'm not Jewish," Helga protested.

"Your husband is. As a Jew lover you should know the law: if the husband is Jewish, the entire household is. It doesn't matter that you aren't, as long as you take your husband's side over the well-being of our nation, you belong to them. I, for my part, don't want any of your riff-raff in my house. There are plenty of hard-working, faithful, Aryan tenants wanting to live in this house. You have until the end of the month to evacuate your apartment." Frau Bohlen shoved the envelope into Helga's grocery bag. "Have a good day!"

Helga stood dumbfounded in the hallway, hearing the soft clicking of doors being shut. It was the neighbors closing their apartment doors when the hoped-for spectacle didn't manifest, yet each thud sounded like a punch, reverberating through the staircase until it reached Helga's ears. There, it felt like the proverbial doors in life, shutting her out.

But in her case, there were no other doors opening instead. Throughout the last year, her life had been a succession of blows. First, Heinrich had lost his citizenship. Then the Falkenstein bank had canceled his bank account on the grounds of him not being a Reich citizen, even as—at the personal request of Julius Falkenstein—he'd stayed on as an accountant. Not as head accountant anymore, but demoted to a member of his former team. At least he still had a job, which couldn't be said of many people in his synagogue.

Defeated, she trudged upstairs, fumbling for her keys to unlock the door to the apartment she'd considered home for such a long time. She walked into the kitchen, where she left the grocery bags on the counter, not bothering to unpack as she usually did.

Turning around, she leaned against the counter, looking through the kitchen door into the living room. As if magically drawn to it, she walked into the living room, touching the sofa where she and Heinrich had sat so often in the evening, enjoying each other's company. Talking, laughing, cuddling.

A tear slipped down her cheek. She turned toward the wooden wall of cupboards, bought with his Christmas bonus a few years ago. It was filled with their belongings: books, the good china, glassware, pictures of her family, her deceased parents, Felicitas and Ernst, Heinrich's parents, his brother, cousins.

Almost without realizing it, she walked into the room David and Amelie shared. Amelie's half was neat and tidy. Books stored in order on the shelf next to her clothing, her favorite doll, a yo-yo she used to perform many tricks. David's half was in careless disarray. Schoolbooks and clothes had been shoved into the shelf, next to a football and an array of stones, sticks and carving tools. The top shelf hosted his collection of valuables, apparently useful to repair anything mechanical, although to Helga it looked like trash.

She bit her lip. Of her two children she worried most about him. Amelie was softly spoken and able to cope with every situation, however grave. A caprice of nature had given her the most beautiful light-brown hair, whereas the rest of the family's was pitch-black. Amelie looked nothing like the caricatures in the Nazi's newspaper, *Der Stürmer*, depicting the greedy Jew with black hair, unshaven, beaked nose, protruding eyes, crooked legs and flat feet.

Her essentially German looks helped her immensely these days, since strangers never expected her to be a *Mischling*. David, though, looked like a typical Jewish boy. Not the one from the caricatures obviously, but from the raciology books that had been introduced into all public schools and whose pictures were often reprinted even in reputable newspapers.

Furthermore, her eldest was a rebel. He never backed down when he felt treated unjustly—which these days occurred more often than not. She feared for him getting into a serious altercation, with the SS roaming the streets, intent on harassing every Jew they spotted.

A leaden fatigue overcame her and she leaned against the door frame, wishing she could leave all these hardships behind. She'd never felt this desperate, not even during the Great Depression, when she often hadn't known how to put food for her children on the table.

She dreaded the moment when Heinrich would come home and she'd have to tell him what had happened. With a deep sigh, she returned to the kitchen to unpack the grocery bags.

On top of the bag sat the brown envelope with the termination notice taunting her. She didn't have the courage to open it. Not now. She cast it aside onto the pile of the other mail that had arrived that day.

Perhaps after dinner she would have the strength to see written in black and white what she already knew from nasty Frau Bohlen's words. An hour later, Heinrich returned home, looking rumpled.

"Whatever happened to you?" Helga asked.

"Nothing." Heinrich's lips were a thin, stubborn line.

"Did those blackshirts harass you again?"

"No."

She didn't insist. It was so much harder on him than on her

or even their children. She was still German, a citizen to the oh-so-glorious Reich, harassed only due to her affiliation to him. If he wanted to talk to her about what had happened, he would do so. After dinner, on their cozy sofa. When the children had retreated to their room and they were alone.

Lately, the cuddles they exchanged weren't promises of love and passion anymore. Their sacred hours alone had become a lifeline of compassion, a way to stay sane in a world gone mad, a last resort, a retreat to recoup the strength and determination needed to face yet another day of constant barrage.

"Mutti, what's for dinner?" David peeked his head into the kitchen, smeared with motor oil from head to toe.

"For you nothing, if you don't get your dirty self out of my kitchen and into the bathroom!" she scolded him with a smile.

"I helped one of my classmates to fix up his motorcycle to sell. They're emigrating to America next month," David said.

Her son was a wizard for all things mechanical. He could repair anything from a broken alarm clock, to household utensils, bicycles and apparently now motorcycles as well.

"Well done. But you'll still need to scrub that off before sitting down at the table."

"I'm hungry as a wolf," David said, trying to peek into the pot on the stove.

But his father blocked the way. "Do as your mother says and get washed."

Grumbling, David retreated into the bathroom. Before locking the door behind him, he called out, "Don't start dinner without me!"

"Always hungry, he must be growing again," Helga said. David had recently turned sixteen, and the cute boy had changed into a burly, strong young man, surpassing even his father in height by a few centimeters.

"Mutti, I'm home!" Amelie shouted, taking off her shoes

and storing them neatly on the shelf next to the door. "I got an A in my English test."

"Well done," Heinrich praised her.

The Lemberg school put great emphasis in learning languages, especially English, French, and Hebrew, to prepare their students for emigration. About a third of Amelie's class-mates had left the country in the past year, and many more were queuing in front of the foreign embassies to obtain one of the scarce visas.

Later that night, Helga handed her husband the dreadful brown envelope. "Frau Bohlen has terminated our lease."

Heinrich looked up at her, his brown eyes defeated. "How long do we have?" He didn't have to ask the reason. Everything these days happened because of him, or rather, because he was Jewish.

"Until the end of the month. That crone considered herself generous giving us so much notice." Helga couldn't help the bitterness creeping into her voice.

"We'll find something else."

"Oh yes? And where? Who's going to rent an apartment to Jewish tenants?"

"Someone will. All the Jews in Berlin have to live some-where, don't they?" Heinrich pulled her closer, stroking her shoulder. "We'll manage, somehow."

The silence hung between them for many minutes, before Helga finally responded. "We will. Like we always do. I'll start looking for apartments first thing in the morning."

"You do that. I wish I could help, but I can't possibly ask for a day off at work."

"I think I'm better off talking to landlords myself, they'll find out about you being a Jew soon enough."

"It shouldn't be that way. I should take care of you, not the other way around."

Helga pressed a kiss on his lips. "Nonsense. In a marriage

each cares for the other. You keep earning the money and I mind the rest."

"I love you. Every day more."

"I love you too." She snuggled into his embrace, forcefully pushing all worries from her mind. For that, she would have enough time in the morning.

33

David hated their new apartment. Mutti's optimism had turned out to be completely uncalled for. On one occasion he had accompanied her to sign a lease contract.

"You are married, aren't you?" the gray-haired landlord in a business suit had asked her.

"Yes, but the application will go in my name only," Mutti had said.

"Look, ma'am, a married woman needs the approval of her husband to rent an apartment. Therefore, we'll need his signature on the contract as well."

"That won't be a problem. He's very much on board with this, since we'll both move in together with our two children."

"This young man is your son?" The landlord pointed at David.

"Yes." David didn't dare utter another word, because Mutti had instilled in him to keep his mouth shut and let her do all the talking.

"What is your name again?" The landlord asked.

"David Goldmann."

"Well, isn't that a Jewish name?"

Mutti intervened. "As you can see from my application, I'm not a Jew and neither is my son."

The landlord pursed his lips into a smug grimace. "Is it pure coincidence that you have a Jewish surname *and* want to keep your husband off the application for the rental lease? Or is it rather an effort to delude me into believing you're an Aryan household, Frau Goldmann?"

David's fingers itched to strangle the obnoxious man.

"I will be the renter, not my husband, so what he is or isn't doesn't matter," Mutti said with her firmest voice, the one she used to make sure David took off his dirty shoes before entering the apartment.

"It does matter. A lot, actually. Because this building is Aryan-only. We do not want any Jews in here, whether they be renters, family members or just visitors. If your husband is a Jew, which I highly suspect, then there's no place for your family in this building."

David observed—half in awe, half humiliated—how his mother straightened her shoulders, looked the unpleasant man straight in the eye and said, "Well, if you don't want us, we certainly don't want you either. Have a good day." Then she turned on her heel, striding out of the office with her head held high.

David followed her, not without glaring furiously at the stocky man. If it weren't for his mother's presence, he would have gladly smashed a fist into the landlord's plump face.

After weeks of unsuccessful searching, they had finally found a place in a rather run-down apartment building in a run-down neighborhood, where the landlord didn't care who lived in the building as long as they paid the overinflated rent in cash.

The new place was about half the size of their old one: a tiny kitchen and a bathroom that was scarcely big enough for one person to turn around, one bedroom for him and Amelie and the living room that doubled up as bedroom for his parents.

In contrast to the modern building they'd previously lived in, this one didn't have toilets in the apartments, but a shared toilet squeezed into a broom closet on each landing.

What bothered David most wasn't the discomfort of traipsing down a drafty staircase and waiting in front of the broom closet for another tenant to finish his business. It wasn't the moldy stench in the rooms either, which Mutti couldn't get rid of, even after airing the place for days on end and spraying every cleaner she owned onto the humid walls. Or the fact that water didn't flow regularly, and they often had to walk down to the backyard to fetch it from the pump.

No, it was the openly hostile glances he received from the other tenants, who whispered behind his back. "Jewish riff-raff! Never clean after themselves. How come we have to share in their dirt? They'd rather go and live with their kind. Other swine won't mind."

More than once David was tempted to make his opinion known with a fist to the mocker's jaw. Only the thought of his family dragging their belongings out onto the street searching for another place to live kept him from doing so.

But the rage bottled up inside him was boiling hotter with every passing day, ready to explode. His saving grace was the Olympics, because suddenly the open harassment stopped.

Berlin wanted to present her best side to the many foreign visitors for the games. Olympic flags replaced the swastikas hanging from every building, and the horrid signs *Jews not welcome here* or *Germans! Fight back! Don't buy from Jews!* had come down.

Even the innocent description *Jewish business*, which a foreigner might find offensive, had disappeared from sight and given way to happy posters welcoming the world to a modern, progressive capital of a Germany nobody had to fear.

David didn't trust the Nazis as far as he could spit, not even when the vile magazine, *Der Stürmer*, was banished from the newsstands, replaced by newspapers featuring images of happy Olympic winners.

David spent hours searching for a job. Despite everyone's efforts to turn the Lemberg school into a safe haven for Jewish students, he was happy when his last day had arrived shortly before the beginning of the Olympic Games.

Mechanics of all sorts were sorely needed to meet thriving demand, and he was taken up as an apprentice in a workshop providing various types of mechanical repairs, mostly for the steam locomotives of the Reichsbahn and the wearing parts of Berlin's trams. It was work after his fancy, since he'd been tinkering with machines since he could remember.

On his first day of work he arrived well in time, washed and shaved—not that the shaving was necessary since there was barely a hint of fluff on his cheeks.

"You are early, Goldmann," the foreman said, then furrowed his brows. "That name is much too Jewish, don't ya think?"

David gulped. "I'm only a half-Jew and the owner, Herr Mayer said..."

The foreman stopped him with a wave of his hand. "For my part you could be a Jewish Gypsy born from Satan and the bad witch, as long as you do your work well, I don't care."

David sighed with relief.

"But not everyone is like me. Sure, most of the lads used to be communists and hate the Nazis as much as you probably do, but none of them will tell you that. And some are snitches, always eager to please the government, ratting out their comrades to garner favors for themselves. Therefore..." The older man scrutinized David with squinted eyes. "What's a good name for you?"

"David, perhaps?" he answered.

"Nonsense. That's a first name and much too Jewish, too." The foreman roamed his eyes across the workshop until it fell on a huge boiler belonging to a locomotive and grinned. "I'm gonna call you Kessel, that fine with you?"

"Kessel," David tested the sound of the German word for boiler on his tongue and shrugged. As long as he was allowed to keep the job, he didn't care either way. "Kessel is perfectly fine with me."

"Well then, Kessel. I'm giving you a run through the workshop before everyone else arrives. For today, you shadow me, because tomorrow I expect you to start working on your own."

"Yes, sir," David said.

"No 'sir' nonsense here, I'm Baumann."

"Yes, Herr Baumann."

"Just Baumann. And don't forget: you're Kessel. Never mention you're a *Mischling*, better yet, steer clear from politics and the topic of Jews. Talk about your work, the weather and girls all you want, avoid the rest. Understood?"

"Yes, si— Baumann." Inwardly David relished the chance to start with a clean slate. Baumann was right: the fewer people who knew he was a half-Jew, the better.

34

"Frau Falkenstein, a summons has arrived for you," the butler announced.

"Summons by whom?" Edith asked, despite a sense of foreboding.

"By the Gestapo." He held out a paper with the black stamp of the Imperial Eagle carrying the Swastika in its claws. The civil servant stamping it must be a stickler for accuracy, because the eagle was throned in the upper left corner, his head pointing straight upward. Above the eagle, the dreaded words *Geheime Staatspolizei* caused a shiver to run down Edith's spine.

She held out her hand to take the paper, noticing the slight tremble and advising herself to do better. She had nothing to fear; she had done nothing wrong. Except, of course, marrying a Jew decades ago when nobody imagined the way things would change.

"Thank you," she told the butler and retreated into the library, before she dared to read the summons. It didn't reveal the reason, simply stated date and time of her appointment with some Kriminalassistent Becker at the Gestapo headquarters in

Prinz-Albrecht-Strasse. Another, more violent shiver raced down her spine, pressing the air out of her lungs.

A knock on the door tore her from her stupor.

"Come in," she croaked, half-expecting a man clad in a long leather coat to jump at her.

"May I serve you coffee?" the young maid asked. Edith had employed her two years ago after her predecessor had resigned because she'd fallen pregnant, and Nazi ideology had no place for women who worked instead of caring for their offspring.

"Yes, please." Edith slipped into one of the armchairs, eyeing the sheet of paper on the coffee table. Again, her heart throbbed painfully in her throat at the prospect of having to go to the Prinz-Albrecht-Strasse. She'd heard so many rumors of people disappearing there.

The maid, Anni, returned with coffee and a sweet bun. "You look pale, *gnädige Frau*, shall I get you smelling salts?"

"No, thanks. This'll do." Edith shook her head. For what she was going to face, she'd need something stronger. A lot stronger. She stared at the back of the young woman, wondering what the Gestapo could want from her.

In the evening she told Julius about the summons. He shrugged and said, "Probably some formality. Nothing to be worried about."

"How do you know?"

"If they had accused you of a serious offense, they'd be here swarming the place and not summon you to visit them next week."

"You're probably right." Despite his reassurance, her anguish increased over the next few days until her driver stopped in front of the impressive gray building, with the beautiful ornamental window frames and pompous entrance.

Straightening her shoulders, she pulled open the huge entrance door. The magnificence took her breath away. It looked exactly like she remembered it from several occasions when she and Julius had visited exhibitions in what used to be an arts and crafts school before the Gestapo had turned it into their headquarters in 1933. The shining beauty of the marbled floor and the high ceilings decorated with delicate stucco art soothed her anxiety.

"How can I help you?" A young woman behind a rather modern-looking desk asked, reminding Edith that this place wasn't any longer what it used to be. Instantly the prickling in her neck returned.

"I have an appointment with Kriminalassistent Becker." Edith showed the summons.

"Second floor, third room to the right." The receptionist waved her onward.

Hesitantly, Edith took the first step onto the broad wooden stairs, polished by decades of use. Despite the warm late summer day outside, in here it was chilly enough to make her shiver.

Kriminalassistent Becker was already waiting for her when she knocked on his door.

"Frau Falkenstein, exactly on time. Punctuality is a characteristic trait of the Germans." He was giving her a friendly smile, which she prayed was genuine and not a trick to make her feel secure before unpacking the thumbscrews or whatever other tool of torture he preferred.

"Herr Kriminalassistent, you summoned me."

"*Ach ja*, I did," he said, almost as an afterthought, as if he was just remembering. "You must be wondering why."

"Indeed I am, since I don't recall breaking any law." The panic threatened to suffocate her, yet she somehow managed to sound her normal self.

He clucked his tongue, seemingly enjoying this conversation. "Then I must alert you to your transgression. Isn't it true that your household employs several staff?"

"It is." Edith's entire being stiffened, since she knew full well where he was going with that overture. "I hadn't realized this was forbidden by law."

Again, he clucked his tongue. She couldn't tell whether it was in amusement, anger or simply disinterest.

"Shall I remind you of the law you're deliberately breaking?" His eyes bore into her.

Edith wondered what would happen if she said *no, thank you, I'm not interested in your ludicrous laws*. Since she'd rather not find out, she bowed her head slightly. "Please, enlighten me."

"I had pegged you for a more intelligent woman, one who knows the rules of the country she lives in."

"Herr Kriminalassistent, I'm very sorry to disappoint you, but with new laws coming out almost on a weekly basis it is difficult to keep track for a simple housewife like me."

"At least you're open to learn. You must have heard about the law for the protection of German blood, considering that you are married to a Jew." Becker stapled his hands on his desk, looking at her expectantly.

"Of course I am. Is this about my marriage? The law also said that existing marriages don't have to be dissolved." By now her heart was beating like a pneumatic drill, and she was astonished at herself for outwardly keeping her aplomb.

"No, it's not, at least not today." He seemed to expect a reaction from her. When she didn't indulge him, he spoke again. "I've summoned you, because you are in violation of article three of said law, which stipulates that Jews may not employ female citizens of German blood who are under forty-five years old in their households."

Edith had argued with Julius about this exact article back when it went into law on January 1st, 1936, so she was forearmed. "Our housekeeper turned forty-five last year."

"I do know that." Again, he cast her a benevolent smile. She almost wished he would bare his teeth instead of showering her with false friendliness.

"Then, what is the problem?" she asked.

"Ach, Frau Falkenstein. You can't seriously have forgotten about your maid, Anni?"

"Anni is my personal maid. I employ her and since I'm an Aryan, that is perfectly legal." She waited for his answer to see how he would twist the case, because one thing was sure: after this conversation was over, she'd have to let Anni go.

He shook his head, sadness in his steely-gray eyes. "It aggrieves me to see not one but two good German women under the spell of an enemy of the Reich. We all know how devious the Jews are. Don't you worry at all for the well-being of an impressionable, beautiful and innocent girl of twenty-two, forced to live in the same household as a Jew?"

The implication was obviously that Julius would seduce or rape the German girl, possibly even impregnate her with a Jewish bastard. *Rassenschande*, as the Nazis called intercourse between Jews and Aryans, was now one of the gravest crimes one could commit.

It was a crime Edith herself committed every time she let her husband touch her, the only saving grace that they were married.

"I can assure you, my husband is a man of honor and would never—"

Becker stopped her with a wave of his hand. "Frau Falkenstein, a Jew, however much you're deluded about his character by blind love, does not and never will have honor. So please, do yourself a favor and adhere to the existing laws." He smiled again. "Because you've been so accommodating, I'll give you until the end of the week to let your maid go."

Even as she considered whether she was expected to thank him for his generosity, he continued, "Consider this a favor.

And don't make me summon you again. The next time you won't get off so lightly."

"I will oblige you in this matter, just like any good German would." Then she stood up, gathered what was left of her courage and fled from the room before he could change his mind.

Compared to the nightmare she'd expected—from being whisked away to a concentration camp, to being tortured, to facing her execution—she truly had gotten off lightly.

Walking down the hallway toward the stairs, a door in front of her opened and a man in the black SS uniform walked out. She recognized him before he turned to face her.

"Edith, what are you doing here?" her brother Joseph said, surprise written on his face.

"Apparently I'm not allowed to employ a German maid anymore," she answered, giving him a once over. He looked good, although she disliked his set jaw that gave his face an unfamiliar hardness. It made him look so different from the hotheaded brother she'd admired and loved all her life.

"That's something you can easily fix," he offered, his features relaxing. Despite their differences he seemed relieved to find out she wasn't in serious trouble.

"How is Sandra? And your boys?" Edith inquired, politely ignoring his suggestion.

"Ach..." He made a dismissive gesture. "I had to divorce her."

"You divorced her? But why?" Edith was genuinely struck by his words. She had suspected his philandering ways, yet she'd never expected him to leave Sandra and his boys.

"You wouldn't believe how she betrayed me."

"Sandra cheated on you?" Edith couldn't fathom the docile, obedient woman engaging in an illicit affair, no matter how often her husband had done the same thing to her.

Joseph gave a cackling laugh. "Certainly not. After the passage of the Nuremberg racial laws, all SS men were encouraged to dig deeper into their family history and present the *Grosse Ariernach-weis*, a certificate of pure-blooded German genealogy going back all the way to 1750. You'd be shocked to hear what I found out."

"I'm sure you'll tell me." Edith could barely hide the sarcasm from her voice. To her, it was clear enough what he must have discovered.

"Turns out that devious shrew hid a Jewish great-great-great-grandmother from me all these years!"

"How inconsiderate of her! A Jewish great-great-great-grandmother? What does that make Sandra? One twenty-fourth of a Jew?"

"One thirty-second to be precise. But however little Jewish blood runs in her veins, it's unacceptable for the wife of an SS man, aspiring to make a career within the organization." Joseph gave her a hard stare. "You wouldn't understand that, though."

Edith raised her chin. "I understand perfectly well. You have put career above family."

"Wrong, I have put my duty to our nation above a woman poisoned with venomous blood. And if you were a patriot, you'd do the same!" he said, challenging her.

She wasn't about to stand for his ridiculous insults. Nobody else might stand up to him these days, but in contrast to Krinminalassistent Becker, she didn't fear Joseph, SS officer or not. "You mean I should be making a career for myself in the SS as well? I'm not sure your Führer would approve of that notion," she said in her sweetest voice, relishing in the appearance of hectic red dots on his cheeks.

"The Jewish pest must have poisoned your brains a lot more than I thought! Take my advice and save all that is left in your grasp: divorce that man sooner rather than later and I'll make sure you'll be welcomed back into our people's community with open arms."

"I hadn't noticed that I wasn't a member of the German people anymore," she answered, not wanting him to know how much truth lay in his words. Ever since Hitler had become chancellor, the situation had gradually deteriorated—even for a woman in such a privileged position as herself.

He stepped nearer, putting a heavy hand on her shoulder. "Edith. Please, you need to listen to me. Things will only get worse for you if you don't choose the right side. I implore you, get a divorce. It's the best for both of you."

"Really? How is a divorce best for Julius?"

"For starters, he's free to marry someone else. One of his kind. Two Jews can still be legally married and seek their luck elsewhere, if you know what I mean."

"Emigrating, you suggest?" Edith almost broke out into laughter, since this was the first point they agreed on. "Why shouldn't I go with him, if that is the solution to all of our problems?"

Joseph sadly shook his head. "You still don't understand it, do you? After all these years? Hitler is going to make Germany great again. Our nation will be the envy of the world, the closest thing to a paradise on earth. You just wait until we have conquered Lebensraum in the east."

She put a hand on his arm, her red varnish contrasting starkly with his black uniform. "You're not seriously advising me to become a farm woman and move to the country of the barbaric Slavs, are you?"

He groaned. "Why do I get the impression you're not taking my warnings seriously?"

"Perhaps, because all you spew is the deluded racial nonsense of your oh-so glorious Führer." The moment she said it, his face turned crimson red and she knew she'd gone too far.

"Don't you ever slander the Führer again!" he spat out between gritted teeth. "You may be my sister, but I won't hesitate to have you thrown into a reeducation camp if I ever hear such vile words from you again."

"I'm sorry, Joseph," she answered ruefully. "It won't happen again."

He nodded, mollified. "As soon as you are divorced, contact me. Despite your age, you're still quite good looking. Thus, it shouldn't be hard to find you a suitable husband among my comrades. Especially with the hefty settlement you're likely to receive."

"Now that is a relief," she said with a sour smile.

"See, there's a whole world of opportunities available to you."

35

BERLIN, JULY 1938

Helga lay on her knees scrubbing the floor as she mused over the recent months. One horrible event had followed another, completely obliterating any semblance of normalcy in her life.

The euphoria of the Austrian Anschluss and the invasion of the Sudetenland shortly thereafter had emboldened the Nazis to unleash a wave of public discrimination and brutality onto unwanted parts of the population—foremost the Jewish population.

The terror culminated last month in the so-called June action or *Aktion Arbeitsscheu*, supposedly to arrest work-shy elements of the population, those not pulling their weight. In fact, it had turned out to be an anti-Semitic measure, arresting in one fell swoop about two thousand three hundred Jews across Germany.

Apparently most of them had been shipped to the concentration camp in Dachau, to be used as cheap labor for the expansion of the camp, which wouldn't be necessary if the Nazis didn't arrest anyone they disliked.

"Can you move away from the entrance?" a deep voice said.

Helga looked up to see a man in a suit pointing at the door.

"I'm sorry, of course." She quickly moved further down the hallway, scrubbing away the grime of hundreds of dirty shoes walking in and out of the huge building.

She had considered herself lucky, because neither Heinrich nor David, grown up to a man with his eighteen years, had been arrested during the June action. A week later, their luck had run out. Heinrich lost his well-paid job at the Falkenstein bank because of yet another new law. This one restricted Jews from working in most professions, and David had suddenly become the sole breadwinner of the family.

Despite finishing his apprenticeship with stellar grades, he earned half of what the other men in his workshop received. The owner of the company jokingly said, since he was only half-Aryan, he deserved only a half-salary.

Helga grabbed the rag tighter, furiously swabbing the already polished floor. As much as she'd wanted to burst into the workshop and tell its owner that her son deserved more than all the others who weren't half as good, she had to grin and bear the humiliation in David's eyes. Decent paying jobs for a *Mischling* had become increasingly rare.

The very next morning after Heinrich had lost his job, she walked the streets in search of employment for herself. It turned out that decently paid jobs for the wife of a Jew were almost as scarce as they were for the Jewish husband.

After five days of canvassing, she finally found employment as a cleaner for an insurance company, albeit at half the going rate, because of her marital status.

When she came home in the evening, she flopped down onto the bed that now served as a sofa as well, her hands, knees and back hurting from the work her body was still adjusting to.

"How was your day?" Heinrich asked, handing her a cup of hot coffee.

"Don't ask." She looked at him, trying to come up with the energy to walk into the kitchen and make dinner.

"Stay right where you are, dinner is almost ready," he said as if reading her thoughts.

"You? I didn't realize you knew how to cook."

He grinned sheepishly. "Actually, I bought the groceries. Amelie did all the cooking." Seconds later, their daughter stepped into the living room and announced, "Dinner is ready."

"Hmm, that smells good," Helga said, sniffing the aroma of mashed potatoes and caramelized onions. Taking Heinrich's hand, who pulled her up, she came to stand on her feet and walked into the kitchen. The room was barely big enough for a table and four chairs.

David rushed in from his room. "God, I'm hungry as a wolf. At work they won't let me eat in the canteen anymore. I'll have to bring my own food from now on," he complained.

A heavy burden settled on Helga's shoulders, threatening to squash her. What had become of her country? Making the life of a part of its population a living hell? Worst of all, she didn't have a sliver of hope that this would come to an end anytime soon. Not as long as Hitler was in power, which she feared would never change.

During the last elections, from which Jews had been excluded, the Nazi party had received 99.1% of the votes. Helga had snorted; that result was a sham. She'd gone to the elections, in accordance with the Nazi slogan, "The Führer calls you! Do your bit!" Not because she wanted to, but because all non-voters were chased by SS into the polling stations anyway.

There, she'd dutifully received her ballot with only two choices. The first one a huge circle beneath a Yes, the second one a tiny circle beneath a No. After risking several glances over her shoulders to make sure none of the SS soldiers were looking at her as they stood in intimidating poses in every corner of the room, she defiantly put her mark into the tiny circle and quickly folded it.

"Let me put this into the urn for you," the friendly election helper said.

Helga, though, had seen her unfold previous ballots. Once she discarded one and alerted an SS man with a nod toward the man who'd given it to her. The poor sod then had to defend himself, babbling something about having lost his glasses... So now Helga smiled at the helper, saying, "Thank you so much," while quickly shoving her ballot into the urn.

Then she strode from the room, leaving the dumbfounded woman behind. She knew full well that her small act of resistance didn't change a thing, yet it felt good to put her opinion on paper. At least the ballot-counters would see in black and white that people existed who hated the Nazis and everything they stood for.

"Mutti?" Amelie raised her voice. "I asked you three times already whether you want mashed potatoes."

"Sorry, I was daydreaming." Helga shrugged off her thoughts, looking at her daughter, who held a ladle in her hand. "Yes, please."

Halfway done with her portion, Helga set her fork aside and said, "We need to leave the country."

"Mutti."

"What? How?"

"That's not possible."

Everyone spoke at once. After the first stunned reaction, Heinrich ordered, "Everyone quiet." He paused for a few seconds before he continued. "We have discussed this, Helga. It's simply not possible. We lack the funds needed to be granted a visa, and neither do we have someone to vouch for us in the receiving countries."

"We can't stay here either," she said with a deep sigh. "It's getting worse for Jews on a daily basis, and I don't see how or when this is going to end."

"Perhaps Frau Lemberg can help?" offered Amelie, who

was attending her last year of school. The Lemberg school had made it their mission to prepare students in the best way possible for emigration.

"I don't think she can provide funds or an affidavit for us," Heinrich said.

David cocked his head, looking into his mother's eyes. "We could go to Palestine."

"Palestine? But that's only for..." *Jews*, she wanted to say. Not even the most benevolent British bureaucrat would give one of the scarce immigration spots to a non-Jewish person.

"I'm not going to leave without your mother," Heinrich said, reading her thoughts.

"They won't take us anyway," Amelie objected. "We recently talked about this in school. You need to either have a lot of capital or an in-demand profession."

"My skills are very much in demand," David insisted.

"You want to go all alone?" Helga asked, her stomach tightening into a huge knot.

"I'm old enough, Mutti."

"But it's so far away. We wouldn't see you perhaps for years." Her heart broke at the prospect. Like every mother in the world she dreaded the day her children would leave the house to live on their own, but she'd never imagined David might move beyond Berlin, or abandon Germany altogether.

"I'm not leaving yet. It's rather difficult to get one of those visas. You need to stay a year or so in a special training estate, taking part in a *hachshara*, a preparation course for life in Palestine, run by the Zionists. Even then it's not a sure thing, because the British control all visas and have restricted immigration to a minimum. The only way for those without Zionist connections to enter, really, is illegally. They call it *Aliyah Bet*. But that's quite dangerous because the refugee ships can be apprehended anytime by British patrol boats guarding the Palestinian coast. They usually send the refugees back or intern them. Depending on circumstances, you never know which one is favorable."

Helga's eyes flew wide open. "Where did you learn all this?"

"Here and there."

"Have you been seriously considering emigrating to Palestine? You don't even speak Hebrew," Helga protested.

David held her gaze. "I can learn it. And one thing is for sure, Mutti, I'm not going to sit here like a sheep and wait for the Nazis to come and slaughter me."

"David. You're exaggerating," Heinrich jumped into the conversation. "Things may be difficult for us, but there's no need to meet trouble halfway. The Germans are a civilized nation. They'll soon get tired of Hitler's antics and everything will return to normal."

"I wish I had your optimism," David said.

"Frau Lemberg said, with the Evian Conference, other countries will finally agree on much higher immigration quotas for Jews. They know all about our plight and have come together to discuss how they can help us." Amelie sounded full of hope.

Helga looked at her daughter, knowing that the school had employed language teachers from France and England, who might know more than what was publicized in the German news. "It seems to me that the delegates have all been very concerned about the refugee crises, but they've not actually *done* anything yet."

"They will, Mutti, they can't just stand by and watch. Someone has to take all the refugees. Frau Lemberg said the foreign governments might put pressure on Hitler to pedal back his anti-Semitic actions," Amelie said.

"As if that would work," David interjected. "The only language Hitler understands is force."

Helga cast an inquiring look at her son. "You better not be planning anything foolish."

David's ears turned bright red. "I'm not, Mutti."

"So, where did you get these ideas?" she insisted.

"Nowhere."

Heinrich, who had been unusually silent, raised his voice. "He's been making friends with communists."

"I haven't." David's ears burned brighter, a clear sign that he was lying.

Helga's heart tightened. She knew her son well. He'd always been a rebel, involved in many fights at school. If he flirted with communist hoodlums, it would lead to a bad end for him. She said in her sternest voice, "David. You need to stay away from these people, they will only get you into trouble. And if you're arrested, God only knows what the Nazis will do to you."

He gave a shrug, apparently believing—like the youth often did—that he was invincible. A sense of foreboding struck Helga and she closed her eyes for a moment, the images of her son being beaten to death on the open street sending icy chills down her spine.

Several days later the Evian Conference ended, shattering all the hopes of Jews desperately needing to leave Nazi Germany. Just one of the thirty-two countries present generously offered an extra quota for "refugees wanting to leave their country of origin", as the delegates euphemistically called the Jews prosecuted by Hitler's regime.

Not only was there only one offer, that offer came from Rafael Trujillo Molena, the ruthless dictator of the tiny Dominican Republic out in the Caribbean. The mighty United States of America claimed to be too weakened by the consequences of the Great Depression to increase the quota of

27,370 refugees from Germany and Austria, whereas Lord Winterton claimed England not to be a country of immigration, conveniently not mentioning the many colonies of the vast Empire or their mandated territory in Palestine.

Meanwhile, the delegate from France lamented that the *Grande Nation,* likewise omitting to refer to their many colonies, was beyond capacity with the foreigners already accommodated.

The end result was nothing but a few warm words, and the designation of an Intergovernmental Committee of Refugees, which was to negotiate with Germany the modalities of an orderly exodus of Jews, including permission to take their possessions with them.

The very next day, Helga passed the newspaper kiosk to gloating headlines. The NSDAP mouthpiece *Völkischer Beobachter* was jubilant. "No one wants them," adding sardonically that other countries had protected themselves from an influx of Jewish immigrants because the disadvantages of Judaization were clearly recognized.

A caricature caught her eye, expressing the results of the conference better than a thousand words could. A Jewish man with two suitcases in his hands, footprints with swastikas on his back, looking in hope at the doors of foreign countries, just to be confronted with the sign "Closed" on all of them. The caption sarcastically wished the refugee, "Bon voyage". Helga's blood chilled as she forcefully tore her eyes away from the powerful caricature. In that instant she realized there was no way out, and it would fall on her shoulders to protect her husband as well as her children.

She straightened her back, determined to fight. If Hitler thought she'd let anything happen to her family, he was very much mistaken.

36

Julius called his deputy, Herr Dreyer, into his office. He hated to admit it, but the Nazis' slew of regulations for Jews had finally made it almost impossible to run a profitable business.

In April, he had been forced to register all his assets with the government. It was a measure nothing good could come from, and he was glad he'd taken precautions by safekeeping some of his wealth in Switzerland as well as transferring their home into Edith's name.

Then, in June, thousands of Jews had been snatched from their families and sent to Dachau, never to be seen or heard of again. Open terror like the June action, supposedly purported against work-shy individuals, alternated with more subtle harassments, including a law about prohibited professions for Jews in July.

That particular law had impacted the Falkenstein bank quite severely, since a local bureaucrat had taken the absurd stance that all bank employees were somehow involved in the now forbidden mediation of real estate contracts, because the bank gave credit to buyers.

Julius knew that the civil servant's interpretation was untenable in a law suit, but, on the advice of Herr Dreyer, he'd shelved that idea and instead had let go all of his Jewish employees, including Heinrich Goldmann. He felt a twinge of guilt, remembering how Edith had asked him to hire the man and all the good work he had done. Though he tried to convince himself that his actions had been necessary, if just to protect the majority of his employees, and himself.

For so many years he'd prided himself in working within a legal framework, but now doubts crept into his mind. Limitation of damage by adhering to every ridiculous new law might be needed for the bank to stay in existence, but didn't he have a responsibility to protect *all* of his employees? Especially those whose life was cumbersome enough due to Nazi law?

He inhaled his cigar smoke, the taste of wood and coffee lingering on his tongue, as he reminisced. In July, the Nazis had issued an order to obtain an identification card for all men turning eighteen, and Jews of all ages.

Julius weighed the cigar in his hand. It was an annoyance, for sure, and he secretly feared this might be used to cause further grief. Starting next year, every Jew, even newborns, had to apply for a *Kennkarte*, and male Jews above fifteen had to carry it with them at all times.

That wasn't the worst though. Merely a month later the Nazis had seen fit to segregate the population into Jews and non-Jews by name alone and released a list of approved first names for Jewish offspring. True to Nazi nature the so-called Jewish names weren't famous, biblical ones like David, Jacob, Jonas or Benjamin, but obscure, horrible, even insulting names.

For those already born, the government had a solution ready: adding Israel for a male and Sara for a female as second name. Furious at this derision, Julius had refused to go the city council to apply for his new *Kennkarte* under the name of Julius Israel Falkenstein.

Edith had begged him to go and comply, anguished something bad might happen to him if he was apprehended on the streets without mandatory documents. In hindsight, it had been a good decision not to join the endless queues in front of the registration offices, but not for reasons Julius could have imagined in his wildest dreams.

On October 5th, two days before a planned trip to visit Adriana in London, the Nazis had launched the next strike against Jews and revoked their passports. Julius had a fit, venting his anger on Edith, but there was no way around it: they had to cancel their trip and he had to go to the registration office and apply for his passport to be reissued by adding the humiliating second name of Israel, and, worse still, stamping a huge red J across the front.

God, how he hated to be singled out as a Jew. He didn't even speak Yiddish, for heaven's sake! With the new passport he would be looked upon with suspicion every time he wanted to cross the border, possibly denied entrance, because the receiving country feared he was there to stay, or the Germans wouldn't let him pass without paying the ridiculous "exit tax" on his entire wealth.

A knock on the door saved him from dwelling on those miserable thoughts.

"You wanted to see me, Herr Falkenstein?" Herr Dreyer said.

"Indeed. I did. Please have a seat." Julius pointed at the conference table in the corner of his office and used the intercom to order coffee.

They talked about day-to-day business, until his secretary had delivered the coffee and closed the door behind her. Then, Julius took a deep breath and broached the topic that caused him so much anxiety. "With all the new rules against Jews, I believe it's time to take precautions to keep the bank safe."

Herr Dreyer nodded. He, too, had heard about the voluntary and not-so-voluntary Aryanization of businesses. "What's on your mind?"

"Transferring the bank to Edith's name."

Herr Dreyer shook his head. "I don't think that'll do now. They'll accuse her of misleading the public and hiding the true, Jewish, owner out of personal interest. It has happened to others."

Julius frowned. "It's not foolproof, I agree. Rather, it depends on who the responsible civil servant is. Since we have very good relations with the one in charge, it shouldn't be a problem."

"Unfortunately, this has changed. Just this morning I received a note informing us about the new SS-Ober-some-thing-or-other in charge. The note advised us to await his visit." Herr Dreyer gave a sheepish look.

"Do you know the new man?" Julius emptied his cup of coffee, leaning back in expectation of the answer.

"First thing I did was to telephone around. All my contacts agree on one thing: this new man is a two-hundred-percent Nazi and a stickler for rules regarding Jews, often going overboard, interpreting the laws in the strictest mindset possible."

Julius groaned. "Any good news at all?"

"I'm afraid not. Therefore, I believe the ruse of transferring the bank to your wife will not bear weight under his scrutiny."

The words left a bitter taste in his mouth, because Julius knew what that entailed. If one of the more pompous bureaucrats felt they were being made to look foolish, they tended to dole out rather nasty retaliations. He didn't even want to imagine how that might end for his family, and the bank. "What do you suggest then?"

Fidgeting in his seat, Herr Dreyer finally said, "I'm afraid you'll have to sell."

"Sell the bank! Never!" Julius jumped up from his chair so

violently, the water carafe toppled over and would have doused everything, had it not been for Herr Dreyer's quick reaction catching and stabilizing it.

"It might only be in name. Find a trustworthy Aryan to keep it safe for you."

Julius furrowed his brows, thinking. "What about you? I'll sell it to you."

"Me?" Herr Dreyer shook his head in disbelief.

"Yes. You know the business in and out, and I trust you."

"Thank you for your confidence, but I don't have the money."

"Well, that is a problem. Though not one that cannot be solved. We'll need a bit of time to come up with a plan." Together they mused how they could best arrange the deal so both sides were protected and the government wouldn't suspect foul play, when the splintering of glass caught their attention.

A second later, the alarm bells rang, and employees raced through the corridors to shut the safe in the basement.

"A robbery?" Julius asked, more to himself than anyone else. It wasn't the first one that happened at the Falkenstein bank, although it was the first he witnessed.

He was pondering whether to go into the cashier's room and get involved or not, when several men in SS uniform stormed his office, shouting "Down with the Jews!" and using their batons to shatter the windows.

"Stop this right now!" Julius raised his voice, using the authoritative tone that usually got him what he wanted.

Today though, it had the opposite effect. One of the men, apparently their leader, slowly turned around, giving Julius a cold stare. "And you are who exactly?"

"I'm the owner of this establishment and I won't allow this behavior." Julius slowly rose to stand opposite the SS man. Beside him, Herr Dreyer seemed to have turned into a statue.

"Oh, you won't allow it?" the SS man said, looking around at his comrades. "Did you hear this? He won't allow us? Show him how much we care!"

On his command, the rest of the bunch continued trashing not only the windowpanes, but also the furniture, the telephone, and—oh no, please—the cabinet with the expensive cognac bottles. Julius was so caught in the spectacle, observing the brown liquid running onto the wooden floor, that he was completely shocked when the end of a baton connected with the skin below his chin.

Under the pressure of the baton moving up, Julius had no choice but raise his eyes to gaze into the mocking face of the SS man.

"What else do you want to forbid us?"

"N-nothing..."

"Speak up, we're all ears! A fine smoke, perhaps?" Before Julius could say a word, the SS man retrieved a cigarette and a lighter from his breast pocket, lit it, inhaled and delicately exhaled, puffing the smoke directly into Julius' face. Then he flicked the burning cigarette onto the puddle of spirits on the floor, smiling when it immediately lit up. "I reckon we'd better leave."

"You... you... fascist bastard!" Julius shouted indignantly, despite Herr Dreyer pulling at his sleeve to get him away from the SS. But Julius' brain filled with red-hot rage, making him oblivious to anything but the *chutzpah* of the SS, setting the office ablaze. Not even the heat emanating from the fire caused him to back off and seek salvation.

"Insulting a government official," the SS man said, grabbing Julius by the collar. The fine material of the expensive tailored suit tore under the pressure, making a ripping sound that pierced Julius' ears as much as the crackling flames licking at his antique furniture. "You're under arrest."

The next thing Julius knew, he was being dragged behind

the SS man out of his bank, and maybe toward the end of his life. For the first time since Hitler's coming to power, he was afraid. Deathly frightened.

Seeing his hapless deputy lingering, he shouted at him, "Call Edith and tell her to inform our lawyer."

37

Edith was a bundle of nerves ever since she had been listening to the radio, and heard about the spontaneous retaliations for the murder of Ernst Eduard vom Rath by the Polish Jew Herschel Grynszpan.

Tucked away in the safety of their mansion on Schwanenwerder Island, she worried about Julius, whose office was located in the center of Berlin. She had put her hand on the telephone a hundred times. Every time she stopped herself from dialing his number, because she knew how much he hated to be disturbed at work.

Then, the telephone rang. Shrill. Menacing.

The sound reverberated through the entrance hall, echoing off the walls, magnifying her fear.

It could be anything, she told herself, striding in measured steps toward the telephone, not wanting to show her inner turmoil to the new maid—a young Jewess. Jewish women apparently weren't in danger of being violated by their employers, or perhaps in the Nazis' minds, it didn't matter if they were. Edith pressed her lips together when she realized that, indeed, a Jew had no right to be protected from harm.

"*Gnädige Frau,* for you." The maid held the receiver toward Edith.

"Who is it?"

"I didn't catch his name." The maid gave a helpless look and, once again, Edith wished for Anni back, who'd never made such a blunder as not to ask for the caller's name. At the same time, she pitied the new maid, a former prima ballerina, who'd been forced to take a job she clearly had not been trained for.

"Edith Falkenstein," she said into the receiver, fervently praying Julius was on the other end, despite knowing this wasn't possible. He would have asked to speak to his wife, which even the ballet dancer couldn't have mistaken.

"Good evening, Frau Falkenstein. This is Herr Dreyer. I'm sorry to disturb you..." She didn't hear the rest of what he said, because she had to fight against a wave of nausea. Julius' deputy at the Falkenstein bank had never asked to speak with her before.

She composed herself, rearranged her face into a semblance of calmness, and said into the phone, "Please hold for a moment, I'll take the call in the library." Then she turned toward the maid and ordered, "Take the receiver and hang up once I speak from the other line, understood?"

"Yes, *gnädige Frau,*" the maid answered on a curtsy. She was quick to learn, but lacked the years of experience Anni had possessed.

Her heart thumping wildly against her ribs, Edith entered the library, where she settled into the armchair and picked up the phone on the small table beside it. For a split second she was tempted not to speak to Herr Dreyer, since his call could only mean bad news. Shaking her head at the silly notion, she spoke. "Herr Dreyer, how can I help you?"

Both of them waited for the telltale click indicating the receiver in the entrance hall had been replaced, before he spoke with a strained voice. "I'm so very sorry, Frau Falkenstein, to be the bearer of bad news—"

Her sharp intake of breath interrupted him, before she forced herself to ask him to continue. "I'm sorry, please go on."

"You may have heard about the upheaval. It is horrifying, there's looting and burning, destruction everywhere you look." He waffled on and on, giving Edith the impression he was avoiding telling her something.

So, she finally interrupted him again. "What about my husband?"

He let out a groan that sounded like a wail. "Oh, Frau Falkenstein, it is a disaster! The SS came here, smashed the windows, the furniture, everything. Then they spilled his collection of spirits and set the office ablaze."

Edith's hand flew to her throat. "Dear heavens! Is he alive?"

"I'm afraid—"

Edith let out a bloodcurdling yell, so loud it alerted the staff. The butler, the housekeeper and the maid all came rushing into the library to find out what evil had befallen their mistress.

"*Gnädige Frau.*" The housekeeper rushed to her side, picking up the telephone receiver, which dangled from the cable tethering it to the apparatus on the side table.

"Julius. He's..." Edith croaked, a thousand emotions washing over her. They had had their differences in the twenty years of their marriage, but confronted with his possible demise, the shock paralyzed her.

The butler took the receiver from the housekeeper's hand and spoke into it. Edith lay in the armchair, oblivious to what happened around her until the housekeeper held something beneath her nose.

The smelling salts reinvigorated her spirits and she sat up straight, just in time to see the butler nod with a serious face.

"Herr Falkenstein has been arrested," he said, handing her the receiver once more.

Edith wanted to laugh and cry at the same time. Julius was not dead. But he'd been arrested and God only knew how the SA, SS, Gestapo, whoever had done the arrest, was treating him. Leaning on whatever little aplomb she had left, she held the receiver to her ear. "Herr Dreyer, please excuse the interruption."

Herr Dreyer gallantly pretermitted her lapse and continued as if she hadn't just made a fool of herself. "Herr Falkenstein tried to argue with the SS. He may, in fact, have shouted at them. They were not amused and arrested him, dragging him out of the building in, if I may say so, a rather harsh manner."

"Where is he now?" Edith waved at the housekeeper to hand her the smelling salts, sensing she might need them.

"I'm afraid I don't know. They dragged him out without explanation. Only after I managed to put out the fire in his office did I hasten downstairs."

"Thank you," Edith said, thinking he should have left the darn office burning to the ground and gone after her husband.

"One of the security guards at the entrance told me the SS had put Herr Falkenstein onto the back of a truck with a couple dozen other people."

Edith got the impression he was carefully avoiding the full truth and inquired, "Why didn't the guards do something?"

"I'm afraid..." Edith wished she could jump through the line at his incessant and annoying use of *I'm afraid* "...the guards share the sentiment that Jews are responsible for so many problems in our society. Herr Falkenstein is their employer, but, between us, many of the men have discussed on the quiet that the bank should be in proper Aryan hands."

Herr Dreyer's remark felt like a slap in the face, a harbinger of evil. It was a development she had feared for many years, even as she had begged Julius to leave the country. Yet, he had always brushed off her fears as unfounded. At first insisting he was not a Jew—until the infamous Nuremberg laws, which turned thousands of converted Christians back into Jews, along with thousands who became Jews only after digging into their genealogy and finding—much to their dismay—that they had one or two Jewish grandparents.

She shrugged. Now was not the time to reminisce. She had to find Julius and bail him out.

"So, do you have an idea where the truck took him?"

"I'm afraid I don't. Herr Falkenstein instructed me to call you and ask you to contact his lawyer."

"That is very helpful indeed." Edith rather wanted to slap Herr Dreyer for being so unhelpful. Now that she knew whom to call, she couldn't get rid of him fast enough. "I'll do that right away. Thank you for informing me." Without waiting for his answer, she replaced the receiver.

"Please, get me my husband's little black address book from the desk in his office," she asked the butler.

"But..." The old man raised a brow, since nobody was allowed to touch Julius' desk, much less his address book.

"This is an emergency," Edith insisted, looking him straight into the eyes. "Make it quick."

The butler seemed to realize the urgency and trotted off without further objections. When he returned, he handed her the little black book, wiping his hand as if he could brush off the committed sin.

Edith didn't pay him any more attention, dismissing the entire staff with a wave of her hand. Dr. Petersen had been lawyer to the Falkensteins even before Edith married into the family. She located his number and dialed it with trembling fingers, praying he'd be in his office—and that he would know how to find and free Julius.

The receptionist answered. "I'm very sorry, Dr. Petersen is occupied at the moment, there have been quite a few—"

Edith had no time for pleasantries, so she interrupted the woman. "My husband, Julius Falkenstein, the owner of the

Falkenstein bank, has been arrested for no reason at all and I need Dr. Petersen to find out where they are holding him. Please tell him to call me back at the Falkenstein residence at his earliest possible convenience."

Edith could imagine how the receptionist would have straightened her spine to sit upright as she realized to whom she was talking.

"Yes, certainly. I'll tell Dr. Peterson to give you a call. Would you like to give me some more details? It might help to get things moving faster."

A relieved smile on her lips, Edith recounted what she knew, ending with, "We're prepared to pay any bail the authorities ask for, as long as they release Herr Falkenstein."

"Please rest assured, Dr. Peterson will work on your case with priority," the receptionist said and hung up.

Edith leaned back in the armchair, relieved the issue was now in capable hands. Yet, she still feared that even Dr. Peterson might not get the desired results—with the Nazis one never knew.

Suddenly, Helga's rebellious expression at the opening of Silvana's school came to her mind and how she'd stated, "I'm prepared to do anything to save Heinrich. Absolutely anything."

New energy coursed through Edith's veins and she decided to do the same. She'd eat humble pie and visit the only person who was in a position to help.

"I'm going out. Bring me my coat, please," she asked the maid.

"But *gnädige Frau*, isn't it too dangerous?" Both the maid and the housekeeper protested after they had come running.

She didn't dignify them with an answer. "My coat, please." Consulting her watch, she instructed the driver to deliver her to Joseph's office in the Prinz-Albrecht-Strasse. As she arrived there, she had to force down the urge to bolt and entered the menacing building she'd been summoned to two years ago.

"Edith? You surely were the last person I had expected to see today," her brother said instead of a greeting. His expression didn't show whether that was a good or a bad thing.

Capitalizing on his pride, she said, "I came here, because you were right all along. Things have become so much worse."

"Better late than never." His face softened into a complacent smile.

"I've come here to ask for your help." She was prepared to throw herself at his feet, if need be, and beg. "Julius was arrested today."

"So, you haven't come here to tell me you divorced him?" Joseph's face turned into a stony mask.

Thinking quick on her feet, she answered, "I have thought about it, but his arrest... it complicates things. Please, for the sake of our family, can you help me to get him free?"

He pursed his lips. "I would do you a disservice. You'd be so much better off without him."

"I know." Edith racked her brain on how to mollify her brother. "And I'm so very sorry. I know I must be a disappointment for you, but not everyone is as strong and heroic as you are. My weakness is that I still love Julius and can't bear the thought of him suffering."

Her speech seemed to have reached Joseph's heart, because he said, "Alright. I'll do what I can. But it will have a price."

"Anything." A huge rock fell from her shoulders.

"First, you must consider divorce."

Edith swallowed hard. How could she promise this, when apparently being married to her was Julius' only saving grace in Hitler's nation? Then she slowly said, "I will consider it," thinking to herself that she wasn't promising the outcome of her considerations.

"Second, he'll have to pay a fine in lieu of a jail sentence for his crimes."

She didn't think Julius had committed a crime—apart from

being a Jew, of course—but she wholeheartedly agreed. "We're prepared to pay any amount requested."

"Good. I'll do what I can." Joseph furrowed his brows. "I don't want it to look like a personal favor though. Perhaps it's best if all further dealings in this issue are handled by someone else."

"Our lawyer, Dr. Petersen, perhaps?" she asked.

"Yes, that will do."

"Joseph." She looked up to him, for a fleeting second seeing the brother she used to love so much and not the hardened SS officer he'd become. "I thank you from the bottom of my heart."

"Don't forget your promise," he said.

"I won't."

Two days of constant phone calls later—and a hefty fine for Julius' crimes—Dr. Petersen personally delivered Julius to the manor.

"Thank God you're back!" Edith forwent proper behavior and fell round Julius' neck.

"Please, you're going to knock me over." Despite his words he pressed her against him for a few seconds, before he let her go to thank Dr. Petersen. "Would you like a drink?"

"No, thank you. I am in a hurry—so many more cases waiting for me. You were incredibly lucky that Herr Hesse vouched for you."

After the lawyer's departure, the two of them settled into the library and Edith asked, "Shall I get you a brandy?"

"I'd rather have a coffee, please." He nonchalantly overplayed his flinch at her question, but Edith knew him too well to be fooled.

Julius might look unscathed outwardly, but there was a hollowness in his eyes, a hidden terror. As soon as the maid had delivered coffee and buns, he gazed at Edith. "I guess I must thank you for getting me out of prison."

She blushed slightly, trying to downplay what she had done.

"I was so worried about you, so I visited Joseph and asked him for help." She half-expected him to hold his standard speech of how important it was to have good relations and how needless her worry had been, but he kept silent, sipping his coffee with a pensive face.

"Does that mean I'm not anymore a persona non grata to your family?"

Edith shook her head, musing whether now was a good time to tell him about the conditions Joseph had requested. "In fact, I had to promise him that I would consider divorce." With bated breath she waited for an outburst of indignation, which never happened.

"I'm so sorry, Edith. I never wanted to cause you harm. If you believe you're better off without me—"

She cut him right off, surprising herself with her boldness. "I don't." A part of her heart filled with sadness, because she would never have the passionate love Helga and Heinrich had, but, for better or worse, she would shield Julius, who had protected her during all these years. "But I'm afraid the next time Joseph won't be willing to help. And then, what will we do?"

"How much worse can it get?" His shoulders crumpled.

Shrugging, she searched for an answer. After a long pause, she said, "Perhaps we should consider emigration after all."

His face was a grimace of misery. "Perhaps we should."

They both fell silent, eating their sweet buns and drinking coffee, while each was lost in their own thoughts, unsure what the future would hold for them.

A LETTER FROM MARION

Dear Reader,

Thank you so much for reading *The Berlin Wife*. If you enjoyed it, and want to keep up to date with all my latest releases, just sign up at the following link. Your email address will never be shared and you can unsubscribe at any time.

www.bookouture.com/marion-kummerow

This book took me both into known and unknown territory: known because it starts out in my hometown Munich, and unknown because the story took me back to 1923, whereas my other books take place in the 1930s and 1940s.

I had such fun writing the scenes in Munich, having been to the places mentioned so many times, it was almost like a walk through the city. More than once I admired the precious mansions along the Königinstrasse, wondering what it would be like to live there.

As always when writing I get new ideas, so it won't surprise you that I initially outlined and wrote the draft for what will become book three in this series. Getting to know the main characters takes some time, just like in real life, and the more time I spent with especially Helga and Edith, the more I was intrigued. What made them stick with their husbands? How did their relationships develop over the years? How did they feel when their entire worldview was upside down? When suddenly they became the person to protect their husbands, when traditionally it had been the other way?

All the main characters in this novel are entirely fictional, although they have been inspired by real people, whose memoirs or eyewitness accounts I have read. The events they experience, however, have all happened and I have tried to depict them as historically accurately as possible. Since the book spans a period of fifteen years, I have only picked up a few of the most prominent happenings, such as the beer hall coup, the fire at the Reichstag, the Night of the Long Knives, and at the very end of the book, the Night of Broken Glass.

Rumor has it that the Nazis themselves set the Reichstag ablaze, using Marinus van der Lubbe as a convenient scapegoat, which could never be proven true. Historians disagree as to whether van der Lubbe acted alone, wanting to protest the condition of the German working class, or if he was involved in a larger conspiracy as the Nazis claimed.

It's a topic that has not been fully concluded. William Shirer wrote in *The Rise and Fall of the Third Reich* that van der Lubbe was goaded into setting a fire at the Reichstag but that the Nazis had set their own more elaborate fire at the same time. I have used this notion and have planted Joseph as one of Lubbe's co-conspirators, so we can be privy to the planning.

Many people believe the persecution of Jews started with the concentration camps, but in fact it happened much earlier. Anti-Semitic sentiments had been present for centuries in European countries and were in the ascendant after World War I, which Hitler capitalized on.

During my research I was surprised about the swiftness and efficiency with which he changed the political landscape after being nominated Chancellor in January 1933. It took less than three months before he had abolished free elections, removed the opposition from political positions and renounced civil rights. The Nuremberg laws in 1935 were the culmination of years of anti-Jewish rules and regulations, stripping them of their Reich citizenship.

Emigration happened in three waves: The first wave began immediately after Hitler's seizure of power and continued into 1935. It was mostly a hasty emigration, hoping the near end of Nazism would allow for an early return. In 1934, this first great wave of emigration ebbed away because of the apparent easing of anti-Jewish terror and hopes for calmer times after the killing of Röhm in the summer of 1934.

The second wave began after the Nuremberg laws in 1935 when Jews had been denigrated to second-class citizens, or rather non-citizens. It was much more organized than the first wave and oftentimes the emigrants didn't have illusions of ever returning to Germany as the first wave had.

The third wave finally took place from the time of the June action in 1938, where thousands of Jewish men were sent to concentration camps and their only chance at freedom was a concrete plan for emigrating with the entire family. After the Night of Broken Glass pogrom in November of the same year, most Jews in Germany were seeking emigration—just to find that this way of escape had been closed down by virtually every receiving country, as referenced in Chapter 35 about the Evian Conference. German Jews had high hopes at the start of the conference, believing that other countries would finally not only realize their plight, but also act upon it.

Again, thank you so much for reading *The Berlin Wife*. I hope you loved it and, if you did, I would be very grateful if you could write a review. I'd love to hear what you think, and it makes such a difference helping new readers to discover one of my books for the first time.

I love hearing from my readers—you can get in touch on my Facebook page, through Twitter, Goodreads or my website.

Marion Kummerow

KEEP IN TOUCH WITH MARION

https://kummerow.info

 facebook.com/AutorinKummerow
twitter.com/MarionKummerow

Made in the USA
Middletown, DE
06 January 2024